'No painted doxy, but very pleasing.'

Sir Dominick put out his hand and pushed back her linen cap.

'A nut-brown maid, like the one in the ballad. More and more to my liking. I've seen too many dark, buxom Burgundian girls lately.'

Aleyne felt herself trembling as he loosened the waves of her brown hair, fingering it gently, then he lightly ran one finger down the fine bones of her cheek.

'Please let me go, sir. I am not willing.' If her lips were trembling in her terrified effort to hold back her tears, it did not reveal itself in the steadiness of her voice.

He ignored her and bent to kiss her.

No man had kissed her so, full on her lips. This man's kiss, without being openly brutal, was demanding, inexorably forcing her lips apart. Horrified, Aleyne found herself almost responding.

She made a little moan of protest and, as he bent close, he saw tears furrowing her cheeks. He murmured a soft soldier's oath and, placing both hands on her shoulders again, held her from him, eyes narrowing thoughtfully as he gazed down directly into her fearful little countenance.

'You really are not anxious for my attentions, are you?'

Joanna Makepeace has written over thirty books under several pseudonyms. She taught history, English and drama at a large comprehensive school where she was head of English before leaving full time work to concentrate on her writing and research. She was born and continues to live in Leicester with her mother and a Jack Russell terrier named Dickon. Her enthusiasm for the theatre and music is unabated and her greatest enjoyment gained from visits to old houses, ruined castles and battlefields. She began to write when still very young after seeing delightfully romantic historical films which she still finds more exciting and relaxing than newer ones.

Previous Title

THE SPANISH PRIZE

BATTLEFIELD OF HEARTS

Joanna Makepeace

First published in Great Britain 1991
by Mills & Boon Limited

© Joanna Makepeace 1991

Australian copyright 1991
Philippine copyright 1991
This edition 1991

ISBN 0 263 77376 0

Masquerade is a trademark published by
Mills & Boon Limited, Eton House,
18–24 Paradise Road, Richmond, Surrey, TW9 1SR.

Set in Times Roman 10 on 10¼ pt.
04-9108-85996 C

Made and printed in Great Britain

CHAPTER ONE

'YOU sent for me, madam?'

Lady Maud Risby looked up coolly from the black velvet frontal she was ornamenting with tiny seed-pearls. Aleyne approached, her black velvet skirts swishing over the flagged floor, and stood awkwardly, her hands tight clasped at her sides.

Lady Risby always overawed her. Perhaps it was her stepmother's beauty, still so apparent in her mourning black, one pale band of fair hair smoothed decorously back from her head-dress shining in the firelight, for it was still chilly on this late April day of 1471. Her stepmother had never been unkind to her, would have sought her friendship had Aleyne had a mind to grant it, for as a bride of eighteen she had come to Risby three years ago to assume a mother's rights over Sir Godfrey's thirteen-year-old daughter. They were near enough in age, but Aleyne had never truly liked her. She knew the feeling was rooted in natural resentment, for her love for her father had been all-consuming and for all of those thirteen years they had been all in all to each other. Now he was laid to rest in Risby church and his wife widowed at twenty-one.

'Yes,' Lady Risby's blue eyes passed over her tense figure, 'it is much too cold for you to remain up there in your chamber. Do sit down near the fire.'

'I had thought to go to the church,' Aleyne stammered, her eyes averted from her stepmother's gaze that she might not see how red-rimmed they were from weeping.

Lady Risby had wept dutifully at the funeral, but she appeared to have that remarkable faculty of retaining her beauty throughout her grief, tears merely serving to

5

enhance those lovely blue eyes and sorrow to emphasise
the fine-cut lines of that glorious high forehead, nose
and mouth.

The sombre hue of Aleyne's gown served only to make
her olive-tinged complexion look sallow and her grey
eyes ugly and puffed from frequent bouts of weeping.
She had not Lady Risby's height, though she was slim
and fine-boned, her youthful body not yet having blossomed to the full splendour of womanhood. Her hair
was brown and pushed well back under her frontal.

Her stepmother appeared to be appraising her. She
sighed and indicated a stool close by.

'Do not go yet. I wanted to talk to you.'

'Yes, madam.' Aleyne sank down obediently. She had
never been able to bring herself to call Lady Risby
'mother' and it had not been expected or demanded of
her.

'Child, you must try now to control your grief. Sir
Godfrey has been buried over two weeks ago and it is
time we considered our situation. Your good appearance,
not helped by weeping, will prove essential to our plans.'

Aleyne's chin jerked towards her stepmother. 'I do
not understand.'

'Tush, girl, you're no fool. You know well enough it
is vital that you marry and soon.'

Aleyne's pale cheeks darkened angrily.

'Marry, madam—how can you countenance such a
suggestion so soon?'

'Nonsense, this is an excellent time to consider the
prospect. You are an heiress. You need a good man to
defend your interests, considering the state of the realm.'
She raised her black-clad shoulders in a little shrug of
distaste. 'The sooner the better.'

'Two weeks only.' Aleyne's grey eyes were stormy and
bright now with threatening tears. 'We are waiting still
for the stonemasons to begin on the tomb and the image-
makers are not yet summoned.'

'Aleyne, your father would have been the first to
commend me for thinking of your welfare. You are now

sixteen. Had he not been ailing this last year he would have seen to the matter himself.'

'I am surely a ward of the Crown. To marry without the King's consent would be tantamount to treason.' Aleyne sought desperately for some means to delay discussion of such a momentous decision.

'Which king?' Lady Risby smiled derisively. 'Poor Henry, only recently brought from the Tower by my lord Earl of Warwick to ride through the London streets and he blinking like an owl, not knowing why all the pother? They say he has so neglected his person during his stay in the Tower apartments that it was necessary to have him bathed and deloused before robing him in his state apparel. Will this so puissant lord rouse himself to consider arranging a suitable marriage for you, mistress? I think not. As for Edward of York, who knows if he will ever regain the crown? And, even were he to do so, his hands will be full enough with affairs of state. Warwickshire is far from the capital and your welfare of little moment to him. We need to shift for ourselves. My kinsman, Sir Thomas Stoodley, is well set up and thoroughly capable of defending you and your property from molestation, whatever the fortunes of war.'

Aleyne held out her icy fingers to the blaze. Lady Risby had spoken many times of her cousin and, only recently, had met him when she and Sir Godfrey had journeyed south to attend the baptism of Maud's sister's son. Aleyne had declined to accompany them. Now she wished she had done so, for it would have been some comfort to have at least glimpsed the man.

'You have heard from him, then?' She tried to keep her tone casual.

'This morning. He sends his condolences and regrets that he was unable to attend the funeral.' She hesitated. 'He is already at Wellesbourne and anxious to wait upon us later today. I took the liberty of summoning him the moment your father died.'

Aleyne faced her angrily. 'You had no business to do so or to offer him any encouragement.'

'As your guardian, until the King's wishes regarding you are known, I thought it only sensible. Aleyne, don't you understand you could be in danger, unprotected here? The country is involved in bloody civil war and to whom could we appeal, should we be threatened by land-hungry neighbours? You know well enough your father was on ill terms with the Forsters and they only six miles distance, and the Vaughans are staunchly Lancastrian. Young heiresses have been abducted and forced into wedlock before now. Of what avail would it be to complain to the King afterwards? A fine would be levied on the offender, and you left an unwilling bride, your lands sequestered. Sir Thomas is little more than thirty and considered a fine-looking man, as you shall see for yourself. Naturally I shall not attempt to over-persuade you, but I do ask you to consider the merits of the case.'

'I am sure Sir Thomas has considered the advantages of marrying me,' Aleyne said bitterly. 'Is he not "land-hungry" as you so bitingly castigate the Forsters and Vaughans?'

'I'll not deny that Sir Thomas would deem a marriage with you advantageous, yet he is no pauper. His manor in Hertfordshire is small but excellently run and it would please you, would it not, if he were prepared to continue to live here? The plan has the merit of ensuring the welfare of our retainers.'

'And you would stay here with us until you remarry?'

A suspicion of surprise—or was it doubt?—crossed Lady Risby's usually unruffled features.

'Certainly, in all events I am too new a widow to consider remarriage for some time.'

'Equally I consider myself too recently bereaved to think of marriage yet.'

'At a more settled time I would agree, Aleyne. Under these circumstances I urge you to lose no time. I say again, you could do far worse than to take Sir Thomas.'

'He hasn't seen me,' Aleyne said wearily. 'He may yet wish to change his mind.'

'Why should he do so? You are not ill-looking when you choose to take pains over your appearance. Marriages are made with legal contracts, not in heaven. You are not foolish enough to harbour romantic notions, surely? Your father and I dealt well enough together for all that I had never set eyes on him until the day he came a-wooing, and he some thirty years my senior.'

'Your father insisted on your accepting him?' It was the first time in their acquaintance that Aleyne had seriously considered Maud's situation, looked at from her own youthful viewpoint.

'He betrothed me to Sir Godfrey. I made no objections. I had no cause to complain. He treated me well, despite my failure to conceive a child, which must have disappointed him sorely. You'll have no such problems, I imagine. Sir Thomas already has two daughters by his first marriage, but fortunately no son to dispute your own child's claims.'

Aleyne nodded, avoiding her stepmother's gaze. She rose to her feet, shaking out her skirts.

'Well, since he is to visit, I'll have opportunity to judge for myself. I'd like to go to Father Robert now, unless you wish me to assist with preparations.'

'Of course not. I can manage. Off you go. Seek Father Robert's advice. I doubt if it will be different from my own.'

'Perhaps. I wish——'

'Yes?'

'Nothing. I feel so alone. I had hoped that Ellis would return when—when he heard how ill Father was.'

'You have me to advise you. How much practical assistance could you have gained from your cousin Ellis? He's scarce a year older than you are and his mind filled to overflowing with notions of chivalry and honour, more fool he. Little he'll find of either when he meets the enemy face to face. Your father warned him of that often enough.'

'Ellis had no choice but to follow my lord Earl when the Earl of March and the Duke of Gloucester landed at Ravenspur.'

'Earl of March, forsooth! Your father would whip you to the bone for daring to call your King that, and he would never have countenanced Ellis's support of the Lancastrian cause.'

'But Ellis was squire to my lord Earl at Middleham.'

'And so were the King's brother, the young Duke of Gloucester, Sir Robert Percy and many more, yet they remain loyal to the Yorkist King.'

Aleyne sighed. She had long given up trying to assess the rights and wrongs of Ellis's conduct. Her father had fought with the Duke of York in the French Wars as a young man. In those days Nevilles had fought to defend the Duke's claim, for was he not descended royally from King Edward III and, on his mother's side, from an older son than John of Gaunt, from whom King Harry descended? The Great Earl of Warwick was cousin to York's sons, Edward, George of Clarence and Richard of Gloucester, yet after this terrible quarrel over the King's marriage to Lady Elizabeth Grey the breach had widened, and now the Earl had publicly denounced his fealty to York and, with his son-in-law, George of Clarence, had declared his support for Margaret of Anjou, poor mad Harry's warlike queen, and her young son, Edward of Lancaster.

Aleyne's father had shaken his head gravely over the folly of it all. This last year he had ailed, coughing away his life until forced to take to his bed. A pike-thrust through the lung at Towton had never truly healed, and had saved him the necessity of taking sides. Two years ago he had begged his old companion-in-arms, Great Warwick, to take young Ellis Dyer, her second cousin, into his service. Ellis had lived with his widowed mother in penury near Gloucester, but had learned skill at arms under her father here at Risby. Aleyne had come to regard him as her brother and missed him sorely. Now Ellis was embroiled in this sorry affair, linked by a sense of gratitude to the Earl, yet pulled too by old loyalties towards his former companions who now supported King Edward.

She had sent a groom south with the news of her father's mortal sickness but had heard no word. It had been rumoured that the Earl's forces had already met those of King Edward's near London, but, cut off by bad weather in this quiet corner of the Cotswolds, Aleyne was still unsure of how matters stood, and her grief had placed her apart from all other concerns. Now a cold chill struck through her as she thought Ellis's failure to reply to her message might mean that he lay wounded or even dead on the field of battle. She thrust the fear aside. Surely God could not have been so cruel? Likely her messenger had not been able to contact his young master speedily, and when he *was* able to do so Ellis would come to her side.

She pictured him, auburn-haired, sturdy, wide brown eyes aghast at her tidings, anxious to ride to Risby yet unable to leave his post. Ellis lived still. He must come home to her—soon.

Despite the solar's fine appointments, carpets from the East, and tapestries which kept the chill from the walls biting into their bones in icy weather, Aleyne was glad to leave it. She was always relieved to be free of her stepmother's presence. She hurried to her own bed-chamber and removed her hennin, donning wimple and hooded cloak for the short walk to the church.

The manor house was not large, nor crenellated. Here in the heart of England Sir Godfrey had seen no need to defend his property, yet now Aleyne glanced back at the house, biting her lip doubtfully. It was dear to her, lying between rolling hills near the old Roman fosse, squat-built of mellow Cotswold stone, surrounded by acres of good sheep pasturage. A small pleasance had been built for the convenience of the ladies beyond the courtyard, which housed barns and stables at the rear of the house. Soon it would be bright with flowers. A mile distant was the village, clustering round the grey

stone Norman church, and here the three-field system
still flourished for all that the villagers worked mainly
for Sir Godfrey, tending the manor sheep. Maud Risby
had put a finger squarely on the point of pain. Aleyne
had every wish to remain at Risby and it seemed marriage with Sir Thomas would allow her that at least.

Father Robert found her kneeling beside her father's
tomb to the south of the altar.

'I expected you earlier, Aleyne.'

'Confess me, Father. I harbour undutiful thoughts.'

He shook his head gently to comfort her distress and,
after listening attentively to her stumbled confession, led
her to the little house by the church.

'Is there further news of my lord Earl' progress,
Father?'

'Still unconfirmed rumour, but it seems sure that the
Duke of Clarence deserted him near Coventry, and on
the eleventh Edward entered London, where he was received joyfully. His Queen has borne him a son in sanctuary. Since Easter there has been no news, but whisper
says the two great armies met near St Albans on April
sixteenth.'

'Over a week ago, and still no word from Ellis. Father
Robert, don't spare me. You *have* had further indica-
tions, even if not confirmed. Has my lord Earl been
defeated?'

'It seems so, Aleyne.' The old man was cautious. 'Dirk
Grantry arrived yesterday from Oxford. It's being said
there that the Earl and his brother were both slain and
their bodies exhibited at St Paul's.'

'Dear God, then Ellis too may have perished.'

'You must not lose heart. The battle for the crown is
not over yet. Queen Margaret landed at Weymouth with
Prince Edward. Warwick's men, those who escaped the
field, would more than likely attempt to join her.'

Aleyne could take no comfort from that. If Warwick
was dead, she was sure Ellis would make every effort to
return to Risby, particularly if he had received her
message and knew he was needed.

'Aleyne, my child, I know how you grieve for your father, but something else is troubling you—apart from these fears for Ellis Dyer.'

She told him quietly. 'What have you heard concerning Sir Thomas, Father? Did my father speak to you of him?'

'Yes. He was, it is true, considering the match. He met him that once at the baptism but wished to know more. I understood he planned to dispatch Ellis to London to make enquiries, but, as it turned out, that proved impossible.'

'His sympathies are not known, then?'

'It appears that Sir Thomas Stoodley stands aside from Court bickering.'

'How can you call it that, Father Robert,' Aleyne rebuked him gently, 'when you yourself served in the Duke of York's train as chaplain both in France and Ireland?'

'I did, Aleyne, but I honour no man who presses his own advantages to the disruption of the realm.'

'But my father said poor King Harry was unskilled to rule.'

'Alas, we cannot deny that it seems so.'

'Then the Duke of York's son, King Edward, should be our King.'

'If God wills it so, Aleyne.' The old priest sighed. 'Until this is decided, no town or village in the land will be safe from plundering.'

'Risby too—particularly if I remain unwed. Oh, Father, how can I give myself to this man while I grieve for my father and live in dread of Ellis's loss?'

'I don't know how to advise you, child, but Lady Risby is right in her avowal that even should you place yourself in the King's hands you cannot be sure of bettering your position. Kings sell marriage rights and you could find yourself tied to some elderly lecher who'd abandon you to country life while he ruffles it at Court, neglecting the manor.'

Reluctantly Aleyne took her leave of the priest and returned to Risby. It seemed there was no help for it but a hasty marriage. She had no vocation for convent life and she owed something to the manor servants.

As she entered the courtyard she saw grooms rubbing down two mounts before leading them into the stables. For one heart-stopping moment she believed her prayers had been answered and Ellis had returned; then she realised that the animals doubtless belonged to Sir Thomas Stoodley, and went wearily to her chamber to prepare to receive him. Maud would expect her to make the best of her appearance. Mutinously Aleyne was glad that she must appear before him in mourning black.

CHAPTER TWO

JOAN, Maud's serving maid who had come with her from London, came to Aleyne's chamber to summon her to supper. She was a big-bosomed, handsome, though sullen, wench whom Aleyne heartily disliked and suspected of reporting on her behaviour to her mistress. Aleyne's nurse, old Hannah, had been retired from service last winter since her limbs had plagued her sorely with rheumatism. Aleyne missed her and rarely called on Joan's assistance. The girl sketched a hasty curtsy.

'My lady says I am to see that you don your best black velvet, mistress. We entertain Sir Thomas Stoodley, my lady's kinsman.'

'I'm well aware of it,' Aleyne found herself snapping at the girl. She had already changed her gown, knowing the hem to be mud-spattered, and turned to allow Joan to lace up and tie in the sleeves.

She dismissed the girl before descending, noting the gleam of avid curiosity in the wench's prominent dark eyes.

Their visitor had his back to her as she entered the hall. He was warming his hands at the fireplace, obviously in talk with Maud who had drawn her chair close to the blaze. He turned as she evidently warned him of Aleyne's approach.

Rising from her curtsy, Aleyne had a confused glimpse of a big fair man bearing down on her before he kissed her soundly in greeting. Angrily she pulled away from his grasp but he laughed and, seizing both her hands in his, stood back to appraise her as if she were prize flesh for the market, she thought furiously. Maud appeared to find no untoward forwardness in his behaviour.

'At last, Aleyne. Sir Thomas has been anxiously waiting to make your acquaintance.'

'Good evening, sir,' Aleyne said coldly, and pulled impatiently at her imprisoned wrists until he released them with a little flamboyant flourish.

'Praise the Virgin, my impatience is fully justified. My kinswoman has not over-stated your charms, lady. I'm honoured to greet you.'

Aleyne found it hard to restrain her contempt for his fulsome speech, nodded curtly and took the chair he himself drew back for her. She examined him covertly as he did a like service for her stepmother.

Maud had not flattered the man in her description. He *was* handsome. His hair was fair, almost red-gold, and fell on to his shoulders in a thick, wavy mane. He was big in every way, large-boned and brawny, and would probably run to fat in ten years or less. Like Lady Maud he had blue eyes, slightly bulbous, a large fleshy nose and full, sensuous lips. His doublet was of purple velvet trimmed with somewhat tawdry lace, but the chain he wore was genuine enough, as were the gems he wore on those large, unusually white hands. Aleyne averted her gaze from them. Her flesh had crawled when he'd touched her.

During the meal she found his bold stare disconcerting. His table manners were good, if somewhat showy. He helped both women to meat and took care not to dip too deep into the dishes, so as not to offend by marking the wine mazer with grease. His talk was largely to Maud of affairs concerning their relatives. He assured her of the safety of her father who'd joined her sister in Hertfordshire when possibility of attack threatened London. Courteously he sought to draw Aleyne into the conversation.

'Maud tells me one of your kinsmen followed Warwick. You must be concerned for him.'

Aleyne nodded. 'Father Robert tells me it is rumoured that Edward of York was successful in an engagement near St Albans. Certainly I shall be afraid for Ellis till we have definite word of his safety.'

Sir Thomas smiled, revealing large strong teeth. 'Oh, the news is true enough. The Earl took up his position on Hadley Green, just north of Barnet, with a Lancastrian force. Edward, with young Gloucester and Clarence, arrived in Barnet on the evening of the thirteenth and advanced even in the dark hours. I understand the battle was fought early in thick mist, and that young Gloucester distinguished himself in his first command. The lad can be little more than seventeen.'

'Surely the Earls of Warwick and Oxford were experienced commanders?' Aleyne commented, her voice trembling a little as she thought of Ellis's peril.

'There seems to have been more than a little confusion under such bad weather conditions. It's being said that Oxford's men beat back one wing of the Yorkists under Lord Hastings, but his returning men mistook the de Vere star for Edward's sun in splendour and attacked Warwick's centre, spreading chaos and panic. Oxford escaped, I understand, but Warwick and Montague were both killed.'

'Well, I hope this decides the issue once and for all,' Lady Maud declared. 'One cannot feel secure on one's own land for fear of attack and looting. Edward, for all his love of luxury, is a strong and able ruler and I, for my part, wish him well of the crown.'

Sir Thomas smiled at her over the rim of the wooden wine mazer. 'I'm afraid it's not over yet. There's still Queen Margaret to be reckoned with. Likely Oxford will have joined her by now, and she has Somerset and Wenlock in her train.'

'So she's landed at last.'

'At Weymouth, Father Robert said.' Aleyne pleated her napkin nervously, her fears only for Ellis.

'Aye, ill tidings for the lady to hear of Warwick's defeat,' Sir Thomas grinned. 'Like as not she'll wish to set sail again, but her commanders will urge her to give battle for the sake of her son, young Edward. If she moves north west towards Wales to seek Jasper Tudor's support we could see some action in this part of the world.'

'I pray the Virgin not,' Maud said, frowning, 'and Risby without a lord.'

The implication was obvious and Aleyne reddened. She sat with the pair for a while and then, making her excuses, was glad to retire, leaving them to talk more of family affairs.

She was up early next day and overseeing work in the dairy. Lady Maud was sharp with the girls if they chattered and she had no wish for the manor to appear ill-governed before Sir Thomas. She had slept badly, achingly worried about Ellis, and doubtful of her own decisions, knowing she would be pressed to accept Sir Thomas speedily. Certainly affairs in the realm were not easing and Lady Maud's fear for the welfare of Risby was real enough.

Hearing angry voices in the hall, Aleyne paused in the doorway before going immediately to table. Sir Thomas was seated there alone, already dressed for riding. Obviously he intended to make an inspection of the manor without loss of time.

Rob Tranton, their steward's son, was sprawled across the rushes near the high table, shielding his face with his hand as Sir Thomas cut at him viciously with his riding whip, which presumably he'd carried to table with him.

'I'll teach you to spill ale over me, incompetent want-wit!' he snarled. 'God's teeth, the stables and midden would provide more suitable employment for your clumsy fingers. Do I buy doublets at some expense to be so stained?'

Aleyne's voice cut coldly across his tirade.

'Rob, ask your father to come to hall, please, and send me one of the serving wenches with warmed water and a cloth to tend Sir Thomas's doublet.'

The boy scrambled awkwardly backwards, half rose and ducked away out of their presence. Aleyne was horrified to see that one cut had laid open his right cheek. Hectic spots stained her own as she advanced on their visitor.

'I am sorry the boy was clumsy,' she said, her tone tight with anger. 'I am sure we can rectify the damage. I'll see that Rob does not serve you again.'

Sir Thomas's snarl was transformed into a smile of greeting as he rose, his temper ebbing at sight of her.

'My apologies, Mistress Risby. I should not have let fly in your household but the lad riled me. I imagine discipline has become lax since your father ailed. It can soon be put right, I assure you, with a master's hand on the reins.'

'I'm sure it could,' Aleyne returned coldly, signalling to the frightened maid-servant who hovered in the doorway. 'Attend Sir Thomas and send ale and meat to my chamber. I'll breakfast up there this morning. I have sewing which requires my attention. Please excuse me, Sir Thomas. Give my steward, Dick Tranton, any orders you please. He will instantly put himself at your disposal. He's Rob's father.'

If he felt any sting in the tail of her last remark he gave no sign of it. Shaking with suppressed fury at his unmannerly attack on a member of her household, she stalked from the room.

Maud was descending the stair from the master chamber, where she still slept.

'I would like to speak to you privately, madam.' It was the first occasion that Aleyne had spoken to her stepmother with anything less than respect. For one moment the woman was startled, quickly recovered herself, and followed Aleyne to her chamber.

'Please close the door, madam. I would not wish any of the servants to overhear us.'

'Certainly.' Maud complied with Aleyne's request and, choosing to place herself deliberately in a position of command, walked unhurriedly to the one stool in the chamber and seated herself.

'Sir Thomas——' Aleyne fought back angry tears '—how dare the man presume? He has struck Rob with his riding whip!'

Maud's fair brows, which she had declined to shave in accordance with custom at Court, rose in an expression of mild surprise. 'Indeed?'

'What do you mean, madam, "Indeed."'? The man has no rights here and should be made to understand that—by you, since you are his kinswoman.'

'I am sorry it occurred. I imagine the boy deserved it. I have said to Sir Godfrey, often, that the boy belongs to the stables. He'll never do to serve at table. He's clumsy by nature.'

'That may well be, but my servants are not to be berated by a stranger and certainly not physically punished.'

'Sir Thomas is merely indicating how things must change once a master is in command of the household.'

'Then perhaps, madam, there should be no change at present,' Aleyne said frostily. 'I shall not join you at dinner since I do not know how to offer civil words to the man. I trust you will make the situation clear to him and,' as Maud rose, 'discover how long he intends to honour us with his presence.'

Bess waited on her in her chamber throughout the day. When Joan tapped, asking if her services were required, Aleyne tartly told her they were not. She sat for hours at a time, her embroidery neglected in her lap, chilled and miserable.

This would never do. However her stepmother pressed this match Aleyne would never accept Sir Thomas Stoodley as her lord. She could not bear the touch of those large white fingers, nor countenance the impudent stare of his bold blue eyes. The incident this morning had brought home to her her responsibility for the members of the household. Bess had brought up a charcoal brazier which she'd placed near the window, but it gave little warmth and at last Aleyne knew she must go down to the solar. Nothing could be gained by shunning their visitor. He must soon be made aware that his suit was not welcome.

'Mistress,' Bess said awkwardly, 'Rob says as how he must see you, not in the house—that is, not where he can be overheard.'

The girl was simple-witted but worked well. Her brown eyes were rounded now with anxiety lest the message should not be well received. Aleyne patted her hand gently.

'Reach out my cloak from the chest, Bess, and then go down and tell Rob to wait for me in the stables. Do not let Lady Risby or Sir Thomas's man see you go there.'

'No, mistress.'

'Go, then. Tell Rob I shall be a few moments only.'

She allowed the girl sufficient time, then donned the dark cloak and hood, thanking the Virgin that she wore no white veil to betray her presence in the gathering darkness. As she sped down the stair she heard the mutter of voices in the solar and reflected on the fact that her light kid slippers would become hopelessly muddied since she dared not clatter about down the stair or across the courtyard in patterns. Angrily she castigated herself for behaving in so secretive a manner in her own house, yet inwardly knew a desperate need to keep both Maud and their visitor from overhearing her talk with young Rob.

The boy drew her self-consciously but courteously into the stable.

'Thank you, mistress, for coming without question.'

'Rob, are you badly hurt? I regret——'

'That's not important, mistress. My hurts soon heal. I had to tell you. Father sent me to Wellesbourne to order malmsey. There were thirty or more of Sir Thomas's men in the village and more sent for. Did you know?'

She peered at his youthful face distractedly in the gloom.

'But that is ridiculous. He's here on a simple visit. Are you saying he's planning to join either side in the conflict or——?'

The information registered even as she spoke.

'You are sure?' she asked briskly.

'Yes, mistress; they wear his livery—corbets sable on a shield vert.'

'Dear God.'

Rob moved clumsily away, concerned lest he should witness her despair, yet uncertain how to avoid it.

'They will force me to this match. Sweet Virgin, to whom can I turn?'

'It's a pity as how Master Ellis ain't here.'

'Ellis; yes.' Chill struck through her shoulder-blades as she thought how vulnerable he would be to Sir Thomas's power, even were he safe and free to come to her assistance; then it appeared to her that her prayer had been answered, for immediately a picture of Ellis's mother, serene and gentle, flashed into her mind.

'Mistress Dyer—I must go to her. She will advise me. Rob, I must go to Gloucester.'

'They'd not let you go, mistress,' he said gruffly.

'Then I must not ask them.'

'But you need an escort, Mistress Aleyne. You cannot ride for Gloucester alone. It's not safe nor seemly.'

'True, Rob; as you say, unseemly for Mistress Aleyne Risby to ride alone, but not for a maid on her mistress's errand.'

'I'd not trust Joan, mistress, and Bess hasn't the wit to find her way or deliver your message safe,' Rob said bluntly.

'I know it, Rob: I must go myself, but in Joan's clothes. It will serve that jade right if I borrow them without her permission. I've missed one or two things of late and allowed them to pass without comment.'

'It's still not safe for you alone,' he insisted, and swallowed, 'not with bands of soldiers roving the countryside. You'd be right game for them, excuse my saying so, but——'

'I know, Rob,' she said quietly, 'but it seems I'm right game for Sir Thomas too, and sure to fall prey without so much as a chase if I remain here. I would rather chance my fortune in open ground than be cornered so easily.'

'Then, if go you must, take me with you.'

'Rob, your father—there could be dangers.'

He flushed in the faint light from the doorway. 'I know I'm not trained to arms, but as escort I'll afford you some protection from insult and in the wrestling ring I can hold my own. Size ain't everything, Mistress Aleyne.'

'No more it is. Dare we wait till morning, Rob?'

'I think not, mistress. You let Sir Thomas see how the land lay this morning. He'll bring up reinforcements soon.'

'I shall be ready to leave in an hour, even less.'

'Aye, mistress. I'll saddle up two hacks for us, not bloodstock—too obvious—but we'll need some speed on the journey.'

She nodded. 'If you can manage to see your father privately get some food for the journey. Take care to let no one else hear you, not even Bess.'

'I know that, mistress. If Joan gets to hear of your plan you'd not get so far as the gate. I think, even so, it were best if you meet me outside the courtyard——'

'In the churchyard by the lychgate,' she said, nodding.

'That's a fair step for you alone in the dark.'

She smiled grimly. 'It's a fair step we're taking, Rob. Pointless to be afraid of the first move in the game; I'll manage.'

She hurried from him up to her chamber and had hardly taken off her cloak before Joan was tapping again at her door.

'Will you be down to supper, mistress?' The girl's eyes tried to penetrate beyond the half-opened door.

'Certainly, but I've still a headache. Go to Lady Risby and ask her for some of her herbal infusion. If I take some before supper it should ease the pain. I must try to join them since Sir Thomas is here.'

She watched the girl scurry about her errand and quickly took the opportunity to root in her chest for a change of linen and one or two pieces of jewellery. She had three gold nobles which should last her throughout the journey and she tied these securely in a cloth which she would wear under her clothing; the silver could be displayed in her purse secured from her girdle. Sure now that Joan would be occupied about her errand, she slipped from her room and into the maid's. In a rough wooden box near the truckle bed Aleyne found a green wool kirtle and blouse. She stripped off her own gown and threw it on to the bed. Joan could take it as payment for her mistress's acquisition of her property, though, as the girl had a liking for bright plumage, she'd take the exchange amiss.

There was no time to look at herself in her polished mirror. Glancing down at the kirtle, she felt suddenly awkward, bereft of her mourning, but she knew Sir Godfrey would understand her need. Joan's brown frieze cloak with its hood completed the exchange, and she stayed only to catch up sturdy walking shoes and her bundle, then tiptoed, still in her slippers, down the stair.

The solar door was ajar and she heard the mutter of voices. As Aleyne slipped from the back door into the darkened courtyard, Joan emerged from the still room and stopped to re-lock the door. Aleyne drew back behind the rain barrel while the maid passed her and entered the house again. With her heart in her mouth Aleyne sped to the stable, where she changed her shoes, then sallied out again, her cloak held tightly round her, skirts held high.

It was the first time she'd crossed the manor land in darkness to go to the church, and the going was rough. She'd dared not take a lantern and several times stumbled. Animal noises sounded strange and excessively loud in the undergrowth, and she gave a startled cry as she came up to the churchyard wall as an owl hooted derisively only feet from her and took off in flight. Crossing the graveyard was the worst bit and she gave a gasp of relief at the sight of the boy waiting near the lychgate holding the reins of two sturdy mounts.

'Rob,' she panted, 'thank the Virgin. I feared you might have been stopped.'

'No, mistress, I took every care.' He cupped his hands for her to mount. 'Will you head for an inn or the convent at——?'

'No. No delays. We ride through the night.'

Once mounted and with Rob for company she felt only a sense of great relief at having escaped from the manor. Whatever faced her on this journey could not be worse than finding herself a prisoner on her own land, and she knew with the clarity of fear that, had she stayed till the morning, she would have wakened to find Sir Thomas's men occupying Risby.

CHAPTER THREE

GUY JARVIS noted with some trepidation that his master's heavy dark brows were drawn together in a scowl. He swallowed a sigh as he followed Sir Dominick Allard meekly into The Green Man in Broadway. It had been bad enough that they'd been delayed at Mickleton when one of the carts had broken down, but now Sir Dominick's destrier had cast a shoe.

'God's wounds,' Sir Dominick raged, 'yet more delay! Has Scroggins managed to find a smith?'

'Yes, sir, but he reports the work will take some time. The man says the stallion should rest up tonight. He'd gone lame before the groom noticed how bad it was.'

'Confounded idiot.' Sir Dominick's dark eyes snapped with impatience. 'There's little point in our pressing on till the morning. But we must be ready to proceed at first light. I'll make to join His Grace's force near Gloucester. Are we still short of horses?'

'Scroggins says we should try to acquire at least two more if possible.'

'Send young Weaver round the town to see if he can beg, borrow or steal mounts. Let him take no excuses from the peasants. Bespeak me a private chamber.'

Guy nodded as Sir Dominick sank down on the window bench, hurling his steel gauntlets on to the oaken table with a clatter. The knight thrust back his mailed coif, revealing thick brown hair. His strong square-cut face, with its dominating out-thrust chin, was still set in a mask of irritation as he gazed round the tap-room.

The place looked clean enough, the furniture rough-hewn but well polished, the floor freshly sanded. Guy stuttered a quick apology as he found his master's angry eyes fixed on him, still hesitating, and shot off to do his bidding. There was no sign of the innkeeper, nor yet any wench, and Sir Dominick was not a man to be kept waiting.

Guy had been in Sir Dominick's service for three years now, the last spent in King Edward's train, forced into exile with the King after Lord Montecute's defection from the Yorkist cause at Doncaster, then during the long, miserable, poverty-stricken months waiting on the Duke of Burgundy's decision to back his brother-in-law, and more recently, this spring, in the triumphant return to England which had culminated in victory at Barnet. Sir Dominick had fought valiantly by the King's brother, young Gloucester, and would be at his side yet, in the King's desperate bid to prevent Queen Margaret joining with her Welsh supporters across the Avon, had not Edward given him special duties in Coventry, to raise more men from the Midlands to swell the royal army on the march from London in pursuit of the Lancastrians. They'd managed a muster of a substantial company, but mounts and carts were in short supply and Sir Dominick was fretting at the need to rejoin the King before the two armies met in conflict.

The innkeeper clattered down the stair and Guy confronted him.

'Your best chamber for my master,' he demanded, 'the finest wine you have, and supper—quickly, man!'

The innkeeper seemed not best pleased to be ordered by some youthful sprig in armour, his fair hair damp with sweat, and still not old enough to require the use of a razor each day.

He was a short man, but stocky, his greasy hair already thinning, though Guy doubted if he was yet forty. His eyes were small, set close together, and his mouth primmed into petulance.

'Wine you may have, young master, and supper, well cooked as can be got anywhere in these parts, but I've but one chamber and that's already taken. You and your master could bed down in the tap-room or in the common-room and welcome.' He broke off and stared through the open door at the rag-tail company now trooping noisily into his courtyard. 'I take it that lot's in your master's charge.'

'Aye, fellow, and they'll bed down in the stables and in the yard.'

The innkeeper sniffed audibly. 'It's to be hoped they'll keep their thieving hands off my hens and——' He did not follow up with the thought that he wasn't keen on his women being accosted either. He cared little for the virtue of his wenches, but far more about the fact that in his experience soldiers meant trouble—they fought among themselves over wenches, which in itself meant damage to his property, and they encouraged the girls to leave service and run off with them, particularly men-at-arms soon to be in battle.

Guy was about to argue, when Sir Dominick strode to the stair foot. One hand twisted the innkeeper's greasy jerkin into a tight knot as he half lifted the man off his feet.

'I do not think you heard my squire well. He said I would need your private chamber. Get up the stairs and see to it that the sheets are changed and fresh rushes strewn.'

The innkeeper tried to bluster and Guy blenched. Sir Dominick Allard was not known as the Wolf merely because of his personal heraldic device. His big body, his arrogant features crowned with a shock of dark hair, unfashionably cropped to wear comfortably beneath mailed coif and helm, his gruff voice, often raised in growls of fury, and his impatience, of poor service and mismanagement of camp-organisation, were character- istics not unlike those of that powerful animal. He was not to be gainsaid. And it was not only men and women who attempted to thwart him who suffered; those who happened to be near could also receive the full force of his wrath.

'Sir, my lord—I've tried to explain. The chamber is taken——'

'Then get upstairs and house whoever it is in the common chamber or barn—I care not.'

'No, but my lord——'

'Sir Dominick Allard, man! I'm simple knight, no lord, but in the King's service and on His Grace's business. I've been in the saddle for hours, must be up at first light, and need to sleep well tonight. Will you deny me?' The knot twisted tighter, the dark brows drew even closer over the hawk-like nose, and the innkeeper's feet rose even higher from the ground.

The sneer with which he'd outfaced the squire had been wiped from his face and he was sweating profusely.

'Sir—er—Sir Dominick, I'm sorry. I'll ask the young lady if she will——'

'Young lady?' Sir Dominick's grip on the man's jerkin slackened momentarily. 'Young lady, is it? Escorted?'

'Er—no, sir. When I say lady I—er—a respectable female, by the look of her, in service, travelling with a groom.'

Sir Dominick shouted with laughter. 'Respectable female, travelling with a groom? In these uncertain times? Man, can you be so easily fooled? Get the baggage out of my chamber.'

'Well, sir...' the innkeeper, once released from Sir Dominick's hold and finding the heavy scowl relaxed into a grin of pure humour, stepped back hurriedly from his tormentor's reach. '...the wench is well-spoken. I doubt if she's——'

'No, now I think of it, *don't* get her to vacate the chamber. Up, man, and invite her to sup with me. I'm sure we can accommodate ourselves handsomely for this evening and for the night.'

The innkeeper swallowed nervously. The wench was not dressed like gentry, yet he had an uncomfortable feeling he would not be well received on such an errand as the knight proposed.

Sir Dominick returned again to the tap-room. A pot-boy came running as he pounded with his dagger hilt on the table-top. Guy was despatched to order his sergeant-at-arms to bed down the men for the night.

Aleyne faced the red-faced innkeeper, anger sparking in her grey eyes.

'Do you dare insult me with such a message? Am I some wanton camp-follower to be so plagued? My mistress sent me on this journey, respectably escorted. Call my groom and get off about your own affairs. The chamber is taken. See that you make it very clear to the knight, if knight he is. His vows should preclude him from such discourteous behaviour.'

The innkeeper moved his considerable weight awkwardly from one foot to the other.

'He is not a gentleman to be trifled with. Mistress, I would suggest compliance.'

Her eyes again flashed fury. 'Compliance? You would urge me to submit to this man? I had mistaken your inn, obviously. Surely it is a haunt of low-born——'

'No more it is, mistress,' the man retorted forcefully. 'I am as anxious as you to have the knight and his rag-tail company gone from here with as little damage as possible. In these hard times I'll be fortunate if he leaves me with a whole building, let alone pays his reckoning.'

Aleyne bit her lip uncertainly as she read genuine alarm in the man's eyes.

'Yes, I understand. For your sake I will vacate the chamber. Perhaps I could sleep in the stable.'

'God's nails, mistress—never that. You'd be better off with the master than the men.'

Aleyne's face paled. She had known the dangers of the road well enough, but, since leaving Risby, had encountered no great problems as yet.

Her nights at Ettingham and Mickleton had been abominable, since no private chambers had been available. At Mickleton her bed-mates had been a stout woman, who stank, and her daughter, who hadn't seemed able to lie still for two minutes together. On both occasions Aleyne had slept badly and woken, frantically scratching from the attentions of the numerous fleas within the bedding. Rob had fared little better, the stables being no more salubrious, though quieter.

This chamber at the Green Man promised a better night's rest. The mattress was hard but the sheets looked clean, and she was so exhausted she desperately needed this respite.

The weather had improved since they'd left Risby, but the dust choked her nostrils, and long hours in the saddle left her thighs and buttocks aching and sore. She was in no mood to counter amorous dalliance with some no-account soldier of fortune, for all the innkeeper reported the man to be in the King's service. She shook her head despairingly.

'Then it seems we must leave your inn. Is Rob out in the stable? Could you provide us with some food, cold bacon, bread and cheese? If our horses have been fed and watered we should be able to press on. I will pay you well, naturally.'

'Aye, mistress.' The innkeeper looked huntedly over his shoulder. 'I think it best if you go. I'll get that man of yours to move your horses before those thieving devils see them.' He shrugged meaningfully. 'In these days mounts be in short supply. I'll serve you some supper up here. *He* should be safe enough in the tap-room for some while yet——' a finger was stabbed disparagingly towards the stair foot '—until he's drunk enough to make him more mellow, at least.'

The man looked doubtfully at Aleyne. She puzzled him. Her dress was of linsey woolsey, suitable for a serving maid, yet gaudily trimmed. The woman's manner went ill with her garments. He could not be sure, but she appeared gentler bred than any servant, yet to be riding abroad with but a boy to escort her... He shook his head as he moved heavily down the stair, his brow furrowed.

Aleyne fretted while she waited for Rob to make his appearance. She looked anxiously out of the window, remaining well back out of view as she saw the men-at-arms settling in below in the inn courtyard. The inn-keeper's worst forebodings seemed about to be realised as she heard the laughing shouts and triumphant whoops of the looters. The stable door was unceremoniously torn down to provide wood for the cooking fire. Aleyne wondered, desperately, if the innkeeper had managed to warn Rob in time that their horses could be comman-deered and that they had been removed to safety. If found in the stable they would be confiscated as simply as the inn's hens and doors.

She listened carefully at her door but could hear nothing from below. It appeared the innkeeper was correct and that wine had mellowed the demands of his customer. She longed to leave the chamber immediately, but dared not go without Rob. In all events, the yard was still crammed with the men-at-arms and she dreaded the ordeal of attempting to leave the inn while they were awake and moving about.

About an hour later the innkeeper returned with a tray laden with hot food, lentil pottage, a roast and vegetables.

He grinned mirthlessly. 'I delivered your message, mistress, in as conciliatory fashion as I dared. Fortu-nately for both of us his sergeant had just reported with information about horses, and the knight seemed preoc-cupied. He waved his hand in a lordly fashion and told me the room and its occupant could wait.'

'But for how long? What of my man, Rob?'

'Off hiding the horses, mistress. He'll be gone some time. I told him to get clear of the town and gave instructions about a little copse about two and a half miles away. The knight's men are scouring the town for extra mounts and supplies.'

Aleyne smiled worriedly and thanked the man. His appearance had not been prepossessing. She had not expected him to be so sympathetic of her plight or so helpful.

As if he read her thoughts he said, 'We've a lass of our own, recently wed.' Peering from the window, he sighed to see the depredations of the men-at-arms. 'I'm right glad she's well away from here at present. If the King's army meets with the Queen's near Gloucester, and talk hereabouts suggests it, there'll be foraging parties and rabbles of fleeing men for weeks to come. You'd best stay here; don't let any of those men see you. The moment your groom sneaks back in I'll try and smuggle you both safe away. The men'll settle soon for the night. Many of them have brought in women from the town, aye, and some of my wenches have joined them.'

Aleyne felt little appetite for the food, though its quality was good and plentiful. She could not dismiss the fear that the knight below would soon come to demand the use of his chamber. But she forced herself to eat a little and drank some ale. Her mouth was dry with fear.

What if Rob were accosted and the horses stolen, or, worse, he were knocked on the head? She shied from the thought of going in search of him, and the idea of pressing on totally without protection terrified her. The noises from below showed her just what she might expect if she were to fall into the hands of men like those of the company who had invaded the inn.

She shivered at the thought of the attentions of the knight in the tap-room. If he allowed his men such licence, what mercy could she expect from him?

At last the sounds from the courtyard began to diminish. She looked cautiously from the window. The cooking fire had been dampened down and men sat or lay in groups about it. A raucous shout of laughter reached her, female. Most of the town women appeared willing enough, she thought bitterly.

But where could Rob be after all this time? They must go, and quickly, sleep in the copse near their horses, under some hedge. This inn was now no refuge. Hastily she began to bundle together her possessions, donned her cloak, her ear cocked to any threatening sound from below-stairs.

Steps came up the stair and she froze, petrified.

Then Rob's voice, in a whisper. 'Let me in, Mistress Aleyne. It's Rob.'

She drew the bolt with shaking hands and he hurried into the chamber and crossed to the window.

'They're settling all right. Now's the time to get you clear of all this, mistress.'

'What have you done with the horses?'

'They're safe enough for the moment, but the good Lord knows whether it's safe to venture with them on the open highway till this company's gone on ahead. They're headed for Gloucester to join the King's force.'

'Then they're Yorkists?'

'Aye, mistress.' He moved back to her and she saw his youthful face strained with concern. 'Are you ready?'

She nodded, breathless with alarm.

He took her bundle and went to open the door for her. He was about to lift the latch when a loud guffaw sounded from below as if the tap-room door had opened, and Aleyne put a detaining hand on Rob's arm.

'When you came up did you happen to see the man in the tap-room?' Her mouth was very close to his ear.

He shook his head and whispered back, 'The door was closed.'

'Let us wait a moment.'

'Mistress, we shouldn't delay...'

But she was looking by him towards the door and the stairway. The innkeeper's voice reached them, obsequient.

'I'm glad we were able to satisfy you with our meagre fare. If you'll wait a moment, sir, I'll find a wench to light you to your chamber. Your men are comfortably bedded down.' He was obviously gabbling now as he strove to delay the knight long enough to allow Aleyne and Rob to escape.

'Nonsense, man, it's light enough yet. Send the wench up later with more of your fine brandy wine. That should warm up the room's occupant. I've never known it to fail yet.' There came a second bellow of laughter and Aleyne felt Rob's young body tremble beside her.

'I'll go down, mistress, and ram the man's words down his evil throat——'

'And get spitted on his sword-point for your pains. No, you will not.'

But his answering whisper was breathy with apprehensive fury and still defiant.

'No, I tell you!' she snapped again. 'How would I fare on the road without you? Stand back from the door; *I'll* manage the man.'

'Mistress, you mustn't.'

His shocked reply was broken off as booted feet ascended the stair somewhat unsteadily, and the door was thrown back on its hinges. Aleyne and Rob were forced to give ground.

Sir Dominick Allard halted on the threshold, smiling a little fatuously. He had eaten well and drunk excessively. He was in a rare good humour and his wine-induced pleasure was heightened by the sudden vision of a young woman peering from behind the protective form of a youth who might have been her brother or her leman. In the golden evening light he saw that she was slim, held herself like a queen, was comely enough, though no voluptuous beauty, and, what was more to the point, clean.

He hooked his thumbs in his sword-belt and grinned down at her.

'Greetings, mistress. I regret I've kept you waiting but I'll make up for it by the munificence of your reward.

You can be assured of that.' His smile hardened as he turned to Rob, who was glaring at him truculently. 'Get off about your business, fellow. Your woman'll come to no harm.'

Rob choked with fury. 'You—you dare insult my mistress——'

'Your mistress?' Sir Dominick's smile broadened. 'I see, I have to deal with a jealous lover.' He shrugged. 'Well, I see that puts up the price. Lucky for you I don't send you off with the flat of my blade about your buttocks for your impertinence. Get out of my sight.'

Aleyne said frostily, 'You mistake the matter, sir. I am no bawd, nor yet a camp-follower. I'm perfectly prepared to vacate this chamber if that is your desire, but be pleased to allow us to pass.'

Head high, she shouldered Rob aside and made for the door again, fully expecting the knight to stand aside, surprised by her anger if for no other reason than her clear rejection of him.

He did nothing of the sort. The smile faded and a sullen line set the firm lips. The thick brows met together in a menacing warning Guy Jarvis would have instantly recognised.

'You're in a hurry, wench,' he said in a voice deceptively mild. 'Where would a respectable wench like you expect to spend the night—under some bush with her leman?' The tone held a distinct sneer.

Aleyne put up a detaining hand before Rob could launch himself bodily at the armed knight. 'That is none of your concern, sir, since you choose to order us from the chamber we bespoke well before your arrival. We fully understand we must abide by the wishes of the gentry.' There was a cutting edge to her retort and Sir Dominick scowled again, by now the pleasant effect of the wine fumes beginning to distil in frustration. Would he allow some chit of a serving wench who was no better than she ought to be, away from her own manor and its lord, to put him out of countenance?

He advanced and, taking her by both shoulders, shook her hard.

Rob let out a yell of fury and fell on him, but the boy's puny blows made no impression on the knight's sturdy body. He released his hold on Aleyne so that she stumbled backwards, and caught Rob in the same hold he'd bestowed on the landlord, one hand gripping his jerkin and lifting him bodily off the ground so that his legs dangled ignominiously. Rob squirmed with wounded dignity, shouting imprecations.

Aleyne recovered herself and started up from her sprawled position on the floor.

'Would you hurt an unarmed boy? Let him go. He means no insult.'

As if he were dealing with a recalcitrant child, Sir Dominick lowered the infuriated boy to the floor and cuffed him lightly twice about the face, blows giving no real pain, the more insulting because of the deliberate leniency. Rob caught back a sob of impotence and was about to launch himself again at his tormentor, when Aleyne ordered him sharply, 'Go below stairs, Rob. Wait for me. I'll not be long.' She added gently after a pause, 'Please.'

Rob stared at her imploringly, then walked obediently from the room. Aleyne heard his feet stumbling down the stair.

Her heart was beating so fast she feared the knight would hear it, and she needed, desperately, for him to believe she had the courage to refuse his determined demands.

'Well, sir,' she said quietly, 'the boy is no true challenge. You have a helpless woman to deal with now. That should prove no danger to you.'

If she had thought to anger him, throw him off balance by her studied contempt, she failed. He threw back his head and laughed loudly again.

'The innkeeper was right. You are well-spoken. Some lord kept you as his leman, did he, cast you out for your insolence? A pity. Now I admire spunk in a woman.'

She bit down hard on her nether lip. She must not cry or plead. Nothing would be more likely to incense this man.

He came towards her but she remained unflinchingly still. He put out his hand and pushed back her linen cap.

'A nut-brown maid, like the one in the ballad. More and more to my liking. I've seen too many dark, buxom Burgundian girls lately.'

She felt herself trembling as he loosened the waves of her brown hair, fingering it gently, then he lightly ran one finger down the fine bones of her cheek.

'No painted doxy, but pleasing, very pleasing.' His words were soft now and his breath reached her, not unpleasantly, but warmly wine-scented, fanning her face.

'Please let me go, sir. I am not willing.' If her lips were trembling in her terrified effort to hold back her tears, it did not reveal itself in the steadiness of her voice.

He ignored her and bent to kiss her.

No man had kissed her so, full on her lips. Her father had done so gently, on her forehead, and Ellis, in the accustomed formal kiss of greeting. This man's kiss, without being openly brutal, was demanding, inexorably forcing her lips apart. Horrified, Aleyne found herself almost responding. He was holding her very close and she felt the hard cold metal of his armour through the stuff of her gown. She leaned back her head with a little sob as he reached out to the lacing of her bodice. Though he did not imprison her hands she felt unable to prevent him. He had been riding hard and still smelt of the stable and the sharp scents of metal-oil and sweat, but there was no rancid stink and she judged he habitually kept his body clean. Her father had smelt so when returning from a hunting expedition or from a journey.

She made a little moan of protest and, as he bent close, he saw tears furrowing her cheeks. He murmured a soft soldier's oath and, placing both hands on her shoulders again, held her from him, eyes narrowing thoughtfully as he gazed down directly into her fearful little countenance.

'You really are not anxious for my attentions, are you?' His tone was dry, not devoid of humour. 'My pardon, mistress. I've taken too much wine, it seems. I'd not wish to press any maid against her will.' He checked the passage of the slow tear down her cheek with his finger. 'Hush, now, there's no call to distress yourself further. I'll call the boy back. Is he your brother?'

She shook her head and he raised one brow significantly. 'No, no,' she choked, anxious he should not further mistake the situation. 'Rob is a fellow servant. He is escorting me to—on an errand for my mistress.'

The knight's lips thinned in a meaning smile. 'I understand, but this is no time for travelling the country. Best to turn back now, my girl. Don't you know armies are on the march?'

She nodded tremulously.

He moved to the door. 'You stay here; bolt up securely. I'll sleep in the tap-room.'

'There is no need. We could leave.'

He grinned, transferring the severe cast of his features to one of boyish amusement.

'As you so rightly reminded me, you bespoke this chamber well before I arrived here. My knightly vows forbid such discourtesy.' He made her a mock bow. 'Sleep well, little nut-brown maid. Shut the door on me before I am tempted again.'

She obeyed him with shaking fingers as he withdrew on to the landing. Then she leaned with her back to the door's oaken stoutness and let her tears have full rein.

He called as he descended, 'None of my men will disturb you. I'll see to that, and,' he chuckled, 'I'll ensure that that fool of a boy comes to no harm.'

She heard him roar a command to the landlord as she sank down on the hard little bed and thrust her fist tight against her lips to stop the weeping.

She was not sure what distressed her so now. He had vowed he would not disturb her again and she believed him. She even trusted that he would see that Rob came to no harm from his men, yet nothing since the death of her father had dismayed her so terribly, not even her fear of Sir Thomas Stoodley's intentions.

This knight was no nobleman. His shabby armour and accoutrements told her that, yet the landlord had said he was on the King's business, the Yorkist King's. Possibly he owned some small manor but needed to recoup his fortunes by serving one of the antagonists in this war. A mercenary? No, he was not quite so low, but of little more account. He was not handsome, a big, domineering dark bear of a man who had left her breathless and shaken.

The rose light from the window was fading now as the sun went down. In the morning she and Rob must press on to Gloucester. Uneasily she wondered if Mistress Dyer would approve of her conduct in flying in the face of such danger, and she also knew she would not tell Ellis's mother about this encounter. All seemed quiet below, except for the odd suppressed chuckle and the movement of booted feet as if the knight had posted a guard to keep necessary watch on his equipment and horses. She had the privacy she had longed for, yet sleep evaded her for some hours until, in the dawn, she managed to fall into an exhausted doze.

CHAPTER FOUR

ALEYNE started awake next morning at Rob's urgent call. Her heart thumped wildly as he beat on the door.

'Mistress, we should be moving soon. The men are already on the move.'

She scrambled out of the bed and dressed hastily. How could she have slept so late and over the noise of departure? For it came to her clearly enough now: the cheery whistles and shouts of men, rattle of iron cartwheels and the yelled commands of the sergeant-at-arms. Her cheeks burned at the thought of their commander. He might look for her, subject her to further insult, de-

spite his promises of last night. She thrust open the
casement after shouting a hasty word of reassurance to
Rob and hearing him rush down the stair. There was no
sign of the knight in the courtyard. He would be break-
fasting in the tap-room, doubtless. She must not go down
until everyone had left, yet she would have liked to see
him go, assure herself that she and Rob would be safe
from any depredations of the company.

The landlord called to her from the door and she hastened to unlatch it and allow him to enter with her
breakfast tray.

'God rot those devils. I can't get a word of sense let
alone any work out of my wenches,' he grumbled. 'It'll
take all my powers of persuasion to prevent them following in the baggage train. The saints know what they
see in these fellows, lecherous drunkards and thieves for
the most part. Did you sleep safe and secure, mistress?'

'Thank you, yes.' Aleyne avoided his curious gaze.
She was aware that he must have heard much of what
had passed last night between her and the knight. The
man had been kind to her, but now she felt embarrassed
in his presence.

Rob came up and she insisted he breakfast with her.
He sat down awkwardly, but she ignored his unease—
her ears were pricked to hear the knight's voice as he
took his departure.

The tramping of feet outside had ceased and Aleyne
drew a breath of relief. They must be safe to leave now.
She turned to instruct Rob to pay their tally while she
collected her bundle of possessions, and was startled to
hear the commanding brusque tones of her last night's
visitor. She turned, mouth open, purse in her hand, to
find him, armed, coifed and ready to ride, standing in
the doorway.

'I come to bid you godspeed, mistress.' His dark eyes
flashed to Rob, seated as an equal at her table, and his
brows drew together in that daunting scowl. 'I trust you
will take my advice and turn for home. Both before and
after a battle men-at-arms can be dangerous.'

She flushed, finding herself too dry-mouthed with nervousness to reply immediately.

Now that she saw him in full daylight she realised her previous assessment of his standing was not totally correct. His squire had polished his armour, and he wore his padded gambeson depicting his coat of arms—a black wolf, rampant, on a field of silver. It was unlikely he was noble-born, since he was not attended by lesser knights, but he made an impressive figure as the early sun glinted on his polished gorget and greaves. A knight bachelor probably in the household of the King himself or more likely one of his royal brothers, George of Clarence or Richard of Gloucester. Quickly she bobbed her head to acknowledge his rank.

'Thank you, sir. We—are—considering——'

'Don't consider. Do it. You,' he barked at Rob, 'see your companion gets home safely.'

Rob nodded.

The knight's eyes roved imperiously over Aleyne, taking in her heightened colour and obvious nervousness in his presence. The moment seemed lengthened unnaturally while he stared at her, his brows still drawn close in what she was beginning to detect as a frown of concentration rather than anger, then he turned and descended the stair again.

She and Rob were on the road again within the hour. To her overwhelming relief they recovered their horses safely from the copse where Rob had tethered them, and he helped her into the saddle.

'Mistress,' he said worriedly, 'perhaps we should heed the Wolf's advice and turn for home.'

'Should we fare better in Sir Thomas Stoodley's hands than in those of marauding soldiery?' she snapped. 'I doubt it. We'll press on and hope battle will be joined in any place other than Gloucester. Did I hear you call him the Wolf?'

'His men call him that, both from his fierceness in battle and——'

'His personal device. Yes, I noted it,' she said shortly. 'At least he did us no harm, unusual in the behaviour of so predatory an animal.'

She waved Rob to mount up and he made no more argument.

They were within three miles of Tewkesbury when disaster struck. It was mid-morning and the road seemed deserted, most field-workers at their labours, when they passed a half-ruined cottage. It was some distance from any other dwellings and Rob reined in, pointing with his whip.

'Should we rest there and eat, mistress, or press on into the town? The landlord provided a meal of bread and cheese.'

Aleyne glanced back at the gaunt shell of the building doubtfully. It looked as if it had been gutted by fire and was somehow forbidding.

'No, let's get on while we can.'

Rob nodded, content, and they trotted on. The mounts could not be forced to any considerable speed but they were comparatively fresh at the moment and it would be sense to rest them later while they ate.

Intent on the road before her, Aleyne did not at first comprehend the sudden whoops and yells behind her. When she did understand their peril it was too late and anyway impossible to do anything about it. There was a thunder of hoofs and she heard Rob give a hoarse cry, then her own bridle rein was seized and she was kicking and fighting to prevent herself being yanked out of the saddle. Her mount reared and came to a bone-breaking, jerking halt, and the man who rode alongside roared with amusement.

'Come, come, my beauty, you'll not be needing so poor a mount. Whoa, whoa, there, give place to Black Dick.'

She was lifted from the saddle on to his horse before him and skilfully he dealt with her own plunging, terrified animal. Her captor wore leather jack and salet, smelt of ale and leather and horse-sweat. She pummelled at his chest with furious fists, the breath taken too hard out of her body to allow her to scream at him. It was all so terrifyingly sudden. She'd had no time to think. While his attention was given momentarily to dealing with the two horses she made a sudden leap from the still-galloping horse, landed hard, rolled over and over and, miraculously, still managed to get to her feet and run.

She was ridden down by a second man, who whooped again loudly as he swept her up and carted her unceremoniously back to his companion, who, swearing by all the saints in the calendar, had brought both horses to a standstill and was inspecting the mare for damage to its legs.

Aleyne found herself dumped down on to her feet. Black Dick seized her and held her tight against him, her wrists caught in a bruising hold.

'Not so fast away, my lass. Why the hurry? Haven't taken such a fancy to Black Dick? Well, there's a pity, then. Many have done in my time, eh, Huw?' He chuckled, appealing to his companion for confirmation of his manly charms.

His accents were unusual. She wondered if he was Welsh. The other confirmed her supposition by growling his answer in a tongue strange to her.

'Let me go,' she demanded, 'let me go at once.'

Black Dick bent his head to leer into her face. 'Come, my charmer, are you saving yourself for the officers, is it?'

Panting, she attempted once more to free herself from his grip. Then, as she half turned, she gave a great cry of horror. Rob lay sprawled in the roadside, his body twisted, and even from that distance she saw a trickle of blood running down his face from a wound on the right temple.

'You've killed him!'

'No, no, he'll have a bad head, my lass. You'll see, he'll mend.'

She struggled helplessly to go to him, but was prevented, and Black Dick's tightening grip on her wrists caused her to gasp sharply in pain, though now she was concerned only for Rob.

'You'll understand, my lass; it's your horses we need—for the army. In short supply they are, so we're foraging.'

These men must be scouts for Jasper Tudor, hoping to join the Queen's force now approaching the Severn.

'Then take them and leave us,' she said shortly.

'And you'll not press us for payment?' he chortled. 'It's generous you are. But it's payment in kind I want of you.'

Huw put in gruffly, this time in English, 'Dick, do as she says, man. Let's take the horses and be off away.' He held up the purse she'd given to Rob to keep for her and jingled its contents jubilantly. 'Man, there's yellow gold here and jewel trinkets. No need we have to tell the captain.' His shrewd glance passed over Aleyne's tense form, and one hand slid to the dagger at his belt. 'Let you not be playing the fool, man. It's best she's not left alive to tell the tale.'

'Destroy such a flower? 'Tis a barbarian you are, Huw Davies, truly.' Dick grinned wolfishly. 'But there, you may well be right, man, but let us sample her charms first.' He winked meaningly towards the ruined cottage. 'Who knows if either of us will be alive tomorrow to know such delights again?'

Aleyne went icy cold and ceased her futile struggling. These men, she knew, were the scum of the armies. They lived precariously from one encounter to another, fighting and risking all for pillage and booty and the savage joys of rapine. If they left her alive after they'd used her she would be fortunate, and, since they'd robbed her and did not wish their captain to know of it, she doubted if they would now allow either her or Rob to survive.

The other man, Huw, muttered again in his own tongue, presumably a comment on his friend's folly, but, as Black Dick lifted her into his arms, he followed them into the ruins.

Aleyne found her voice then, and screamed with all the power of her lungs. Her captor cursed and put a hand over her mouth as he flung her to the ground under the shelter of the crumbling wall. She bit at it savagely and it was his turn to scream in agony. Viciously he caught her a buffet to the side of the head so that her senses swam and she had all she could do to continue her efforts to free herself. Now she could give her attention to nothing but the man who had hold of her. Freeing his injured hand, he crouched for a moment, sucking at it, and muttered an obscene oath. She knew she had doomed herself now, but felt a fierce jubilation at the pain she had dealt him. As she struggled to sit up he was fully on her again, his breath stinking of onions and stale wine, the harsh leather of his jack with its metal buckles bruising her breast.

It was then, as she submitted, fainting, back on to the grass, exhausted by his brutal pushing, that she heard the pounding of hoofs ringing on the flint of the road.

The man called Huw dashed to the ruined opening and shouted hoarsely back at his companion, 'Men-at-arms, a troop of them, and pack-horses. Leave her, man! We must get away, now.'

Dick grumbled irritably, even now unwilling to relinquish his prey. 'Why should it concern us? Stay still and they'll pass us by. Useless to run now. Too late.'

Aleyne lay passive, panting. She could feel the naked terror in the other Welshman and he crouched close to them, his eyes huntedly seeking for some way of escape.

'They'll be Yorkists, like as not, Dick. In the Virgin's name, why did you dally with the wench? We should have taken her horses and killed both of them. Now we're trapped.'

'Keep your cowardly thoughts to yourself, man, and stay quiet. Why should Yorkists leave the road and find us?' Dick chuckled evilly. 'They'll be in a hurry if they've a captain with 'em, and anxious to join the fray, more then we want to do. The devil give them bad luck in it.'

He lifted his hand to buffet Aleyne into silence when she gathered all her strength, threw up her head and bit him again. Before he could recover himself she had torn free and dashed towards the cottage opening. Huw rose and tried to head her off, but desperation gave her both strength and cunning. She evaded him and was clear of the opening before Black Dick could lumber to his feet and follow. The troop of men-at-arms was coming on fast now, and Aleyne, in her panting run, was practically under the hoofs of the leader's horse before she could check. He pulled in his mount as it rose, forelegs high, in the air, squealing with fear and fury. Aleyne tried to shield her head from those iron-clad hoofs menacing her, but her one thought was that if she died for it she had won free from those devils in the ruin. There was chaos around her, alarmed shouts, oaths from the man above her, desperately attempting to calm his mount, and the terrifying noise of the excited brute's trampling on the flint of the road. Dazed, Aleyne realised that she had escaped death by some miracle, or the skilful handling of the rider, and managed to crawl to the ditch at the roadside, still shaking in sheer panic.

Her breath was coming in great gasps and felt as if it were tearing her lungs in two when her shoulder was shaken roughly and she was drawn to her feet by a devastating grip of an iron-clad hand on her shoulder.

'God in heaven, what did you think you were doing, dashing out into our path like that? Did you want to kill yourself? Worse, did you want to damage my horse? By the Virgin, I'm like to take a horse-whip to you!'

Aleyne was still panting too hard to reply. Her legs were threatening to buckle beneath her. She managed to get out one desperate little panted word. 'Inside.'

'What?' Her rescuer glared down at her, still furious, then turned to look where she pointed. The captain's eyes narrowed and he signalled to two of his men. The troop had dismounted and were watching events in some amusement. Instantly his sergeant-at-arms came to attention and silently he and his fellow cautiously approached the ruin.

Now Aleyne could see that her rescuer was a knight, fully armed, though he wore no helmet, only the mailed coif. Despite her sense of shock at her near brushes with death, both from the marauding Welshman and the rearing horse, her eyes clouded with horror as she recognised the scowling countenance of the knight from the inn. She put a hand to her mouth to check her lips from trembling, and pulled herself upright. He looked down at her, his punishing grip relaxing somewhat on her shoulder.

'Are you all right, unhurt? You deserve to be dead.'

She shook her head weakly. 'No, I—I think—I am unhurt. Men in there, they attacked Rob and me. He's badly wounded. Please—please help him.'

His dark eyes were staring down at her, his mouth held in hard with anger, then recognition dawned and he started suddenly and looked beyond her to the cottage.

'In there, you say? Armed men, or footpads?' He grasped her arm and shook her again, though not so hard this time.

'Men-at-arms, I think, looting for food and mounts.'

He grunted and released her suddenly as his two men emerged, shunting a sullen Black Dick before them. The sergeant aimed a deliberate kick at the Welshman's backside and he landed, sprawling, before the knight.

'One of them managed to scramble over the back wall and away, but this fellow was still trying to do up his points.' The sergeant's amused contempt was obvious in his tone, and Aleyne's face flamed.

The knight looked down at her impassively. 'I warned you what would happen if you stayed on the road. Did he rape you?'

She shook her head, mutely avoiding the Welshman's pleading eyes. 'No—you—you—were in time. But Rob is hurt. He——'

The knight snapped a question at his sergeant. 'Is the boy alive?'

'Aye, sir. He's in a bad way, though. Looks like a broken leg, and his head is bleeding.'

The knight nodded grimly. His gaze passed to the prisoner, who had scrambled awkwardly to his feet and stood, head down, awaiting his fate. 'Hang him from the nearest tree and let's get on.'

Before the two men-at-arms could seize their prisoner Aleyne said, horrified, 'Oh, no, please...'

The knight's thick eyebrows rose in interrogation. 'Oh, you have no objection to his attempted rape? You seemed very anxious to escape him.'

Aleyne's resolve faltered beneath his contemptuous stare and she mumbled, scarlet-faced, 'Of course I object, but—but...'

'But?' He shifted one mailed foot impatiently.

'The punishment is too harsh...'

'You think he should be allowed free to rape other young girls?'

'No, certainly not.' Aleyne's tone was tart, and he flashed a curious glance at her. He had not expected so curt a reply from this serving wench.

She swallowed hard and said, through gritted teeth, 'Judgement should not be so summary...'

The knight said in a steely voice, 'I have no intention of taking prisoners.'

'Oh.' Aleyne bit her lip uncertainly. That the knight was on some mission of importance had not occurred to her in her horror at the thought of the man's immediate dispatch.

As if the Welshman felt the impending noose tightening around his dirty throat he made a sudden desperate move for freedom. One of the men-at-arms was holding him by one shoulder, his eye on his captain, awaiting his decision. For the moment his attention was diverted. Black Dick thrust his free hand into the neck of his grease-stained jack and withdrew it smartly. Aleyne's eyes were drawn to the sudden movement by a flash of steel and she gave a startled cry. As if in answer there came another, answering, flash and the Welshman was down, a grey goose-feather shaft protruding from his throat. The threatened men, white-faced at his realisation of peril, knelt beside him in the road and plucked at the shaft.

The knight shrugged and turned away. 'It seems our problem has been solved due to the quick thinking of one of my bowmen. You see, mistress, you might have cost me the life of one of my best men by this foolish shilly-shallying.'

Aleyne thrust her hand to her mouth against the overbearing need to vomit. The horror of the events of the last hour was beginning to take its toll. She had no brief for the marauding Welshman but his summary sentencing had unnerved her. Never before had she seen a man die without being shriven, right before her eyes, and her attempt to save him from that fate had endangered the life of one of her rescuers. She began to shake uncontrollably.

The knight's voice came coldly to her from the entrance to the ruined cottage. 'I would think you would want to see how your young companion does.'

Aleyne was horrified that she could have forgotten Rob's plight, even under the stress of the recent events. She gathered her skirts and hastened before him into the ruin where he'd been carried to kneel beside Rob. Blood was beginning to seep from the wound on his head, but he appeared to be coming round, for she could hear him moaning softly.

The knight stood looking down at him dispassionately. One of the men-at-arms hurried in with a muttered apology to his captain. He carried two stout pieces of wood. 'Beg pardon, sir. I thought as how I could make the boy a mite more comfortable till we can get one of they monks to see to him.'

The knight nodded, and the man knelt by Rob and began to straighten the limb awkwardly bent beneath the boy's body. The soldier's eyes regarded Aleyne curiously and with a hint of sympathy. Aleyne reddened under that look. She was unused to the marked lack of respect she was afforded. She had not yet accustomed herself to the reaction from others she got, being dressed in Joan's cheaply flamboyant clothing as she still was. Doubtless the man thought, as the knight most likely did, that she was Rob's leman. The man bound the injured limb into a straight position held by the two wooden supports. He appeared to have some expertise. Soldiers were prone to such accidents, Aleyne thought. The man stood up and dusted down the knees of his hose.

'He should do all right now, sir, unless the break bleeds within.'

Rob had stirred under the rough and ready ministrations. He groaned aloud, opened his eyes for a moment, then closed them again, succumbing to the blackness which claimed him.

'It'll be the pain, sir,' the soldier commented. 'Best he doesn't feel it for a while.'

He saluted and left the cottage. The knight strode to the ruined doorway, summoning Aleyne imperatively.

'Come, we must be on our way. I'll escort you to the Abbey guest-house. The monks will see that the boy is brought into Tewkesbury.'

Aleyne remained stubbornly beside Rob. 'I won't leave him.'

The knight drew a hard, impatient breath. 'Indeed, you'll do as I say. I've wasted enough time over your affairs as it is. I'll not leave you to be accosted again. That fellow's accomplice could easily return. What would you do then?'

'What would Rob do then?' Aleyne returned angrily. 'I tell you, I'll not leave him here.'

The knight walked angrily back to her, leaned down and dragged her ungently to her feet, shaking her quite hard.

'God's teeth, why do I have to be plagued by such stupidity? At any moment His Grace the King will have need of my services, and I am left waiting on the whim of some foolish wench.'

'There is no need for you to concern yourself with my needs, sir,' Aleyne said with as much dignity as she could muster following such summary treatment. 'Rob and I will do well enough. I thank you for the help you have rendered me. If you could request help from the Abbey as you pass through Tewkesbury I would be even more grateful.'

His dark brows twitched together in fury at having his orders questioned. 'Wench,' he roared, 'did you not hear what I said? Like it or not, you'll ride with us into Tewkesbury.'

'Not without Rob.'

She thought for one moment he would strike her; then he bellowed to his sergeant.

'Sir?' The man was there within an instant.

'Detail two of the men to make some rough sort of litter to bring this boy into Tewkesbury. Tell them to leave him at the Abbey infirmary and make haste to join us on the Gloucester road.'

'Sir.'

Firmly the knight took Aleyne's arm in a grip which allowed no further objection and led her outside on to the road. He released her suddenly, so that she almost stumbled, and summoned his horse to be brought up. Quickly he mounted and reached down one arm to Aleyne. 'Mount before me. It's but a short ride into Tewkesbury.'

She looked back longingly to the cottage where the two men assigned to the task were putting together a litter comprising two long sturdy branches over which a horse-blanket had been thrown. Assured that Rob would not be left unprotected, she came close to the nervously prancing charger, stepped lightly up on the knight's mailed foot, and allowed him to settle her before him. His arm closed tightly round her. He gave one brief command and the little troop moved forward.

He did not speak and Aleyne was conscious of his nearness. Memories flooded through her of his drunken behaviour at the inn at Broadway, and she was uncomfortably aware that she had gone down in his estimation now he had found her apparently disobeying his instructions and continuing to ride on with Rob. Did he believe she was on her way to join the baggage company of one of the armies? Her cheeks flamed at the thought. Obviously the notion was well to the fore of his mind and her dress gave evidence of her intention. It was not unheard of for a swain to allow his leman to offer herself for payment while she was youthful and attractive enough for both to gain by the arrangement. She had not pressed to ride her own mount. Indeed, she had not dared to mention the horses; was not sure if the Welshman had not made off with them. If he had not, then certainly these Yorkists would commandeer them. The innkeeper had informed her that the troops' presence in the area was to obtain remounts and supplies for the army. She swallowed painfully. Black Dick had dealt her a buffet to the face, and her teeth and throat ached. Now she was beginning to feel her bruises.

She wondered how it could be that this man who had left before them, presumably on some other road, had now come up with them again. At the time she had thanked the Virgin for her rescue; now she was not sure whether her rescuer would relinquish his own claim on her when they reached Tewkesbury. She must stay at the Abbey with Rob at least until she had consulted the infirmarian about his condition. If then she was sure all would be well with him she must continue her journey to Gloucester. Ellis's mother would surely be able to afford her some protection from the demands of Lady Risby and Stoodley until these battles for the throne were over and she could appeal to the victor for help.

The knight rode at the head of the column, so they were not choked by the rising clouds of dust. It was unseasonably hot for early May, yet Aleyne still found herself shivering violently as the shock of the recent encounter still affected her. As if her riding companion felt her trembling he pulled her yet closer against his mailed breastplate and tightened his grip round her waist.

The road seemed deserted but as they neared Tewkesbury they overtook one or two carts piled high with palliasses and bundles, women and children clinging nervously together on the tailgate or in some cases walking beside the creaking carts. Each company drew in to the roadside and halted while the mailed troop rode by, the drivers touching forelocks in respect and clearly anxious to avoid any confrontation with the soldiers. The people were already deserting the town and villages, knowing all houses in the area would be looted when the warring armies moved in.

A single rider approached the troop and drew rein. The knight apparently recognised him and did likewise, lifting his hand to halt the men behind him.

The youth was panting, so he had ridden hard, and Aleyne recognised him as a youngster she had seen from the window of her chamber the previous evening.

'Sir Dominick.' His words came in gulped breaths. 'It's true what we heard. The Queen is marching towards Gloucester but it's said the King has sent an ultimatum to the governor, Sir Richard Beauchamp, and the man will not dare allow the Queen's force to enter and cross the bridge over the Severn. The King left Sodbury very early this morning and was well on the way to Cheltenham. I heard it from one of the scurriers sent out to Tewkesbury to sound out the feeling of the townsfolk. It seems best we make for Cheltenham and meet him there.'

'Good.' The knight nodded. 'Then the intelligence we had that it would be too late to meet him at Cirencester was true enough and I was right to turn for Tewkesbury.'

This, then, was the reason the knight had changed direction. Aleyne drew in a hard breath. Since he was clearly in haste to join the King's force she would be safe at the Abbey. He could not hope to take her with him. Might it be possible for her to retrieve her horses

and proceed? That was a forlorn hope but she would
pray the Virgin that their mounts remained hidden or
had wandered back to the ruin after the alarm of the
attack.

The squire was chattering as he manoeuvred his mount
into position beside his master's charger.

'Some of the villagers and townsfolk are deserting their
homes and farms. The houses are being boarded up in
Tewkesbury.'

'Yes, we've passed some of them. Naturally they fear
for their wives and daughters.'

Aleyne felt considerable sympathy for them. The
young squire's eyes opened wide at sight of her.

'Sir Dominick, would that be the wench...?'

'Indeed, it is,' the knight returned grimly. 'We encountered her and the boy on the road and in some
danger. I am escorting them both to the Abbey.'

The squire opened his mouth as if to question the decision, then thought better of it and closed it again. He
drew his mount in close behind his master's and the
knight gave the order to advance.

Tewkesbury seemed deserted as they entered, all shops
and houses well boarded against looters. The knight ordered his men to take the Cheltenham road and himself
made for the Abbey. Rob's litter had been left far behind,
and Aleyne could only hope he would be brought in
quickly before any of the threatened action could begin.

The knight was greeted respectfully but with some
signs of doubt by the porter on duty, who looked
anxiously at his mailed presence with alarm. Aleyne was
left waiting at the gatehouse while the knight demanded
that he should be conducted to the Prior without delay.
The porter hastened off, his impatient guest in tow.
Aleyne waited uncertainly. Several monks and lay servants passed by, staring at her curiously. Again she
wished with all her heart that she had not chosen to don
Joan's clothes.

After what seemed an eternity but was in fact no more than half an hour the knight returned with a young novice monk in attendance.

'Now, madam,' he said briskly, 'I have made arrangements for you to be accommodated in the guest-house until I return. I have spoken with the infirmarian personally and your companion will have the best of care. I regret I must commandeer your two mounts but in all events it would be rank foolishness for you to attempt to leave the Abbey until this business is over. I shall be back to see that, this time, you obey me. Afterwards...' he shrugged '...we shall see about returning you to your own manor.'

Before she could utter one word of protest he had turned and passed through the gatehouse, and the young novice diffidently made to lead her to the quarters assigned to her. She stood for a moment, biting her lip uncertainly, very close to tears of frustration, then she, too, shrugged and followed her guide.

CHAPTER FIVE

ALEYNE was allotted a small cell-like room in the Abbey guest-house. It was scrupulously clean and she was delighted to know that in it she could be private. She also realised that the knight had exerted his authority and paid out money so that she might be comfortable. She was not sure if she was pleased by this. His attitude towards her both at the inn and on the road had been less than respectful. He had also ordered her not to leave the Abbey, and she surmised that he was unused to being thwarted. A meal was brought to her, simple but well cooked. Here, in the Abbey, she had not expected sumptuous fare and when the young lay servant called to remove her platter she asked if an injured man had been brought into the infirmary.

'Indeed, yes, mistress, about an hour ago. He has been made comfortable. The infirmarian has attended him.

Sir Dominick Allard informed us about the attack on him and requested that he be given the greatest care. If you would like to see him I could take you there now.'

'Yes, certainly.' Aleyne stood up at once.

The boy escorted her out into the courtyard, through the cloisters, round the side of the chapter house, through the small private cloisters and into the long room laid aside for the sick monks and some lay townsfolk who needed medical attention.

Rob had been accommodated in a side room laid apart for lay patients. Aleyne was relieved to see him propped up on the straw palliasse and obviously well aware of his surroundings. He looked pale and drawn, but his eyes brightened at sight of her and the lay servant left them alone together.

'Oh, Rob, how are you? Does your leg hurt? What did the infirmarian say?'

Rob blushed fiery red with embarrassment. 'Bless you, Mistress Aleyne, you've no cause to be bothering yourself about me. I'll mend.'

'But the leg is broken?'

'Aye, they say so.' Rob's fair brows drew together as he remembered the pain of the setting. 'But it's not bad, and the monk says I'm not like to lose it, so I'm lucky, though it'll be some days before I can walk again. What shall we do, Mistress Aleyne?' His blue eyes clouded in distress. 'I'm that sorry to be leaving you in this mess. Have you room at some inn? I've been in a rare taking about you, 'cos they say there's like to be fighting here-abouts and soldiers coming into the town after.'

Aleyne put a hand on his sturdy brown arm. 'I'm quite safe, Rob. I have a small room in the guest-house and will have to stay there tonight and possibly tomorrow. You must think of nothing now but getting better. You took a bad beating and in my defence. You must not blame yourself for what happened.'

'I can't remember, mistress. The monks tell me I was brought in by two men-at-arms—surely not they pesky Welshmen?'

'No, no,' Aleyne said hastily. 'The Virgin came to our help. That knight, the one from the inn, he had changed his destination and came upon us on the road. The Welshmen were driven off and he then instructed his men to bring you here and has arranged accommodation for me.'

Rob's eyes showed how troubled he was and he swallowed before trying to put into words his concern for her.

'Mistress Aleyne, you should not—er—trust any man on the road, and that knight...'

Aleyne gave a little bitter smile. 'I know exactly what you mean, Rob, and, indeed, I shall be very cautious in my dealings with that man. I hope and pray I shall be gone from here before he returns, as he has sworn to do.'

'But you cannot travel alone, Mistress Aleyne, especially not with these men troubling the district.'

'We'll see,' she said briskly. 'It isn't far to Gloucester, Rob. Who knows? Perhaps I can send a message to Mistress Dyer and she would send a servant to escort me. For the moment I am relieved to know you are in good hands. Try to sleep now, and I will come early in the morning to visit you again.'

As she emerged from the room one of the infirmarian's assistants passed her. He reassured her further concerning Rob's condition and, taking her to the main door of the infirmary, pointed out for her the way she should go back to the guest-house.

Exhausted though she was, she found it hard to sleep. At intervals she could hear the bells summoning the monks to service in the church, and she tossed and turned on her mattress. She had spoken confidently to Rob. What point was there in worrying the boy? Yet she was extremely concerned about her future plans. If there was to be fighting in the town or nearby it could be weeks before the district was safe to travel in, and she doubted if she would find anyone in Tewkesbury brave enough to carry a message for her to Gloucester. Like it or not, she must make the journey unescorted. She could not risk being found here unprotected and at the mercy of the dark knight's whims.

Despite her promise to Rob it was after midday before Aleyne managed to visit the infirmary again. She fell into a heavy slumber about noon and was late stirring. Since she had no wish to bother the Abbey servants at this hour for breakfast she dressed hurriedly and took herself off to the almonry where she thought doles of bread would be issued to the poor. Surprisingly the place was not as crowded as she expected. A young novice was moving about among the beggars with his basket of bread and she was thankful to obtain a portion and a cup of ale. One or two of the men eyed her curiously but she kept herself apart from them and ate hurriedly. They were obviously excited and, heads close, full of the latest news from the town. Aleyne checked the novice as he prepared to move from the room.

'There seem few poor people here this morning, Brother. Is there trouble in the town?'

The young man shook his head sadly.

'Aye, indeed, mistress. The battle is in progress, so it's said, and people are keeping well away from the town, particularly those who have no real business here. It's quiet enough now, but soon soldiers'll be pouring in. We are preparing to treat some of the wounded.' He crossed himself. 'Aye, and many will need to be shriven and buried before the day is out.'

Aleyne crossed herself also and sat for a moment, staring deep into her ale cup. She wondered about the fate of those men who had come to her rescue on the road yesterday, particularly that of the knight—Sir Dominick Allard, the lay servant had told her his name was. She had no wish to fall into his hands again, yet neither had she any wish for harm to come to him. He had proved himself her protector, though disagreeable and disapproving enough. He had planned to join King Edward's army, she knew. Aleyne had found the motives for all this fighting so confusing that she was unable

to judge the cause or to pray for victory on either side.
Her father had said, sadly, that poor King Henry was
incapable of ruling the realm and she knew he also dis-
approved of the savagery of Henry's consort, Queen
Margaret, yet could Edward Plantagenet, former Earl
of March, have the true right to England's throne? Henry
might be a poor enough warrior and leader but he was
true son to great King Harry the Fifth. Aleyne sighed.
Her father had fought beside Edward's father in France
so he must have had some sympathy for the Yorkist cause
and had stated once that the Lancastrian heirs had
themselves usurped the throne from poor murdered King
Richard the Second. Which army, then, had the right
of it? Would God support the right? Aleyne would like
to think this was so but she judged the victory would go
to the mightiest in battle rather than to the army which
deserved it.

When she reached Rob's side he had already eaten a
good dinner and was delighted to see her.

'You look rested, Mistress Aleyne. Did you sleep well?'

'I was late dropping off, Rob; that's why I was so late
stirring. How are you?'

'My leg still aches a bit but I slept well. It's very quiet
in here.' He leaned forward anxiously. 'These monks
won't tell me anything. Is there news of the armies,
Mistress Aleyne?'

She shrugged. 'The townsfolk are all closeted inside
their properties. There's talk among the poor in the almonry that the battle is in progress. They have so little
to lose, poor souls, that there is no point in their aban-
doning the town.'

She looked up, startled, as the hurried pattering of
sandals could be heard outside the door and a low murmuring as if the infirmarian's assistants had been summoned quickly but instructed not to disturb their
patients.

Aleyne gave a meaning glance at Rob and he nodded.
She rose and went to the door. Two monks literally ran
by her, lifting their habits to aid progress. It was so unlike

monks to hasten anywhere, let alone run, that Aleyne
realised some urgent need had allowed them to dispense
with the rule. She turned back to Rob. 'I imagine
wounded are being brought into the town.'

He nodded soberly.

'I'll go and see what I can discover.'

'Mistress Aleyne, do be careful,' he begged. 'If the
battle is over there'll be trouble in the streets.'

'I know.' She hurried back to the bed and took Rob's
brown hand in hers. 'If that is so I must take my opportunity to get clear of the town as soon as possible. I
leave you in good hands, Rob. You must not stir from
your bed until the infirmarian gives you leave. Promise
me.'

'Mistress Aleyne...' He broke off at sight of her
earnest expression and sighed, sinking back against his
pillow. 'The Virgin guard you. I will do as you say, mistress. Don't worry about me, but take care whom you
trust.'

She squeezed his hand and, smiling at him encour-
agingly, hurried from the room.

As Aleyne raced through the small cloister she saw
monks running from the scriptorium into the south
transept of the church. The clamour met her immediately she left the infirmary building—hoarse shouting,
the clang of armour and horses' accoutrements. The sight
that met her eyes as she entered the church appalled her.
The monks ahead of her had halted in the choir, clinging
together fearfully. Aleyne pushed by them towards the
nave itself. Men were crowding into the great church for
refuge. So great was the crush of bodies that some were
in danger of being trampled underfoot. Some wore
armour but many were simple men-at-arms, all battle-
stained, jacks and breastplates dented and slashed, all
crazed with fear. At this stage it was impossible for
Aleyne to know which army had triumphed. The infirmarian was busy with his assistants, trying to help the
wounded who lay under the great high arches moaning

in pain and terror. The infirmarian's controlled tones
called instructions to his assistants and the lay servants
who had drawn together, as frightened as the fugitives
who needed their help.

Before Aleyne's horrified eyes the huge north door
was thrust open and armed knights were framed in the
opening, light from behind them illuminating the gloom
of the shadowed church. Aleyne cried out in alarm as
some of the fugitives nearest the door were unceremoniously seized and jerked outside. Their screams rent the
air and Aleyne swallowed back sharp bile as she realised
they were being summarily dispatched. Her sense of
outrage at this attack on the sanctity of God's house
displaced her fear. She moved forward and slipped in a
pool of blood. Her hand clutched at the carved rood-
screen for support and she gave a little distressed cry.

Then she saw the great giant of a man in the doorway,
who brandished a huge two-handed sword. He was
flanked by other knights, and Aleyne thrust a hand hard
against her mouth as she recognised one of them as her
rescuer on the Tewkesbury road, Sir Dominick Allard.
His armour bore ominous brown stains and was dented
from force of mace or battle-axe. He was wearing his
helmet, but the visor was up and she could not fail to
recognise those strong, dominating features. Even in the
dimness of the Abbey Church Aleyne could see his heavy
brows were drawn together in a scowl and his attention
was fixed on the giant with the long sword. A great con-
certed gasp went up from the fugitives in the nave, and
Aleyne guessed that she was looking at Edward
Plantagenet himself, the golden giant of the Yorkist
house, the handsome Rose of Rouen. So York was victorious and these poor souls clustered together here were
fugitives from Queen Margaret's army.

Even as she kept fascinated eyes on Sir Dominick, another unfortunate was plucked from near the open door
and dragged outside. A shout of outrage came from some
armed Lancastrian knights near the rood screen.

There came a sudden hush as the Abbot, Strensham, robed in vestments for holy mass, came out from the entrance to the rood screen and stood poised on the steps. He appeared to have been celebrating mass at the high altar, for he still clutched the sacred cup.

He raised one hand imperatively to silence the shouts which defiled Holy Church.

'My lord King,' he enquired in a quiet but commanding voice, 'what do your men do here? They break the laws of sanctuary. I beg you most humbly to order them to withdraw.'

The golden giant's voice rose clear to the roof vaulting. 'Father Abbot, you know well Tewkesbury Abbey has no right of sanctuary.'

'My son, surely you will not continue to allow your men to commit sacrilege and shed blood even beneath the arches of God's house?' If the Abbot was afraid, and he had good cause to be, he gave no sign of it. Aleyne waited breathlessly for the King's answer and it seemed that every fugitive there held his, for there was no sound in that quiet place.

The King turned to the knights who attended him and they conferred in a low murmur, then he turned once more to the abbot.

'I am prepared to concede that this place is holy, Father Abbot, yet I cannot allow these traitors to escape me.'

'At least grant them the mercy of respite, prayers for the dead, and help for those sore wounded. In the end all must leave the church. How can any man escape you?' The Abbot's voice was weary and dispirited.

'It shall be as you wish, Father Abbot. My men will withdraw from the church and I shall forbid any further slaughter within the confines of the Abbey grounds, but my guards will surround the buildings. In the morning every man here must come out and submit himself to judgement.'

The Abbot bowed his head. 'You are the King, my lord, and we your humble subjects.'

There was a stirring among the little knot of knights. One who stood on the King's right hand caught impatiently at his arm as if to object, but the other smaller man beside him put off that arm and the first noble shrugged off his grasp angrily. Aleyne saw Sir Dominick Allard bow to the King in deference, turn, and stride from the church. She thought she heard him ordering men just outside the door.

She clung to the carved rood screen, her knuckles whitening with the strain. She felt very close to fainting. One sight of that blood-stained figure filled her with dread. He had declared that he would be back for her after the battle and there was so little time now. She must escape him. He had fought in this battle, taken part in the vengeful pursuit. She swallowed once again to keep back deadly sickness. She could not fall into that man's hands as these helpless fugitives within the church would do.

There was little point in returning to the guest-house. The Welsh soldiers had stolen her money and her bundle had been lost when Sir Dominick had insisted she ride with him into Tewkesbury and also appropriated her horses. She had taken her leave of Rob, assured he would be safe and well attended until she could make arrangements for him to be conveyed home to Risby. There was nothing to keep her in Tewkesbury—except her desperate fear of setting out on a journey so fraught with dangers for an unescorted woman.

She pushed her way uncertainly through the fugitive Lancastrians in the nave. Many of the wounded were uttering pleas for water, which could not be brought, since no man dared venture out of the church. Others were moaning or muttering prayers. No one made any attempt to prevent her leaving and she slipped out through a side door near the Abbot's lodging. How could she manage now to evade Sir Dominick Allard? Aleyne forced a smile. That, surely, need not concern her. He was much too busy harrying the Lancastrian wounded.

The crowd had grown larger now outside the Abbot's gate, swelled by some of the townsfolk and beggars who had ventured into the streets despite their fear of attack and pillage. So dense was it, and so difficult to fight her way through, that Aleyne could not fear that she could possibly be recognised and apprehended by any one of Sir Dominick's men-at-arms who might have had something to gain by returning their commander's woman to him.

Round the north porch it was densest. Undoubtedly something of importance was happening here. Several times Aleyne was shouted at and jostled hard as she tried to make her way towards the market-place.

The streets were rowdy with laughter and the yells of triumphant men-at-arms, dust-stained, bloodied and mostly drunk, wearing the devices of the Yorkist supporters on their leather jacks. They were staggering about in little raiding parties, laden down with booty taken from the field and also from the houses of unfortunates near to the town: armour, boots, weapons, pewter and silver household goods. Some of the men had gaudily dressed women hanging on their arms, camp-followers reunited with their men after the fighting. Imperative voices ordered the crowd to move and give a little, as mounted men on errands for their lords rode impatiently by, forcing the people almost on to the house walls. Aleyne was nearly knocked over by one such rider and clawed desperately at the person next to her to try and keep her footing.

A stout arm held her up and she hastily murmured her thanks to a young woman little older than herself, perhaps seventeen or eighteen. She wore a bright red kirtle and a blouse which was surprisingly clean, for her uncovered hair, bright red-gold in colour, free from hood or wimple, declared her to be one of the camp-followers. She was comely of features and her long lips broke into a friendly smile as she drew Aleyne nearer to the wall for support. In those movements Aleyne saw that she was lame. She put one hand on her hip, surveying Aleyne keenly as, again, they were jostled together by the movement of the crowd.

'Hey, mind how you go, there.'

'I'm sorry,' Aleyne said breathlessly. 'That rider took me by surprise.'

'They've no patience and no manners, those esquires, cheeky young jackanapes.'

'Yes,' Aleyne agreed ruefully. 'What is happening? I know the King was here a while ago but I thought he'd withdrawn.'

'So he has,' the woman said drily, 'but the crowd are here to witness the prince's body being brought into the Abbey.'

'The prince, one of the King's younger brothers?'

'No, no.' The woman grinned again. 'Gloucester fought bravely and helped bring off the victory, and the King kept Clarence well under his eye, lest he turn tail again. No, this is Prince Edward, Queen Margaret's son.'

Aleyne drew a hard breath. Though she knew Queen Margaret was not credited with a merciful heart, she pitied the woman for the death of her only son. All was lost, then, for the Lancastrian cause. Here, near this little market town, Margaret had lost the heir and the throne. Perhaps the young man had been spared the fate of the other fugitives—death on the headsman's block.

Aleyne could see now the pennants of the victorious Yorkist nobles: the black bull of Clarence, the white boar of Gloucester, the lion of Norfolk, and flying proudly, the lilies and leopards of England beside Edward of York's personal banner of the sun in splendour. Somewhere among them was a banner bearing the device of a black wolf on a field of argent. Aleyne shivered, despite the warmth in the late afternoon of the hot May day.

There came the sound of monks chanting, and the crowd drew back into two columns, allowing the bier of the dead prince to be borne into the Abbey Church.

Aleyne peered anxiously at the knights who followed the covered bier, dreading to see a familiar dark face among those who escorted the monks through the pillaging men-at-arms. Her lame companion glanced at her curiously.

'Are you afraid of someone?' Her fair brows drew together in puzzlement. 'You aren't one of the camp women, are you?'

'No-o,' Aleyne confessed breathlessly. 'I—I was on my way to Gloucester when—when my servant——' she corrected herself hastily '—my companion and I were attacked and our possessions stolen. The worst might have happened but a knight came by with a company of men-at-arms; Sir Dominick Allard, I've been told he is. He—he saved me, but my friend lies injured in the Abbey infirmary and I—I need to get away from Tewkesbury and quickly.'

The woman nodded. 'I think I understand. Now you fear Sir Dominick Allard as much as the men on the road?'

'He brought us here and—he ordered me to wait for his return. I saw him at the Abbey door with the princes. They...' she shuddered '...they were pulling out some of the fugitives...'

The woman grimaced. 'The King is in no merciful mood.'

'No man should shed blood in Holy Church.'

'The victors are unlikely to listen to the strictures of monks or priests tonight; that's why you shouldn't be travelling unescorted.'

'I know, but—I dare not stay here. Could you show me the way to the Gloucester road?' She hesitated. 'I would offer to pay you well, but...'

The woman grinned companionably. 'Of course I will, but it will be no easy feat to go unmolested through the lines of soldiers. Have you food?'

Aleyne shook her head.

'We'll manage. You intend to walk to Gloucester?'

'I have no choice. My horses were—appropriated.' Bitterly she stressed the final word.

'Gloucester is not your home?'

'No.' Aleyne coloured. 'I am—Aleyne Risby. I live near Wellesbourne. I have a friend in Gloucester who, I'm sure, will help me.'

'And you cannot go home?' The question was very direct, and Aleyne flushed again.

'No,' she said evenly. 'I cannot go home.'

'In that lies the bond between us.' The other woman was skilfully impelling Aleyne through the crowd, impervious to the angry curses and jostling of those she thrust aside. 'I, too, cannot go home.'

Aleyne looked at her closely. The woman's features bore nothing of the coarseness of expression she had noted in the faces of the other baggage-followers. Seeing her glance, her companion gave a short brittle laugh. 'I am Kate Shepton. My father is a prosperous wool merchant in Barnet. As you see, my expectations are somewhat limited.' She glanced meaningly down at her right leg. 'My parents were ready to consign me to a convent but——' she grinned crookedly '—I've no vocation for the contemplative life. So far my face has proved my fortune. I found a protector in a sergeant-at-arms in Gloucester's train and stayed with him after the victory at Barnet. It's a tough existence with the army, but preferable to being bounded by convent cell-walls.'

'And you don't know if—if your man is wounded or...?'

Kate shrugged. 'Not yet, but if I know Will Scroggins he'll have guarded his own hide well enough. It's getting dusk now and we'll have to cross the battlefield. I hope you've a strong stomach. Some of the sights you'll see on the field aren't for the squeamish.'

Once clear of the Abbey, Kate Shepton drew Aleyne across the fields towards Swilgate Brook. The ground had been churned into a morass by the trampling of men and horses and the passage of the heavier guns. Here there were few men-at-arms to be seen, most, as Kate predicted, having joined the pursuit up to the Abbey door. Kate stopped at a broken-down wagon and seized a sack which she threw towards Aleyne.

'Keep hold of that. We'll fill it with supplies for your journey.' She shaded her eyes against the rays of the dying sun which gave a reddish glow, causing Aleyne to shiver. The ground, she fancied, must be slippery with blood, but she set herself to be guided by her companion. Kate set a fair pace, and her progress, though ungainly, did not seem too much impeded by her lameness.

'The worst of the rout was over towards the river,' Kate indicated, with a wave of her hand, 'but we'll be coming soon to the Lancastrian lines and we'll see the bodies of men and horses, so be ready for them.'

Soon the more ominous signs of the recent combat became apparent: abandoned weapons, mostly pikes and bows, for the pursuing Yorkists had snatched up the more valuable hand-guns and swords, then the bodies of men, and, further on, of two horses. Aleyne averted her eyes and Kate stopped and put an arm round her shoulders.

'It won't be pleasant, but not as bad as it will be tonight when ghouls appear to rob the bodies and dispatch those still alive. We must be clear of the field by then so keep going. Try not to look. Most of these are at least out of their misery. It's the ones back there in the Abbey and those on the run who'll be hunted down relentlessly.' She gave that familiar shrug which Aleyne knew to be an expression of pity for those defeated unfortunates. 'If the King demands the full penalty for treason the living will wish they had died on the field.'

'Did you hear news of Queen Margaret,' Aleyne asked as they struggled on, 'and of the Princess of Wales?'

'It's rumoured they made good their escape. Lord Wenlock was killed. He had charge of the Prince during the battle.'

Kate waved and called a greeting to two leather-jacketed men who trailed a serpentine back towards the town. 'If these wars are over it will mean lean pickings for the likes of me.'

Aleyne considered what little she had known of the harshness of life for people like Kate. What terrible things

Kate had seen and endured while life had cushioned
Aleyne from reality on the manor at Risby, yet they both
had in common their reasons for fleeing their homes.
Both objected to being forced into marriage; Aleyne with
Sir Thomas Stoodley, whose very image filled her with
abhorrence, and Kate dreaded her marriage with the
Church to such an extent that she had sold herself for
only an illusion of freedom. If they came safely through
this she would try to find some means of helping Kate
when she came into her own again. Surely Kate would
not want to continue this precarious and degrading way
of life?

Abruptly Kate pulled up short and motioned for silence. Some little distance ahead two men emerged from
a tent and carried equipment to a waiting wagon: a
folding table, camp stools, mattresses. One man stood
back and called to the other.

'Hurry, Mat, we may not yet have missed all the
entertainments the town has to offer.'

The younger man paused doubtfully in the tent's entrance. 'We should finish the job, take down the tent
and——'

'We can do that later. Sir Dominick will be fully occupied waiting on His Grace of Gloucester at his lodging
for hours yet.'

'But to leave the equipment entirely unguarded... He'll
have the flesh from our backs!'

The older man laughed. 'Lad, who's likely to steal
such stuff when there's real loot to be had in the town?
Am I to leave you, then?'

Aleyne had stopped short at that dreaded name. She
saw the boy look shudderingly over the field, now greying
in the twilight. 'No, I'd not want to stay here—alone.'

'You'll have company enough,' the other quipped,
'and some more, living and more dangerous, by and by.
Come, then; we'll be back at first light to finish, and no
one the wiser.'

He strode off purposefully and the boy was forced to
almost run to keep pace with him.

Kate turned to Aleyne, her eyes gleaming. 'This is Allard's tent. There'll be wine and supplies in the wagon, never missed. Sir Dominick will be feasting his victory with the King in the Abbot's lodging tonight.' She checked at sight of Aleyne's frightened expression.

Aleyne said slowly, 'Do you know this knight?'

'Only by reputation. My protector, Will Scroggins, is one of his sergeants. Is he the man...?'

Aleyne nodded and shivered again.

'Right; well, all the more need for me to get you supplies and set you on your way. Hold the sack open for me.' She grunted her satisfaction as she took from the abandoned cart a leathern wine-skin and a loaf of bread. 'This will do for a start, and there's a cold capon here and a cheese.'

Aleyne was white-lipped, her cheeks scarlet with shame. Never in her life had she stolen so much as a sugared plum from her own kitchens.

Kate chided her laughingly. 'There's no one to see except the dead and they aren't likely to talk; but I speak foolishness to keep up my own spirits. You must not feel guilty. These Yorkist knights won't ask where their food at tonight's supper comes from, or if the donor was willing to give. Our men are too busy to provide for us, and I'm not prepared to go hungry. I have done too often.'

'But you will take nothing but food?'

'Nothing. If I were caught with pewter or plate they'd hang me out of hand.' Kate have a hard laugh. 'It's amazing what liberties the King will allow his men, yet hold to a strict moral attitude against the likes of us. We have our uses, but only within limits. It's from our ranks that he can afford to take his examples to quell the murmurs of the townsfolk when the worst of this is over.'

The field was becoming more and more ghastly as the light faded. Already they had company. Through the greyish light which gathered like a mist over the grass Aleyne saw forms creeping and bending over the bodies of the slain. Kate stiffened and caught at Aleyne's arm as a stifled cry came to them out of the darkness.

'Keep very close to me now. If we are caught here those devils cannot afford to let us live as witness to their deeds.'

'They are murdering the wounded.' Aleyne tried to pull free, anxious to give the alarm, make some desperate effort to prevent the perpetration of such ungodliness.

'They're human scavengers, jackals on two legs, and they'll pick their victims clean of all clothing and valuables. Aleyne, would you draw them to us? I've seen this, after Barnet. We'd get short shrift. You can't stop it. No one would heed you or care.'

Aleyne swallowed her disgust and horror. Would she ever forget such sights if she lived to be a hundred?

They had crossed the terrible field now and had reached the road. It was then, near the wall of a barn, that she recognised the tethered horse.

Kate stared at her in alarm as she went up to it and began to stroke its nose.

The horse was no destrier, but a sturdy hack, and she knew how difficult it could be to handle. Had not Sir Dominick Allard found it hard enough to stay in the saddle when she had fallen almost below its plunging hoofs in her desperate flight from the marauding Welshman? The same hack had carried the double load of its master and Aleyne when they had ridden into Tewkesbury. Aleyne's lips set in a mutinously stubborn line. Sir Dominick had stolen her horses; why should she not borrow his to get her to Gloucester in safety? She looked back at Kate and bit her lip at the other woman's undoubted terror.

'This is Sir Dominick Allard's horse?'

Kate shook her head uncertainly. She did not know, but the animal was a thoroughbred, a knight's horse, and even to be caught near it was to place themselves in peril.

'Aleyne, come away at once. I can't imagine who could have been careless enough to leave the animal unattended here, but he's likely to lose his ears in the morning if his master finds out.'

'Then he will indeed do so,' Aleyne declared, 'for I intend to borrow the horse.'

'No...' Kate let out a wail of terror '...Sweet Virgin, no! Food is one thing. To take a horse, a *knight*'s horse, is rank folly. Even the thought of it brings the feel of a hempen rope tightening on my neck.'

'But I've no intention of stealing the horse. The moment I reach Gloucester I'll send the animal back with a groom.'

'You would never reach Gloucester. If you know the animal, others will, and you'll be challenged before you've gone a mile.'

'If I'm caught I won't involve you.'

'Aleyne, you mustn't, it's certain death.'

Aleyne was examining the horse for any sign of injury. She knew well enough that the knight would have used his destrier during the combat but the hack might well have strained itself while carrying them into the town or during its frantic struggle earlier.

Kate was gazing huntedly round, then, recognising Aleyne's determination, she thrust the sack of food into her friend's hands.

'Then go, if you must, but hurry. At any moment we could be caught.'

Aleyne had some difficulty mounting. The nobly bred animal was restive and blew loudly through its nose, tossing its head at the feel of unfamiliar hands upon the bridle rein. Kate cupped her hands to help Aleyne into the saddle. In the dim light her face looked drawn and pale. At last Aleyne was up, and Kate patted the horse's withers.

'Where can I find you, Kate?'

'Who knows?' Kate grimaced comically. 'I shall be following the army when it leaves.'

Aleyne struggled to hold in the plunging animal and leaned down to shout, 'I'll try and find you, I promise. I owe you a great deal.'

She was about to ride off when a small group of mounted men appeared from the direction of the town and almost rode her down. Her mount whinneyed, reared, and almost threw her. In attempting to run clear, Kate stumbled and fell heavily. Aleyne strove to calm her frantic animal.

A harsh, hatefully familiar voice roared, 'By St Michael, that's my horse! Here, one of you, stop that girl!'

Aleyne panicked, dug in her heels and tried to steer the plunging horse by him, but Sir Dominick rode his destrier skilfully across her path and snatched the reins from her. She sat, uncertain, for one valuable split second, whether to try to jump clear and run or stay and attempt to help the captive Kate who had been seized by one of the dismounted men-at-arms. Circumstances decided for her, for, while she tried helplessly to disentangle her leg from her torn skirt, Sir Dominick dismounted, walked to her, and jerked her quickly from the saddle.

It was clear that in his fury he did not recognise her, for he said coldly, 'Perhaps, girl, you would like to say where you were off to on my horse.'

He towered over her, unhelmeted but still in full armour. She stared, fascinated, at the oil gleaming on tasset and breastplate. His mailed coif was thrust well back, revealing the shoulder-length dark brown hair, and the strong square-cut face with its dominant jutting chin. His grip on her shoulders was painful as he regarded her out of fierce dark eyes under those heavy level brows.

'Well, answer me. Your kind usually manages to find some excuse, however lame.'

Aleyne strove to find her tongue as he gave her shoulders another irritated shake. She needed to plead Kate's innocence but could find no words. She was too confused and frightened to even struggle.

As he continued to scowl at her recognition struck, and his eyes positively bulged with temper. Abruptly he said over his shoulder, 'Bring the other one to my headquarters. Pass this girl up before me. I shall want an explanation later of how Roland was left unattended.'

He mounted his horse and Aleyne was lifted bodily up before him; then he put spurs to his destrier, after issuing some command which sent his men riding hard across the fields towards the river.

She was so horror-stricken she could not think. Slow tears coursed down her cheeks and splashed on to her hands. Realisation of her plight sharpened her fear for Kate. By her foolishness she had doomed the woman.

Her captor pulled up before one of the houses near the Abbey wall. An archer in the blue and murrey of the House of York came at his order and helped Aleyne down. She looked anxiously round for Kate but the knight seized her elbow and jerked her ungently into a stone-flagged corridor through to a rush-strewn solar at the rear. The place gave the appearance of having been recently evacuated, and she thought it probably belonged to some wealthy merchant, for she caught a glimpse of a well-waxed court cupboard laden with pewter, a bright tapestry on one wall and one or two chairs as well as the stools. An archer kept guard at the door as Sir Dominick let go his grip on Aleyne's elbow and stalked to the table to pour wine for himself.

'It might assist your cause, just might,' he flung over his shoulder, 'if you told me to whom you intended to sell my horse.'

Her voice seemed unusually breathy and husky. 'You know well I had every intention of returning it.'

'Don't play the madam with me, wench. You forget, I heard different tales from you before. I want the truth. What man put you up to this? Understand me well: stealing is a hanging matter and your youth and sex won't save you if you keep up this stubbornness. I'll not have thieving and conniving among my men. Someone told you where the horse would be left unguarded and gave you instructions about where to deliver it.'

'I am not to be held responsible for the carelessness or dishonesty of your men,' Aleyne snapped. 'You appropriated my horses so I saw no reason why I should not borrow yours. Of course it would have been returned to you in the morning.'

Her genteel tone caught him on the raw and he swung round furiously, his hand upraised to strike.

'God's teeth, must I be constantly plagued by you? I thought you a respectable serving wench in trouble and worthy of my consideration. Now I find you, red-handed, in the act of stealing my horse.'

Aleyne's mounting anger had almost overlaid her fear.

'You will not listen!' she roared back at him. 'Do you never listen? No, I imagine you think that by storming at all your inferiors you will force them to bow to your will. I'll say again, I don't know any of your men. I needed the horse to continue my journey. The woman with me had no hand in this. She tried to stop me. If you must hang someone let it be me alone.'

He almost choked in his fury. 'Never have I met such insolence. Your powers of story-telling take my breath away. If I didn't know what kind of wench you are I'd be inclined to believe you. Do I have to beat the truth out of you?'

He advanced on her and Aleyne withdrew a step from the naked fury in his eyes. Reasoning with this man was impossible. It had been difficult enough at the inn when he had been deep in wine, but, sober, he could be equally intimidating.

His arm was lifted to deliver the threatened blow when a cool youthful voice arrested him in the act.

'The lady looks exhausted, Dominick, and very distressed. Terrifying her further might well have the effect of restraining her from telling you what you are so anxious to discover.'

Sir Dominick jerked about to face the newcomer, who had paused in the act of entering the room. Aleyne, also, turned startled eyes on him.

Slim, rather below average height, he was fully armed but unhelmeted, like her captor. She judged him to be in his early twenties, though the serious expression on that narrow, clever countenance and tight-held mouth might have belied that assertion and he could be even younger than he appeared at first glance. His grey-green eyes met hers in a steady, detached fashion and she dropped hers beneath his appraisal. Suddenly she felt deep embarrassment for her dishevelled appearance and, worse, for the circumstances in which she found herself. Instinctively, she knew she was in the presence of one of the great nobles of the realm.

Sir Dominick confirmed her opinion by the deference he afforded his visitor. He bowed very low.

'Sir, forgive me; I did not know you required my services.'

The young nobleman sauntered to the table and nodded at the archer, who, at a signal from Sir Dominick, shot forward to pour wine for him. Seating himself on one of the chairs, the young man looked thoughtfully at Aleyne and held out a bejewelled hand for the proffered wine goblet.

'Well, what has she done?'

'I found her stealing my horse.'

The newcomer's level brows were raised slightly and a glimmer of a smile twitched the tight-held lips.

'The famed Roland?'

Sir Dominick's cheeks flamed with anger and Aleyne stilled the explanation she was about to make.

'Indeed, sir.' Sir Dominick's tone was frosty and the nobleman suppressed a chuckle.

'My pardon, Dominick, for my flippancy. I know how much you prize the beast.'

'Roland or no, I'm determined to get to the bottom of this continual thieving. I'd say little to the occasional misappropriation of supplies—all armies are prone to that—but I'm concerned that some of the men are going into business with outside buyers, and that cannot be tolerated.'

The young man took a swallow of wine and frowned as his appraisal of Aleyne passed from her uncovered hair to her ruined gown and shoes.

'And you think this young woman is involved in these proceedings?'

Sir Dominick shot Aleyne another glacial glance. 'I'm at a loss to know what to think. She's no ordinary camp-follower. She speaks well, gives herself airs, and also appears to ride with some skill. I encountered her first at an inn in Broadway. She gave me some tarradiddle then about being on an errand for her mistress. There was a groom with her. They appeared to be runaways with a way to make in the world...'

Aleyne decided now was the time to make a decisive plea before she was condemned out of hand and Kate with her. She faced the nobleman, feeling instinctively that he would give fair consideration to her case. 'Sir, I am not with the army, and my servant and I are no run-aways, at least, not in the sense Sir Dominick here implies. I did try to explain to him. I needed urgently to complete my journey to Gloucester. After I left the inn at Broadway Rob and I were set upon, and he was injured. Sir Dominick came to our assistance and es-corted us into Tewkesbury but he comandeered our horses for army service, and now the battle is over I saw no harm in borrowing his horse. I had every intention of having it duly returned to him.'

The nobleman's .grey eyes regarded her intently. 'Mistress,' he said quietly, 'how is it you came to be travelling so far from your own manor, especially at such a time?'

'I...that is...' she stammered, 'I am in service at a manor near Wellesbourne and was on an important errand for my mistress to a friend of hers who lives in Gloucester.'

Sir Dominick snatched at one of her hands before she guessed his intention. 'These are not the hands of a serving wench. Look at them, my lord; dirty, true, and blistered, but uncalloused. They never did work in kitchen or even at the wash-tub, cleaning and pressing clothes. They are white and smooth, not red and work-worn. She is telling us a parcel of lies.'

'I've no doubt of it, Dominick. Her speech and bearing tell me she is no servant and certainly no camp-follower. I think it is time you told us who you really are, mistress,' the nobleman said sternly.

Aleyne drew a hard breath. She was still not sure if she could trust this courteous but perceptive stranger. At last she put back her disordered hair with a resigned gesture. 'I'm Aleyne Risby,' she said tiredly. 'Most of what I said is true. I am journeying to Gloucester and I do need to get there quickly.'

The drawing together of Sir Dominick's heavy dark brows heralded his bemused comment. 'Risby? The name seems familiar.'

The nobleman nodded. 'Certainly it is. Sir Godfrey Risby supported the Earl of Warwick, I believe.'

'That is so,' Aleyne said proudly, then her voice broke a little. 'My father died less than four weeks ago. I am a ward of the Crown and I claim the King's protection and,' she added hastily, 'for my maid, Kate, who was arrested with me.'

'That wench with the lame foot is your maid? She was not with you at Broadway nor on the road,' Sir Dominick snapped suspiciously.

'But she is with me now. Why should she be if she is not my maid? She joined me in Tewkesbury.'

'Sir, this woman is incapable of telling the truth for two minutes together...'

'But she is Mistress Aleyne Risby?' The nobleman stared at Aleyne challengingly.

She dipped in a curtsy. 'I am, indeed, my lord. My groom is in the Abbey infirmary and will bear out the truth of my story. I request, formally, that I be allowed to present my case before His Grace the King, to whom, I am sure, I can give proof of my identity.'

The younger man's eyes twinkled as he rose to his feet. 'You cannot, in courtesy, refuse the lady's request, Sir Dominick. Perhaps her maid should be summoned to attend her. It seems sensible that she be kept here under protective surveillance until His Grace is less involved with affairs of the realm.'

'Why cannot she be packed off home to Risby where the facts of this matter can be ascertained?' Sir Dominick said testily. 'I, for one, do not accept this tale so easily, and Tewkesbury, just now, is no place for a ward of the Crown. I could send two of my men to escort her. I've no wish to be her gaoler.'

Aleyne recognised the younger man's authority and appealed directly to him.

'I was forced to leave Risby because I was being pressed into marriage, sir. Again, I plead for your protection until the King is able to make known his wishes concerning me.'

'Indeed?' The grey-green eyes narrowed. 'If that is so, the offending gentleman must be called to account. To force the hand of one of the King's wards is an act of overt treason. See to this lady's well-being, Sir Dominick, until I can look into this affair.' Once more his lips twitched faintly as he viewed the sorry state of Aleyne's apparel. 'Perhaps it might be possible for one of your men to... appropriate——' he stressed the word mockingly '—clothing more suitable in which Mistress Risby might appear before His Grace.'

Sir Dominick bowed stiffly in acknowledgement of the command as he accompanied his noble guest to the door. The young man's shoulders shook as he glanced back to where Aleyne stood forlornly in the centre of the room, her back turned from them.

'Poor Dominick. Surely you did not really believe her to be a camp-follower? Aleyne Risby is an extremely wealthy heiress, and her marriage, within the King's gift, will be a fine inducement to some fortunate gentleman

and encourage him to remain loyal to the Yorkist cause.
His Grace will not take kindly to your forceful treatment
of the lady. You were not unwise enough to thrust unwelcome attentions on her, I trust?'

Sir Dominick swallowed, avoiding the noble's eyes.

'I see you made that grave error too. Dominick,
Dominick, when shall we make a courtier of you if you
will mistake ladies for women of easy virtue?'

This time Sir Dominick's furious dark eyes met his
grey ones and did not falter.

'We must see to it that the maid is summoned to
chaperon her mistress,' the nobleman said hastily, recognising the signs that his victim was rising to the bait
and would soon choke on his own temper.

'I'll see to it.'

The nobleman bowed to Aleyne, who turned and
curtsyed low.

Her legs were shaking beneath her as they had at her
first encounter with Sir Dominick Allard. She took the
opportunity to seat herself on a stool while he bade his
visitor farewell. When he returned, and stood gazing
broodingly over her, she said haughtily, 'Please send my
maid, Kate, to me.'

He scowled and inclined his head. 'I'll also arrange
for food and wine to be sent in to you both, and water
for bathing.'

His parting shot, aimed at her unkempt appearance,
sent the hot blood to her cheeks.

'Excuse me, mistress.'

After he had left she leaned back, physically and
emotionally exhausted, as his mailed shoes rang hol-
lowly on the stone flagging of the corridor. The arrival
of the unknown young nobleman had saved her from
suffering at the knight's hands.

That he was still extremely angry with her he had made
very plain, and she realised she had exacerbated the
situation by unwittingly making him appear foolish in
the eyes of his lord. If the King did not accept her story,
and handed her back to Sir Dominick for summary

justice, she did not believe he would be merciful. She was very close to tears, her hand pressed to her fast-beating heart, when Kate came in, wide-eyed and bemused, and they clung together, laughing and crying at the same time, hysterically.

CHAPTER SIX

LATER that evening Sir Dominick's sergeant-at-arms self-consciously brought Aleyne a simple blue wool gown and an outdated hennin and white veil.

'It's the best we could do, my lady. One of the town merchant's wives sold us the gown and there's a gilded leather belt to go with it.'

Aleyne nodded at him graciously. 'Thank you. This will do very well.'

Warm water and clean towels were sent in and Aleyne scrambled thankfully out of the torn and muddied clothes she had borrowed from her stepmother's maid, and Kate helped her to change. The gown was over-large and required some pinning, but Kate was able to supply what was necessary and she washed and combed out Aleyne's soft brown hair into damp tendrils. Then the two of them sat down before the smoky fire a servant had kindled, because the room was thought to be clammy and damp. Indeed, after the unseasonable warmth of the day, it had turned chill, and they were glad of the fire's sulky glow while Aleyne dried her hair.

Kate also managed to wash, and brushed off the worst of the dust then sponged stains from her own scarlet kirtle, and set to with a will when a cold capon, loaves of fine white manchet bread and wine were brought in to them. Aleyne was too anxious and excited to eat, but she managed to consume a slice of breast of fowl and some bread at Kate's insistence.

'How quick-witted of you to tell Sir Dominick I was your maid,' Kate said thankfully. 'When those men seized me I thought my last hours had come.'

'I had to think very quickly. It was the least I could do. I got you into the mess. I can only hope my story will be believed.'

'Why should you think your story will not be believed? Won't your man bear it out for you?'

'I'm not sure if Rob will know quite what story to tell.'

Kate's eyes opened wide and Aleyne hesitated, then proceeded to tell her new-found friend who she was and the circumstances that had forced her to flee from her home.

Kate looked very grave at its conclusion. 'Can you be sure you will not be pushed into the arms of this Stoodley, whom you distrust so much?'

'I doubt if the King would do that. Sir Thomas has not supported His Grace in these last two encounters.' Aleyne gave a little shiver of apprehension. 'True, I might fare even worse; though, knowing Sir Thomas, I think that is hardly possible.' She shot a quick glance at Kate. 'You have followed this army. What can you tell me about this man who arrested us, Sir Dominick Allard?'

'Not very much. He's in the household of the Duke of Gloucester, a good commander, so they say, but stern and hard to please.'

'I can believe that. Do you know anything of his fortunes?'

'He's a Yorkshireman like most of the men in Gloucester's household. They call him the Wolf for his badge of the wolf rampant and because of the ferocity of his fighting skill in the charge.'

'Yes, I've heard that.' Aleyne thought again that the man resembled the animal with that shock of shaggy brown hair and snapping, angry eyes.

They sat on before the fire after a man cleared away the food, washing bowl and towels. Aleyne plucked at the wool of the gown nervously.

'I hope if the King receives me he will give me an escort and leave to continue my journey to Gloucester. Kate, would you consider entering my service permanently? I need a maid, a companion I could trust.'

'Willingly,' Kate replied without hesitating.

Aleyne was comforted by the simple reply. She had known the lame girl for only a short time, yet she felt, instinctively, she had found a true confidante.

They were both startled when a faint knock came at the door and Guy Jarvis put his head cautiously round it. He blushed awkwardly and avoided Aleyne's gaze, obviously recalling what he had heard about the embarrassing scene at the cottage near Tewkesbury.

'Sir Dominick sends me to inform you that he will escort you tonight to the Abbot's lodgings, where the King will dine with his commanders. He will take only a short time to change his clothing and will be at your service.'

'Thank you.' Aleyne paled. So she must face the King very soon now and explain herself. Had Rob borne out her tale? She was about to enquire as to his welfare, then decided better of it. Her pride would not allow her to question Sir Dominick's squire if his master was prepared now to accept her identity. Surely, if she was summoned to dine at the Abbot's table, all must be well? Yet, even so, her difficulties were by no means at an end. They could be just beginning. What if the King's plans for her indeed proved more horrifying than the threats she had already fled from?

She dismissed the squire and turned, flustered, to her maid.

'Kate?'

'Your gown becomes you well, mistress, or it will do when I've adjusted the belt and the hennin correctly.' Kate deftly placed the white veiling and stood back, smiling. 'There, you are quite respectable and could by no means be mistaken for...' She broke off and Aleyne laughed.

It was then that Sir Dominick broke in on them and made Aleyne a stiff half-bow.

'Good evening, Mistress Risby. I see my men managed tolerably well in the task I set them. It was hardly to be expected that Tewkesbury could produce without warning a court gown for you.'

Aleyne flushed darkly. The remark was churlishly uttered and hardly designed to give her confidence.

'I am most grateful, Sir Dominick,' she said, curtsying, but the edge of frost was still on her voice. She had not forgiven his earlier cavalier treatment of her.

He was plainly dressed in a brown velvet doublet and grey hose, which made him even more resemble the Wolf his men termed him. His thick dark hair was combed and smoothed back now, but she thought it unlikely it would ever appear completely tamed. Unlike Sir Thomas Stoodley, he made no effort to impress. She wondered at his apparent closeness to the young nobleman who had come to her rescue earlier. His large brown hands were unadorned by gems, and the single decoration of his plain attire was a heavy gold chain, fashioned with enamelled white York roses and the engraved likeness of a heraldic wolf rampant in solid gold hanging from it. It occurred to her that the costly chain had been a gift, possibly offered in payment for some special service or even from a lady.

'The infirmarian informs me that your groom's leg is broken and will need care. Naturally, the boy was very anxious about you but I was able to assure him that you are in safe hands.' His tone was ironic and Aleyne bit her lip uncertainly, knowing that Rob would recall what had happened at the inn and be most disturbed at again encountering Sir Dominick.

'Again I must offer my grateful thanks for your prompt care of him.'

He nodded. 'Did my squire inform you that you were to be received by His Grace the King?'

'I am so unprepared—have I a choice, Sir Dominick? Could I decline?'

'Since you are a declared ward of the Crown I fear not.' The steel had come back into his voice, which had softened slightly, as if in apology, when they had spoken of Rob.

Aleyne turned questioningly towards Kate.

'Your maid will accompany you, certainly. It would not be fitting for you to be without her in attendance. There will be few women present, one or two merchants' wives...' He hesitated and she lowered her head that he might not see the sudden gleam in her eyes. It was more than likely that the more attractive women had been invited by command of the King, and possibly to the discomfort of their husbands, who were forced to a show of compliance. Though it was never voiced openly at Risby, Aleyne was aware of her father's opinion of the handsome King, 'the Rose of Rouen', whose Queen was as beautiful as she was discreet concerning her husband's amusements.

Guy Jarvis waited in the hall with cloaks for both ladies, apparently procured, as the gown had been, from some lady of the town. Sir Dominick paced silently beside Aleyne the short distance to the Abbot's lodging. The market square and streets were lit by brands set in sconces on house walls, and she paused momentarily as they passed the Great West door of the Abbey at sight of the company of armed men grouped around it on guard lest the defeated Lancastrians attempted to escape the King's vengeance during the hours of darkness. Pity at their plight overcame her.

'Will the King execute all the captured Lancastrian commanders?' She looked up into Sir Dominick's stern features, limned by the flickering light from the pitch torch which Guy Jarvis held to light their way.

'The ringleaders, doubtless, and any traitors who have changed sides recently to gain advantages. The men serving under them will more than likely be allowed to go free, but Somerset must die if there is to be any lasting peace in the land.'

'I heard that the Prince had been killed.'

'Yes; his body is awaiting burial in the Abbey chancel.'

'How his mother, poor Queen Margaret, will suffer when she hears the news,' Aleyne sighed.

'Poor Queen Margaret, as you term her, has been responsible for most of the atrocities in these wars,' he retorted. 'Had she been willing to accept the decree making the Duke of York, our King's father, heir to King Henry's throne, the conflict would have been at an end a decade or more ago.'

'You could hardly expect her to tamely submit to a truce which disinherited her son,' Aleyne said sharply. 'No mother would agree to such a thing. Prince Edward was King Henry's only son and had a right to succeed.'

'If he *was* the King's son,' Sir Dominick muttered, and Aleyne reddened angrily. It would be like this boorish knight to believe what suited his purpose. He appeared to have no good opinion of women and had immediately chosen to believe the worst of Aleyne, not only at their first meeting, but this afternoon also, over the matter of the horse.

They were received by the prior at the entrance to the Abbot's lodging and escorted into the parlour. A large board supported on trestles had been set up along one complete length of the room with a shorter one at right angles to it near the centre. To this high table Sir Dominick led Aleyne and waved Kate and Guy to a place at the bottom of the long trestle.

Several of the Yorkist knights now began to filter into the parlour. One or two curious glances were cast at Aleyne, and Sir Dominick curtly introduced her as the King's ward. Immediately she found herself treated with marked respect, though she caught one or two critical glances at her somewhat unsuitable gown. Now the company was joined by the King's more senior commanders accompanied by several ladies. Sir Dominick acknowledged their presence with several frosty bows and forbore to make Aleyne known to any of them. She deduced that she had been correct in her earlier surmise and that His Grace had requested the presence of several of the town's more notable ladies. The two or three sombrely but richly dressed merchants who escorted their womenfolk looked decidedly uncomfortable.

There was a hasty scramble to stand as the Abbot entered with the King and the two royal brothers, the Dukes of Clarence and Gloucester. The Princes took their places of honour at the high table and, to her acute embarrassment, Aleyne found herself placed beside the King. Behind this resplendent company came the prior, the town Mayor and the ladies of his household, and a handsome nobleman Aleyne later discovered to be the King's chamberlain, Lord William Hastings. Sir Dominick bowed and made to withdraw to a seat at the lower table. Aleyne gave a sudden gasp of panic at being so abandoned. The young nobleman on the King's left made a discreet signal for him to remain and indicated he should seat himself by her side. Instantly she recognised him as the young man who had come so promptly to her rescue and given imperious instructions about her safe-keeping. She flashed him a glance of profound gratitude. Why she was so relieved to have the surly Sir Dominick beside her she couldn't have said, but she told herself that this was natural, knowing no other in this intimidating and splendid gathering.

The King, resplendent in scarlet velvet, greeted the company jovially, and Aleyne could detect in his smiling countenance no sign of displeasure with the Abbot, Strensham, for having actually dared to reprove him.

As her father had said, the King was handsome, though Aleyne considered his complexion somewhat florid. Her youthful rescuer looked even slighter and rather pale in his splendid court apparel—a blue doublet edged with marten fur, embellished by a fine bejewelled gold chain. Next to him sat a heavily built young man with the same reddish gold hair as the King's, falling to his shoulders in long curls. He eyed the company with haughty disdain. Aleyne guessed him to be the King's brother, George of Clarence, who had been son-in-law to the Earl of Warwick and abandoned him at Coventry, returning his allegiance to Edward only shortly before the decisive battle of Barnet had doomed his father-in-law. He was gorgeously dressed in a doublet of purple-figured velvet.

Noticing her glance towards her rescuer, Sir Dominick bent towards Aleyne and whispered, 'His Grace the Duke of Gloucester,' then confirmed her earlier surmise as to the identity of the florid Duke of Clarence.

Aleyne bowed her head as she caught the smiling acknowledgement of the Duke of Gloucester. No wonder Sir Dominick had deferred to him so hastily and obeyed his instructions without argument. The King's younger brother could not be defied.

Aleyne was able to recall very little of what followed. Her gaze lowered deferentially to the plate and cup she shared with Sir Dominick, she picked at the rich delicacies the Abbot, despite his hasty preparations, had provided for the entertainment of his sovereign: pike in rich spiced sauce, poultry of all kinds, haunches of venison, followed by eel broth and a dish of bream, then, finally, a plentitude of tarts, jellies and preserved fruits to complete the repast.

At length the trestles were cleared and the King graciously lolled in his chair as the Abbot's singing boys performed for his pleasure, and the Mayor, with his ladies, at last took his departure. The choristers dismissed, the King beckoned to Sir Dominick to approach him. Aleyne was dry-mouthed with apprehension. Until this moment the King had not deigned to utter one word to her and had hardly acknowledged her presence at the feast other than to smile graciously once in her direction.

Sir Dominick led her forward and she sank in a deep curtsy before the King's chair. She was acutely conscious of the interested gaze of the young Duke of Gloucester who stood behind the King's chair. The Duke of Clarence had already lumbered off to his lodgings some time ago, on the King's amused permission. He had taken so much of the sweet malmsey that Aleyne thought his squires would have some ado to keep him on his feet until he reached his own chamber.

'So this is the young lady who travels to Gloucester without escort in time of war, Sir Dominick. The lady shows courage, though her decision might be termed foolhardy by some I could mention,' the King said silkily.

Aleyne dared to lift her eyes and look full at him. 'Your Grace, I beg to correct that assumption. My steward's son, Rob Tranton, rode with me and guarded me well until he was attacked on the road and injured.'

'The man lies in the Abbey infirmary, Your Grace. He has a broken leg but I am informed the bone is not shattered and the limb will heal.' Sir Dominick supported her statement, though grudgingly.

'I am pleased to hear it. Sit, mistress.' The King waved Aleyne to a stool near his chair and she trembled as his bold blue eyes passed over her, taking in the clumsily altered gown and outmoded hennin.

'I understand from my brother Dickon, here, that your haste to Gloucester was to escape an over-enthusiastic suitor.'

'Yes, Your Grace.'

'Let me think. Your father remarried recently——'

'Mistress Maud Stoodley, sire, my stepmother.'

'Could she not have protected you from so importunate a suitor? Has she left the manor?'

'No, Your Grace.' Aleyne hesitated uncertainly. 'The matter was delicate. The man was—her kinsman.'

'Ah.' The King grinned broadly. He ran his finger appreciatively round the jewelled rim of the Abbot's finest wine cup, provided, though reluctantly, for his sovereign's use. 'Well, we cannot allow our ward to be wed to one not of our choosing, however convenient that may be to your stepmother. We must acquaint her with our wishes. I regret the death of your father, Mistress Aleyne. He was my father's friend and mine, and deeply loyal to our cause. We shall miss him. Accept our sincere condolences.'

Tears sparked to Aleyne's eyes as the King's kindly words brought to her mind her terrible sense of loneliness which recent horrifying events had forced to the back of her mind momentarily. She swallowed back the lump in her throat and ventured to plead her cause.

'Since my servant Rob Tranton will be forced to keep to his bed in the infirmary for some weeks, he will be unable to ride with me to my kinswoman in Gloucester, sire. I would deem it a great favour if you would designate one or even two of your men-at-arms to escort me to her home, now that the fighting appears to be over.'

He frowned, considering. 'We must do better for you than that, Mistress Aleyne. It is our duty to find you a husband and speedily.' He bent forward to place a be-jewelled finger beneath her chin at her sudden start of dismay. 'Be assured that we shall have your welfare at heart. Messengers shall be sent immediately to Risby to acquaint your stepmother with our wishes concerning you and to enquire into the state of affairs at the manor. Certainly, in the meantime, you must have adequate protection. Have you a woman in attendance?'

'Yes, Your Grace, my maid Kate Shepton.'

'Good. It remains, then, for me to appoint a suitable guardian. Sir Dominick, I order you to keep my ward in charge over the next few days here in Tewkesbury. You have a suitable lodging in the town?'

Sir Dominick bowed. 'Yes, Your Grace. I have arranged for Mistress Risby to occupy rooms in the house next to my own quarters.'

'Excellent. Provided she is adequately chaperoned and guarded, that should serve until affairs here allow me to proceed to the capital.' The King's lips twitched as he glanced down at her over-large gown. 'See that she is provided with everything for her comfort. It may not be possible to provide you with mourning garments, Mistress Aleyne, but Sir Dominick will do his best, I assure you. I understand the lady will need to be pro-vided with a mount?'

Aleyne saw Sir Dominick's shoulders stiffen and knew that the King had heard from his brother's lips the entertaining story of how she had attempted to steal the

knight's favourite hack. Realising that the tale had made
him appear slightly ridiculous in the eyes of his companion gentlemen, she sighed inwardly. This coldness
between them would not allow her stay within his charge
to be a pleasant one, and the taunts of others would
certainly not ease the tension. He was not a patient man,
Sir Dominick. The tale of how he had taken the King's
ward for a camp-follower must make titillating gossip
to be handed down from nobleman to man-at-arms
throughout the King's camp. Aleyne's cheeks burned at
the thought. Under such circumstances it would not
prove an easy task for the King to provide her with a
husband, unless, she thought bitterly, her considerable
fortune would more than compensate the unfortunate
man chosen for the indignity of taking to wife a woman
whose reputation was so besmirched.

The King graciously dismissed them, and Sir Dominick
led her from the Abbot's lodging and back through the
darkened streets. Kate and Guy padded silently in
attendance.

As they entered Sir Dominick's lodging a man came to
stiff attention in the stone-flagged corridor. Aleyne recognised him as the soldier Sir Dominick had addressed
so harshly when he had found her in the act of ab-
sconding with his horse. It appeared that he held the
man responsible for the incident. Now she saw that he
wore Sir Dominick's badge of the rampant wolf on his
jack, a man with a distinct air of authority, likely one
of Sir Dominick's officers.

The man gave a nervous laugh. 'I'm sorry to disturb
you, sir, but you did ask me to report to you before you
retired.'

'Certainly I did. Are all arrangements completed for
Mistress Risby's comfort?' Sir Dominick led the way into
the parlour and indicated that Aleyne should seat herself.

'Yes, sir. I've made sure, personally, that the upstairs
chamber in this house is clean and that there is fresh
linen provided. A truckle bed has been procured for

Mistress Risby's maid. Your baggage has already been moved next door.'

'Excellent.'

Aleyne said quietly, 'I regret that you have been put to some inconvenience.'

'The King's wish is my command,' he returned suavely.

The officer coughed again as if anxious to be about his business, and Sir Dominick turned imperiously back to him. 'Well?'

'I've made a tour of inspection, sir, and intimated to all your men your orders concerning theft from our supplies and the penalties facing any man who is caught disobeying them.'

'Not before time.'

'The men will settle, sir, after tonight.' The officer cleared his throat awkwardly. 'It is understandable—after the rigours of the march from Windsor——'

'I accept that we must expect some degree of insubordination after a victory, but there is to be no relaxation of discipline tomorrow. There's important work on hand, and I'll not have the men behaving badly before the townsfolk. Any indiscreet incident could spark off trouble and my lord of Gloucester must have our full support in his task of dealing with the Lancastrian prisoners.'

The Duke of Gloucester, despite his youth, was Lord Constable of England. Aleyne shuddered as she thought of his grim task of judging the rebels and overseeing the ensuing executions which must take place over the next few days. That tight line of his mouth she had noted spoke of his distaste for the proceedings. Had she glimpsed, too, a sign of some haunting sorrow in those grey-green eyes?

Sir Dominick prepared to dismiss his officer. 'Report to me at first light. I must be in position at the west door of the Abbey when the prisoners surrender.'

'Sir.' The officer saluted, then hesitated as if he had something further to say. He glanced meaningly at Aleyne as if he would rather not divulge his further information in her presence. As Sir Dominick waited coldly, he added, somewhat lamely, 'The prisoner, sir, the man we took skulking behind our lines...he is insisting on speaking with you. Before committing him with the others, I thought——'

'I've nothing to say to the man.' Sir Dominick gave a wearied wave of his hand.

'He appears to be a gentleman of some standing, sir, no common spy.'

'I'm aware of that. Keep him under guard until I can deal with the matter.'

'Do you wish us to...?' The officer cocked an eyebrow in Aleyne's direction, and she shivered again. Was the soldier asking if he was to put the prisoner to the torture?

Apparently Sir Dominick assumed this to be so, for he said curtly, 'Not until I've had time to examine him myself. Is he injured?'

'Not seriously, sir. He was blooded in the arm when we took him, and sustained some bruises. The men mishandled him. Am I to see to it that he's fed decently?'

'Yes, I suppose that is his right.' Sir Dominick turned from his officer irritably. 'You can go now,' then to Aleyne, 'Now, madam, Guy will light you to your chamber and I will take my leave of you.'

She rose and curtsied. 'Thank you, and goodnight, sir.'

'You do understand that my men have orders to keep you safe? I would be grateful if you would not subject them to harassment. You will not be permitted leave to go abroad without my personal escort.'

Aleyne reddened angrily. She had been grateful for Sir Dominick's care of her this evening and the steps he had taken to ensure her comfort. Now she was reminded all too summarily of her position here. 'I understand that I am your prisoner, sir,' she said frigidly.

'You are my honoured guest, Mistress Risby, and one for whose safety I must answer to His Grace the King.'

She nodded, tight-lipped, and he signalled to the squire to kindle a candle to light Aleyne and Kate up the steep stair. There was nothing further to say. He was determined to show his authority over her and it was best to accept the situation with good grace.

As she swept into the corridor, the uncertain light of the brand set above the lintel of the back door flickered upon the haggard features of a man, wrists pinioned behind his back, who was being bundled unceremoniously through to the rear courtyard. Aleyne's limbs turned to water and threatened to give way beneath her, so that she was forced to reach out for and cling to the wooden stair-post.

Kate, concerned, rushed forward to support her, but Aleyne shook her head and forced herself to mount the steps while Sir Dominick stood, frowning, at the stair foot, watching her.

Once inside her chamber, she gestured to Kate to close and bolt the door. The maid hastened to obey, her expression as bewildered as Sir Dominick's.

Aleyne listened to the sound of the squire's feet descending the stair as she sat unsteadily down upon the bed, her hand pressed to her fast-beating heart.

Sir Dominick's prisoner, he whom the officer had deemed a spy in the King's camp, was Ellis Dyer.

CHAPTER SEVEN

ALEYNE lay for hours, staring up at the roof timbers above her head while Kate, on the truckle bed beside her, fell instantly asleep.

Her mind went over and over Ellis's plight. She had striven to recall in strict detail every word she had heard spoken concerning him. Why had he not taken sanctuary in the Abbey with the other prisoners? Sir Dominick's officer had said he was 'no common spy'. He had said that Ellis had been taken behind the Yorkist lines and that he had specially requested to speak with Sir Dominick. Why? Were they acquainted? Ellis had

been in Warwick's company, so presumably he was now
in the Queen's service. Had he been taken before the
battle?

A cold sweat of fear drenched her. If that was so Ellis
would not be afforded honourable treatment, nor the
mercy of the axe, should he be found guilty of spying.
He could even be tortured. The officer had suggested
such a course last night and Sir Dominick had ordered
him to hold his hand until he had spoken with the
prisoner. That implied that he knew Ellis. She frowned
in the darkness. Sir Dominick had been in Gloucester's
household, Kate had told her, and Gloucester had been
trained to arms by Warwick. It was possible that Sir
Dominick Allard and Ellis Dyer had met during those
early days before the Earl of Warwick had abandoned
his allegiance to King Edward. Then, surely, he would
be kindly disposed towards his prisoner—unless he
despised him now as traitor to the King's cause.

One fact only comforted her: Ellis did not appear to
have been seriously hurt. Yet that too suggested, omin-
ously, that he had played no part in the conflict. He had
not noticed her, she was sure. She had been in shadow
and Ellis entirely concerned with his own possible fate.
And he had not expected her to be in Tewkesbury. For
the moment it was better that Sir Dominick did not know
that she and Ellis were known to each other. There must
be some way she could help him. She would take no
sides nor condemn him for any dishonourable conduct.
She could not understand these wars or the need for
brother to fight brother. It was enough to remember that
Ellis had served her father loyally. Certainly she must
find some way of talking with him. That was going to
prove difficult. Last night Sir Dominick had made it very
clear to her that she was virtually his prisoner, as much
under guard as Ellis was.

She was falling at last into a state of mind-fogged
stupor when the noise began outside her window: the
jingle of horse accoutrements, the creak of saddle leather
and the nervous movements and whinnying of restless

horses. She sat up immediately, remembering Sir Dominick's orders to his officer to wake him at first light.

The Earl of Somerset and the Lancastrian lords had sworn to emerge from sanctuary at sunrise, and Sir Dominick must be at his post with his lord, the Duke of Gloucester.

Kate stirred, thoroughly wakened now by the growing noise outside in the market-place, which swelled by the minute as archers and pikemen formed into companies ready for the grim task of the day. She pushed herself up on the truckle bed and met Aleyne's questioning look with a helpless movement of her hands.

'You had best not be seen at the window. Sir Dominick would not approve. Wait while I dress.'

Hastily she shrugged into her clothes, went to the window and threw back the casement. 'Such a to-do. Half the King's army appears to have mustered. I pity those poor souls in the Abbey.'

'Can you see Sir Dominick?'

'Yes, he's right beside the Gloucester herald. I can see the wolf pennant flying next to that of the white boar. They are forming up in line and making for the west door of the Abbey. It looks as if Norfolk's company has been sent to cover the east front.'

Aleyne slipped her feet from the bed and reached for her clothing. 'How long do you think Sir Dominick will be busied?'

Kate shrugged. 'The proceedings will take some time. It will prove a ceremonious business and the King swore to the Abbot that he would keep firm control of his men after the excesses of yesterday and the slaughter within the nave.'

'Please hook me up, Kate.'

Kate turned, her eyes widening at sight of her mistress so soon dressed.

'There is no need for you to rise yet, better not. I can go to the kitchen and bring up breakfast for you. You should rest. There will be nothing for you to do here, and I doubt if you will be able to visit your servant until this business with the rebels is over. Even then the monks will be confused and overworked, what with the masses for the slain.' She closed the casement as if to shut from Aleyne thoughts of the victors' vengeance.

'I've no time for food, Kate. I need your help and advice.'

'I don't understand.'

'I must act quickly before Sir Dominick is released from attendance on the Duke of Gloucester.'

Kate looked decidedly alarmed. 'Mistress, you are not planning anything which would anger Sir Dominick? I tell you he is a devil to cross, and——'

'Kate, is there any way of discovering where the prisoner who was brought here last night is being held?'

'I suppose I could find out from one of the men, but why? Do you know the man?'

'He is my kinsman, and served in my father's house as page and squire till he entered the service of the Earl of Warwick. I must talk to him, Kate. Can the guards be bribed?' Distractedly she recalled that she had nothing which she could offer. It was just possible that a promise would suffice. The fact that she was an heiress must be now circulating about the camp.

Kate pursed her lips, her hands on her hips. Aleyne noticed that she often appeared to ease her weight on to the good foot by standing with the bad one slightly forward.

'Guards can usually be bribed if the sum offered is high enough. That is one thing we can rely on in a changing world,' she commented cynically, 'though Sir Dominick's men might prove more difficult to handle. You've seen for yourself how stern a disciplinarian he is. If one of his men was caught helping you to see the prisoner it could earn him a flogging or worse.'

'As you know I have no money or jewels with me, but I would see to it that the man will be paid in the future and paid well. You know I would keep my word, Kate. Could you convince one of the men of that?'

Kate gave that habitual shrug. 'You realise you would not escape blame if Sir Dominick were to discover this. It could prove very unpleasant for you. If the man is held to be a traitor——'

'I know, Kate, but this is vital for me. Will you try?'

Again Kate shrugged. 'You know that I am—acquainted with several of the men in this company. One of my—er—friends is in charge of the prisoner, or was last night. He owes me more than one favour. Stay while I go down to the kitchen. While there I'll see what I can find out.'

'Do you think Sir Dominick will have left men to guard this house?'

'Certainly; he is responsible to His Grace the King for your safety and there could be trouble later when the men disperse from their duties at the Abbey. I did not see Sir Dominick's squire by his side. It may be that he has been left in charge here.'

Kate returned quite quickly with the tray, somewhat out of breath.

'It's as I thought. Guy Jarvis is in charge. He is anxious to be of service. If we could find some errand in the town to send him on we could dispose of him for a while and it would be easier to talk with the man.'

Aleyne nodded. 'Send him up.'

Kate called for service below and soon Sir Dominick's squire appeared in the doorway supervising two men-at-arms, who brought up a steaming ewer of water and a basin for Aleyne to make her toilet. He himself carried clean napkins over his arm as he made his bow.

'Good morning, Mistress Risby. I am commanded to attend you in any way you see fit. Sir Dominick excuses himself. As you know, he is busied about the King's service.'

Aleyne forbore to make the comment that the work was grim indeed, and smiled upon the squire more graciously than he had come to expect.

'Thank you. I know you must be hard pressed.' She waited while he dismissed the serving men. 'You must

be over-tired. You will be glad when all this campaigning is over and you all back on Sir Dominick's
manor. And now I have been foisted upon you to require extra attendance.'

He bowed low, his young face crimsoning in embarrassment. 'I am more than happy to be of assistance,
lady. At all events I am well used to campaigning. It has
been like this since we landed at Ravenspur; London,
Barnet, then the forced march here. There's been scarce
time to draw breath.'

'You have been in service to Sir Dominick for some
time, then?'

'Three years. I went with him into exile in Burgundy.'

'Then you have seen more than enough slaughter
during these past months.'

'Aye.' His expression softened. 'My mother will be
glad of a sight of me soon, now.'

'Is she widowed?'

He nodded. 'My father was killed in the Duke of
York's service at Wakefield.'

Aleyne's eyes blurred with tears at the thought of her
own recent loss.

'Is there anything more I can do for your comfort,
mistress? I regret I am not able to provide you with
waiting-women, but the town is in chaos.'

'I am concerned still for my servant.'

'It is not possible yet for you to visit the Abbey,
Mistress Risby.'

'I understand that, but——' she hesitated and turned
the gaze of her lovely eyes upon him pleadingly '—but
could not you go and enquire for me?' Tears glinted on
her long dark lashes and Guy was lost.

He reddened and hedged, remembering Sir Dominick's
precise orders. 'I could send one of the men.'

'I would be much more reassured if I know you had
spoken with Rob personally and you could bring me
word from the infirmarian regarding his condition.
Please, would it take so long?'

'I am commanded not to leave the house.'

'Sir Dominick is anxious to ensure my safety. I realise that, but I assure you I will not stir.' She shuddered, turning from the window where the noise of the victorious army's clamour could still be heard. 'I would be afraid to venture out—until I am well guarded and that, out there, is over.'

He bit his lip; then, seeing her tear-filled gaze, he capitulated. 'Then I'll go. It can but take but half an hour or so, and I can pass easily through the ranks wearing Sir Dominick's livery and with my authority, more simply than any man-at-arms.'

She smiled at him, offering her hand. He bent awkwardly to kiss her fingers.

She was ashamed to use him so and surprised at her own duplicity and how simply it had come to her in her desperate need.

Kate reported from the window when the squire had left the house.

'You must wait now while I go to look for our man.'

Aleyne paced the room in a fever of impatience. Suppose Kate's friend was not on guard? All this must be done in haste. Sir Dominick must not return to the house before she had managed to see Ellis. She had the presence of mind to place a half quartern-loaf and some cold meat within a clean napkin, remembering how coldly Sir Dominick had referred to his prisoner. Any food Ellis had been given was most likely of the poorest quality.

When Kate returned she looked triumphant. 'Put on your cloak and come quickly. There is no one outside the door.'

She drew Aleyne hastily down the stair and out through the rear door of the house into the small garden.

'The prisoner is being held in the store barn next to the house where Sir Dominick is being lodged. I have spoken with the guard. You can have only minutes with him. We can go through this gate.'

A man-at-arms in salet and jack bearing the wolf rampant device saluted Aleyne and stood back from the heavy studded door to the stone-built outhouse.

'You must be very quick, mistress,' he said gruffly, 'unless you wish me a sore back or, even worse, a twisted neck.'

Aleyne nodded grimly and the man unlatched the door for her. She called Ellis's name softly as she entered into the darkened interior. Light filtered only dimly from a slit high up near the roof, and she blinked awkwardly till her wrists were seized and a familiar voice said huskily, 'Aleyne . . . by the Virgin, it cannot be! How can you possibly be here in Tewkesbury?'

She was gradually becoming used to the poor light and could just make out Ellis's features. His lips were warm on her fingers and gently she withdrew her hands from his grasp.

'Ellis, let me look at you. Are you hurt?'

As she had seen last night he looked pale and drawn, his auburn hair dishevelled, but he shook his head at her question.

'No, I'm well enough and happy to see you, but—I don't understand. I thought you safe at Risby.'

They had provided him with sweet-smelling hay for a bed and she sank down on a bale of it.

'First you must eat,' she said crisply, setting out the bread and meat for him.

He reached for it eagerly and she noted how he wolfed down the bread, tearing off strips and forcing it hastily into his mouth. He checked at her stare and broke off, embarrassed.

'Bless you for this. They brought me some slops last night but I've been well nigh starved since the Earl was killed. With armies living off the land, pickings have been poor, especially for fugitives.' He waved towards the hay. 'I was grateful for that. I've slept under hedges since Barnet. But never mind me. Tell me what you are doing here. Is all well at Risby?'

Tears threatened again but, resolutely, she forced them back. This was no time to dwell on her sorrow.

'My father died. Did you receive my message telling how ill he was?'

His brown eyes widened at her news and he reached out again and captured her hand.

'Oh, Aleyne, I grieve for you. No, I heard nothing. If only I could have been with you——'

Hastily she pressed him to reveal the cause of his imprisonment. 'There have been problems. I was forced to leave and seek your mother in Gloucester but——' she laughed shakily '—I have had sundry adventures on the road and now the aftermath of the battle—more about me later. But you, Ellis? I saw you brought in last night. How is it that you were taken? Were you making for Risby?'

'I was captured behind the King's lines.' His mouth was held in grimly, and she sensed his fear.

'I heard what was said. But why, Ellis? Were you acting as scurrier for Somerset's force?'

He gave a barked laugh. 'By God's blood, no. Why should I fight for Margaret? I wanted to join Edward's force. They took me before I could find a way of contacting Gloucester.'

'I don't understand, Ellis. You fought against the Duke at Barnet.'

'I fought for the Earl. When he was killed my allegiance to him was finished. My only wish was to rejoin my old companions from Middleham and offer my blade to His Grace, King Edward.'

Aleyne shook her head, perplexed. She would never understand men as long as she lived. As a squire, trained to arms by the Earl of Warwick, Ellis had considered it his duty to support his lord in whatever course the Earl decided on, but his heart had always yearned for the House of York: for allegiance to his former friends, Robert Percy, Francis Lovell and the youthful Duke of Gloucester, who had each served in the Earl's train at Middleham. Her father had tried to explain how the

King's marriage to Lady Elizabeth Grey had angered the Earl and soured the relationship between him and the young King he had been instrumental in placing upon the throne, but, to Aleyne, the political necessities of changing allegiance had proved impossible to grasp. To her, kinsmen and friends were surely to be supported loyally through good times and bad. Now Ellis wished to change sides once more, a fact she found bewildering.

'Are you in great peril?'

He gave a rasping breath. 'Aye, Aleyne; I'm likely to die a hideous traitor's death at Tyburn if I cannot prove my intentions. That is well nigh impossible now. The battle is over and I've no way of proving my loyalty with my sword arm, and Dominick Allard refuses to allow me speech with His Grace of Gloucester.' The last words were grated out through gritted teeth and she realised his hatred for Allard.

'You think the Duke will believe you?'

Ellis shrugged uneasily. 'Who can tell? We were comrades once at Middleham, but then—so were Allard and I. I can but pray to God that Gloucester will listen to my pleas. It is my last hope.'

'Ellis, he is Lord Constable of England. Even now he is at the Abbey by the King's side, arresting the Lancastrian lords as they emerge from sanctuary. Can you really hope he will accept your pledge of loyalty when you fought for the Queen and King Henry at Barnet?' Aleyne's tone was doubtful.

'I fought for the Earl,' Ellis repeated doggedly.

'But that's all one, Ellis. The Earl was then fighting Queen Margaret's cause. His daughter is wed to Edward of Lancaster.'

'Aye, Aleyne, but what can a man do but follow his lord? That's the way of it. You cannot understand what governs a man's honour.'

'No,' she retorted, caustically, 'I can't, for this honour you prate of is likely to cost you your life. Why couldn't you have gone into hiding after Barnet, or simply gone home to await the outcome of this latest encounter?'

'I wanted——'

'I know,' she said bitterly, 'you needed a new cause to enhance your fortunes.'

'Do you doubt my intentions, Aleyne?' His tone was puzzled as if he was unused to that coldness in her voice.

'I've seen too much lately to trust to any man's honour.'

She had risen as if to leave, and he scrambled up too and seized her hand. 'You have no reason to think ill of me, Aleyne. You were not wont to do so at Risby.'

His tone had softened and she turned to his eager youthful countenance, her lip trembling at memory of the happy times they had spent together. Gently she reached up and touched his bruised cheek.

'Of course I don't distrust you, Ellis. I am rightly concerned for you. Something must be done to get you out of this mess, and soon, for I'm afraid Sir Dominick means you no good. He has been appointed my guardian by the King. I overheard what was said when you were brought in last night.'

His eyes narrowed thoughtfully. 'And his men are keeping guard over you?'

'The Duke of Gloucester was instrumental in placing me in his care, thinking it was best for me.'

Ellis snorted. 'The devil he did! Watch yourself. Allard is a hard man to cross.'

'I am tired of having men tell me so. Why are you at odds with him when you tell me he was at Middleham with you?'

He shook his head wearily. 'I cannot think why he denies me access to His Grace. I can see that he has some reason for bitterness. He followed the King into exile last year and, doubtless, his fortunes suffered for it. My support of Warwick will not have endeared me to him, but, in honour, he should give me leave to put my case fairly now.'

That word 'honour' again! Aleyne bit back her angry response. Little of honour she saw in men's motives. Was Dominick Allard's reason for denying Ellis oppor-

tunity to defend himself an attempt to better his own
standing with the King? His capture of a traitor, and
that felon's hideous punishment, might be proof of his
own stern loyalty, particularly as Ellis Dyer had once
been counted among his friends.

Her heart beat more quickly at thought of Ellis's fate.
He was still holding her wrists tightly and she made a
little movement to release herself. Here, in the shadowed
interior of the barn, she could not read Ellis's expression,
but his own quickened breathing told her he, too, was
overcome by his feelings.

He whispered hoarsely, 'I should never have left you,
Aleyne. If—if I am spared——'

'Ellis, you must not even think the worst. Keep up
your spirits.'

'I must face my danger, Aleyne. Those men in the
Abbey have had the whole night, as I have had, to consider theirs.'

Her voice was throaty with emotion. 'I will find some
way to save you, Ellis. I must.' She pulled her hands
from his grasp and turned, hand to her cheek, as she
heard outside the movement of feet on gravel. He had
caught her close and, for seconds, she had experienced
that strange terror which had first assailed her as Sir
Thomas Stoodley had kissed her in greeting, then that
terrible sense of panic when she had been helpless in the
hands of the Welshman along the road. Surely she could
not be afraid of Ellis, whom she had known and trusted
since childhood? Yet now she had this unaccountable
need to be away from him——

'I must go. Sir Dominick is not aware of your connection with my family?'

'I doubt if he remembers it, if he did so.'

'Then he must not know it if I am to have any chance
of helping you.'

He released her reluctantly. 'You will not alarm my
mother by telling her of my imprisonment?'

'No, that would be cruel until we know more what is
best to be done. Promise me you will not give up hope.'

'I promise. God guard you, Aleyne.' He reached out and, cupping her chin between his hands, he drew her close again and kissed her very gently upon the forehead.

She submitted, and forced a smile. 'I will, coz.'

Hastily she pushed open the barn door to find Kate waiting impatiently. She found herself trembling as Kate led her quickly back to their lodging.

CHAPTER EIGHT

ONCE in her chamber, Aleyne dismissed Kate after thanking her for her help. For the moment she would delay talk of rewarding the accommodating guard, knowing that Kate had that matter well in hand. She had to be alone. Her feelings for Ellis within the barn had been difficult to understand. She had expected to treat him as she always had done, as her childhood friend and confidant. She had sensed that his attitude to her had changed also. His grasp on her fingers and the intensity of his gaze had not been lost on her. For the first time in his presence she had felt embarrassment. She had almost been afraid to meet his eyes. His predicament had filled her with fear for him, but that was not unmixed with some irritation. Why had he behaved so foolishly? Recently she had begun to distrust the motives of all men. She feared now that Ellis too had begun to consider her a prize to be desired.

She told herself that her experiences had left her vulnerable. She must cast such thoughts from her mind as unworthy of the respect she held for Ellis. He was in great danger and she must put her whole mind to helping him escape. She realised now that that was the only solution. Ellis's faith in the friendship of the Duke of Gloucester was, surely, misplaced. The King was not disposed to mercy. Sir Dominick Allard had made that quite clear to her. The young duke would be governed by his brother's wishes. Ellis could expect no help from that quarter, and certainly none from Sir Dominick himself; therefore his only hope was to escape from the barn before he could be brought to judgement.

When Kate announced that Guy Jarvis was back from his errand Aleyne was relieved to hear an excellent report of Rob's progress.

'You should be able to see him, if you've a mind, after the noon meal, Mistress Risby. Things have quietened down in the streets, and affairs at the Abbey will soon be back to normal.'

Sir Dominick did not appear at her lodgings, and dinner was served in her room.

Guy Jarvis offered himself as escort to the Abbey and Aleyne accepted with alacrity. She and Kate were hurried by him through the now deserted streets into the Abbey's domestic buildings.

Rob was propped up on a truckle bed in the infirmary and was delighted and relieved to see his mistress safe.

'I have been half out of my wits with worry, Mistress Aleyne, but the knight, Sir Dominick, told me yesterday you were safe and well.'

'Be easy, Rob. I am now under the King's protection and my stay in Sir Dominick's charge only temporary.' She smiled a little as she noted the boy's suspicion of her new maid. 'This is Kate. She is to serve me and has already proved a true friend.'

He nodded doubtfully.

The infirmarian assured Aleyne that Rob's leg would mend, provided the boy stayed still for a while if the bones were to knit true.

'He should be left here with us for two weeks—longer if possible, lest the limb distort.'

Aleyne smiled at the old man warmly. 'Of course we must be guided by your advice, Brother.' She was embarrassed by her inability to offer coin for Rob's care but he told her Sir Dominick Allard had already made such provision.

Rob promised he would be patient and accept his enforced rest cheerfully and she left, gratified to know he was in good hands.

When she and Kate again entered her lodgings and climbed to Aleyne's chamber she discovered a large wooden chest had been placed there during her absence. Kate jerked open the lid and gave a little gasp. Aleyne approached to find a profusion of silken and brocade gowns in jewel-like colours, together with hennins and veiling as well as several decorative belts and soft leather shoes. Kate exclaimed over the splendour of the materials as she lifted out one of the gowns for Aleyne's inspection.

Aleyne shook her head dubiously, mindful of her mourning. 'It is neither necessary nor suitable for Sir Dominick to go to such expense. For the present I can manage quite adequately with the blue gown we have altered.'

'I doubt that, Mistress Risby, since His Grace the King has consented to sup tonight at my lodging and has commanded your presence.'

Aleyne swung round sharply at the sound of Sir Dominick's hated voice. He stood in the doorway, his lip curling ironically at sight of Kate's evident pleasure in the gowns and trinkets. He bowed to Aleyne. She curtsyed stiffly and signalled her leave for him to enter the chamber.

'His Grace is indeed kind to honour me, but I imagine he must be over-busied with state affairs, and I——'

'Will dutifully accept his invitation,' Sir Dominick said smoothly. He waved his hand irritably as she made to protest. 'He will not excuse you. You must be present.' Moving to the window, he peered down into the street. 'I trust that Guy obeyed my instructions and has seen to your comfort.'

'He has, sir.'

'Good.'

'I have to thank you again for your care of my servant. I have been to visit him—with your squire as escort, of course.'

'Is the boy improving?'

'Thank you, yes, but the infirmarian informs me it will be weeks before he can leave his bed.'

'Annoying for you, but I shall see to it that you are well served in the meantime.'

'I am constantly reminded, sir, that your care of me is something of an imposition.' Her tone was frosty, and he turned from the window to face her, his brows raised as if in astonishment at her angry tone.

She continued. 'I take it that now the business of the rebels is completed you will soon be leaving Tewkesbury. I trust then that His Grace will find it possible to meet my request for an escort to Gloucester and your onerous task will be at an end.'

He smiled faintly as he would to a churlish child. 'You are anxious to be rid of my company, mistress.'

'As I am sure you are to be rid of mine.'

He made no answer but held her gaze steadily so that she was the first to look away from him, conscious of her deliberate rudeness and faintly ashamed of her conduct.

She sighed. 'Sir, I regret the incident of the horse,' she began, and saw him stiffen. How touchy he was at mention of that! She began again. 'What I mean is, I am sorry I placed you in a position that...'

'Yes?' he said harshly, and she swallowed hard.

'No matter. All this will soon be over.'

He regarded her sombrely under those shaggy brows of his. 'We cannot be sure of that for a while. There are trials of the rebels yet to be concluded. I shall be needed at the Lord Constable's side.'

Aleyne caught back a concerned gasp. Was Ellis's fate to be decided soon? In her haste to be free of Sir Dominick's guardianship she had forgotten that her first thought must be to find some way of freeing him. That could not be managed if she was no longer in Sir Dominick's household.

As he moved to the door to take his leave he said, 'His Grace of Gloucester will be present tonight. You can rely on him to see that your interests are protected.'

Aleyne was still concerned that her gown should be suitable for her mourning and finally chose one in purple velvet trimmed with grey fur. While Kate fitted it to her satisfaction, Aleyne thought desperately about Ellis. Should she choose this opportunity to put his case before the King? Or would it be possible to speak privately to the Duke of Gloucester, relying on his former friendship with Ellis? Both courses might well spell his doom. She knew too, instinctively, that Sir Dominick would be furious with her. Might it be possible to discover his reason for keeping his captive from the other Lancastrian prisoners? She always felt so uncomfortable in his presence and seemed always to say the one thing to anger him.

Despite the grim proceedings of the earlier part of the day, the King seemed utterly at ease in the small but comfortable solar of Sir Dominick's lodgings. He greeted Aleyne warmly when Sir Dominick led her into his presence and, as she rose from her deep curtsy, he placed her at table in the seat of honour at his right. His younger brother, Gloucester, took his own place on the King's left. Aleyne was perplexed by the air of deep anxiety she noted in his manner as he ate frugally and drank less, replying quietly but courteously to the King's gallant flattery of his new ward. Sir Dominick, having made the customary expressions of gratitude for his sovereign's mark of favour in gracing his table, made few comments throughout the meal.

'I hear that your servant is progressing well.' The King smiled broadly and turned towards the knight. 'And Sir Dominick is now assured of the truth of your story. God's teeth, Mistress Risby, if you only knew how he dotes on that brute, Roland, you might have understood how very close you came to swinging on a hempen rope as a horse-thief!'

Aleyne felt the hot blood crimsoning her throat and cheeks as she saw Sir Dominick stir rebelliously in his chair.

'I feel we owe the good knight some mark of favour for holding his hand—for preserving your honour, and

for other, more valuable, services he has rendered us
these past months.'

Aleyne met the King's intensely blue eyes with her own
bewildered ones. Of what business was it of hers how
the King chose to reward the knight's loyalty? It was
well she was seated when the blow came, for her limbs
would have completely failed her.

'Sir Dominick has expressed a wish for your hand in
marriage, mistress, which I grant him gladly. Indeed, I
am delighted to do so, knowing you will be safe in his
keeping and your lands and manor excellently governed.'

Her fingers trembled on her wine cup and the red
liquor slopped on to the snowy drapery. She fumbled to
right the cup and found Sir Dominick's hand on hers,
steadying it.

She struggled to find her voice, to protest, beg—to
scream. Nothing came. Her eyes met those of the Duke
of Gloucester and he smiled at her. She would get no
help there. Allard was one of the gentlemen of his
household. It had been more than likely his request to
his brother that had found favour.

She pulled her hand from Sir Dominick's grasp and
turned hurriedly to the King, stammering awkwardly as
she found her voice at last, 'I appreciate the honour Your
Grace does me in seeking to ensure my welfare, but I
am still in mourning. The time is too soon. I beg
you——'

'Time is out of sorts for the usual niceties, I grant
you, Mistress Risby.' He cut short her objections almost
brusquely. 'The realm is still unsettled. We cannot have
you at the mercy of any knave who casts eyes on your
fortune. Sir Dominick is our choice for you. It is our
express wish that you marry before we leave Tewkesbury.
My lord of Gloucester's chaplain will arrange matters.
Eventually we shall be pleased to receive you both soon
at court...'

His words ran on while her senses reeled. So soon?
She had run full tilt out of the frying pan indeed! To
wed this man—this icy stranger—who appeared to

despise her! Why, then, had he sued for her hand? The King's words echoed and re-echoed in her brain: 'Any knave who casts eyes on your fortune.'

She was to be sold, as Lady Risby had foretold, and Sir Dominick Allard's pledge of loyalty to the House of York was to be highly rewarded indeed. Fury strangled further words in her throat. So she was to pay the price of the King's need for security. By all the saints, she would not so tamely submit. She had escaped Sir Thomas Stoodley, she had distrusted him, feared the corrupt rule he would have imposed upon her people; yet Allard, this iron man who dealt out retribution at the Duke's side without fear or favour, this implacable enemy of Ellis Dyer, was to become her husband and control her life.

She was thankful when the King rose from table, yawning noticeably. The Duke of Gloucester attended him, but, in leaving, exchanged a meaning glance with Sir Dominick. Aleyne had risen in courtesy; now she faltered and caught a tight grip on the table edge to steady her. Sir Dominick accompanied his noble guests to the door. Angrily she fought for some measure of control. Her future husband returned and signalled for Kate to leave them alone. Keeping her face averted, she waited for him to speak, but he was silent, and finally she turned back to face him, goaded to fury by his watchful stillness.

'I should consider myself honoured, sir, that my manor and estates are of sufficient importance for you to accept as a bride one who has made you a laughing stock among your companions and compromised herself by wandering about the countryside in war without a considerable escort.'

He sighed. 'If you had no desire to have a husband chosen for you by His Grace you would have done better to stay at home. As it is, you are a ward of the Crown and we are both subjects to the King's will.'

'Am I to suppose this match is not pleasing to you either?' Her voice was steely, and she released her grasp on the table edge to stand upright, her whole body stiff with resentment for this new insult.

He shrugged. 'Certainly the idea was first mooted by His Grace of Gloucester, and I have no objection.' He indicated the chair she had vacated. 'Let us at least be civil, Mistress Aleyne. You knew well enough you would not be allowed free choice. Is the notion so unpalatable? I gathered you had a distinct aversion to Sir Thomas Stoodley.'

She would have preferred to remain standing, but her limbs were trembling again and she sank gratefully into the seat.

'I objected to being forced to the match.'

'Aye,' he said tiredly. 'Though you might not believe me, I can understand your predicament.'

She was startled by the softer note to his voice and stared back at him, bewildered.

He seated himself opposite and fiddled with the handle of one of the newfangled forks provided for the King's feast. At length he cleared his throat. 'We know little of each other——'

'And what we do, we dislike heartily,' she cut in.

Again he sighed. 'There you go again. Will you not give me a chance to explain my position?'

She bit her lip on a sharp retort and turned away from him.

'As I was about to say, we know little about each other, but that is not unusual. Despite your foolishness,' he raised a hand to stem her further angry words, 'and, whatever you might say, your conduct has been arrant foolishness, I find you courageous, mindful of the welfare of your servants, and gently mannered—attributes I find attractive in a prospective bride.' His lips twitched slightly. 'You are also very beautiful.'

She gave a great gasp and he continued. 'I observed that the first time we met. I noted too how promptly you rebuffed my advances so I assume you to be virtuous, mistress.' His eyes now met hers squarely. 'Come now, do you find me less attractive than Sir Thomas Stoodley? I am young, strong, in the King's favour, and prepared to treat you kindly, provided you obey me. Can we not manage to deal well together? Edward could well have sold you to the highest bidder, some elderly lecher at court. He makes no bones about his need for gold to enrich his treasury.'

She dared not look at him, knowing well enough that what he said was true. Yet everything had come upon her so quickly. She was trapped; like a hunted creature she sought still for some escape and, finding none, snapped back at her adversary.

'And I am to be grateful for such a mercy? Do you tell me that you do not covet my lands as Sir Thomas did?'

Her mark had gone home. Angry colour mottled his neck.

'I confess I am no wealthy gentleman. My marriage to you will certainly be to my advantage, as it would to any of the noblemen who would sue for your hand. The King has seen fit to give you to me. I regret the need for haste over the ceremony. I would have preferred, as I am sure you would have done, to have given you time to come to terms with your situation. However the King has commanded that the matter should be concluded before he leaves for London. I have provided you with a suitable wardrobe and it would seem sensible to cut short your mourning. I will dispatch men to Risby to inform your stepmother what is determined. She will, of course, receive her dower share of the inheritance, a third of the revenues from the estate until her death, as is her right. It will be for you to decide if you wish her to continue to live in the manor house. If not, we must make suitable arrangements for her. In all events, I shall be in attendance on His Grace of Gloucester in London during the coming months, so you will be unlikely to return to Risby for some time.'

'And if I should wish to live quietly on my own manor lands,' she said shakily, 'what then?'

'That would be quite out of the question. Naturally, you must take your place by my side. You heard of the King's wish that you should be presented at court. You need have no fears over the running of the manor. If your steward is not considered trustworthy I'll appoint a man of my own choosing.'

'Master Tranton is utterly loyal,' she said quickly. 'He is Rob's father and devoted to my interests.'

'Indeed? Then that is one worry off my mind. I shall be busied about the Duke's service throughout tomorrow. Since the King will wish to leave very soon now, I shall arrange the marriage ceremony for the evening within one of the Abbey chapels. Fortunately you will not have an excess of baggage and can easily make yourself ready to accompany me the following day if called to do so.'

He bent and lifted her limp fingers to his lips. 'You must be very tired. I'll call your maid. Try to rest throughout tomorrow.'

His grasp was strong and it would have been both futile and childish to attempt to extricate her fingers from his hold. When he returned with Kate she curtsyed to him formally and walked as calmly as she could through into her own lodging.

Before retiring she sat by the window, staring down into the darkened street. She was too angry and bewildered to cry. In these few short days her happiness had come so abruptly to an end: her anxiety for Ellis, sharpened now into a desperation of fear; the loss of her father; the duplicity of her stepmother; and then, following swiftly, the harrowing events of the last days. It would be useless to run. She knew that instinctively. There was no one to whom she could turn for help. Ellis's mother could not be reached and would be powerless. Poor woman, she would need all her fortitude to face bravely the probable fate of her son. Aleyne had thought the young Duke of Gloucester sympathetic to her plight, but it appeared that it was his wish that her hand be granted to Sir Dominick.

Kate touched her shoulder gently and the simple, kindly gesture broke down the barrier of pride and reserve, and she sobbed out her story in her maid's arms.

'We are all pawns,' she said bitterly, 'goods to be sold at market to the highest bidder. I thought I might turn to Gloucester, but I believe him instrumental in arranging this marriage and—strangely wrapped up in affairs of his own.'

'It's said about the camp that he loves the Lady Anne Neville, has since childhood.'

'But she is Edward of Lancaster's widow.'

'Bestowed on him as a pawn of *her* father.' Kate nodded. 'The marriage was Margaret's price for his support, a future Queen for the kingmaker's use as power behind the throne.'

'And she has fled with Queen Margaret?'

'I've heard no news of them. The men were saying Queen Margaret would most likely make for Worcester and the West.'

'So Gloucester wishes to have the Lady Anne in his charge. She is a wealthy heiress,' she added bitterly.

'It's more than likely she'll be put in the care of her brother-in-law, George of Clarence.'

'Poor lady,' Aleyne said fervently, recalling the sight of the noble Duke being assisted to bed by his squire after he'd drunk himself under the table.

Kate finally persuaded her to go to bed and, after all the emotional exhaustion of the day, sleep mercifully took her quickly.

The moment she woke she sensed the atmosphere of dark foreboding which shrouded the house, and she looked enquiringly at Kate when she brought up her breakfast.

'Will it be today?'

'The trials of the rebels are proceeding now under His Grace of Gloucester, as Lord Constable, and my lord of Norfolk, the Earl Marshall.'

Aleyne shuddered, her thoughts turning instantly to Ellis's plight. As yet she had thought of no way of helping him, yet even now he might be facing his judges.

Guessing her fear, Kate said, 'It's being said the King intends only the Lancastrian nobles to die. Lesser lords and men-at-arms have already been released.'

Aleyne pushed aside her platter and ale cup. 'It's no use, Kate; I can't eat.'

She rose and, pulling on a bed-gown, went to the window. Already the chamber seemed airless.

'I would come away from there, mistress,' Kate warned. 'They are preparing the scaffold in the market-place.'

Aleyne's fingers trembled on the casement catch as she identified now the sound of dull hammering.

She forced herself to descend to the solar and look through the gowns Sir Dominick had provided. The heavy velvet gown most resembled mourning but was hardly suitable for a wedding, and the increasing heat would soon make it uncomfortable even during the evening hours. Between them they finally decided on a gown of blue and silver thread, the material rich enough to please Sir Dominick and the royal Princes who might attend the ceremony. Kate fitted it and they worked to adjust it to Aleyne's slim figure. She had no jewels so they carefully unpicked seed-pearls from another gown and applied them to a length of cloth of silver to form a vest for the gown's deep low neckline. As Aleyne stitched under Kate's direction, she considered how unreal the whole affair seemed to her. She was sitting, outwardly quite placidly, sewing her wedding garments, and in the evening she would be under the total domination of her husband. No, she could not bear to harbour the thought.

Restlessly she put aside the silver tissue and rose to her feet. As if realising her terrible fascination for the harrowing events outside, Kate rose and the two went silently above stairs when the muffled drums sounded from the market square and the noise swelled of townsfolk pushing by the well-guarded house. The executions would begin very soon now. Aleyne's heart hammered within her breast as she feared for Ellis.

Fortunately for their sensibilities, they were unable to distinguish very much from that distance and especially above the heads of the massive crowd which had gathered. Aleyne saw a blur of colour at one end of the square, which she thought must be the banners of the Lord Constable and the Earl Marshall; also the bright-hued garments of those in attendance. The crowd hushed suddenly and she thought the first of the condemned, most likely the Earl of Somerset as the most noble of the prisoners, was mounting the wooden steps to the platform. She turned hastily from the window, sickened, and Kate caught at her fingers to steady her as the drums sounded again and half covered the dreadful, final thud of the axe falling.

'Oh, Kate,' she whispered brokenly, 'how can we stand here, watching, and all those people with small children?'

'The deadly fascination of horror, I suppose,' Kate sighed, 'and some mark of respect too. Traitors or no, they were all brave gentlemen and, strangely enough, I believe that dying in public gaze gives a special courage of its own and a dignity.'

Aleyne nodded, shuddering. 'Will Sir Dominick be present?'

'I imagine he will be there, in attendance on the duke.'

And from this scene of bloodshed he would come to her side, and soon to her bridal chamber!

'Kate, I have to know if they have taken Master Dyer with the other prisoners. Can you manage to find out for me?'

'I don't like to leave you while——'

'Please, Kate.'

'Then come with me back to the solar. You will not be able to see or even hear so much from there.'

Aleyne nodded and returned to her neglected sewing. She lowered her head over the work, but her fingers were trembling and she was afraid she would prick her finger and mark the delicate fabric with blood.

Kate hastened back to her.

'Master Dyer is still in the barn. Sir Dominick has not yet handed him over for trial. Strange, isn't it?'

Aleyne agreed that it was. Did my lord of Gloucester still not know of Ellis's presence in the Yorkist camp? If so, why was Sir Dominick keeping it from him? Did he fear that the Duke would accept Ellis's word that he was attempting to join the Yorkist force, and so fail in his desire to do Ellis some harm?

The morning appeared to drag until Sir Dominick attended her to enquire if she was feeling well and if preparations were going well for the evening's ceremony. He was coldly courteous as ever, and seemed preoccupied.

Aleyne forced herself to enquire about the day's proceedings, her thoughts on Ellis.

'Are—all the executions over?'

He looked at her steadily. 'Yes.'

'I hear the King has shown mercy to all but the leaders.'

'Thirteen paid the supreme price of treachery,' he said, a trifle harshly. 'They have all been previously forgiven once by His Grace or invited to return to their allegiance.'

'Did the Duke of Somerset make a good end?' she asked timidly.

'He died bravely as we all expected and so did Sir John Langstrother, Prior of St John. They all went courageously. It is over for them now.' He crossed himself. 'That cannot be said for Queen Margaret. She will yet have to bear the news of her son's death.'

'The Lady Anne's husband.'

He shot her an odd glance from beneath those dark brows and said brusquely, 'Prince Edward will be buried in the Abbey with due ceremony,' then, quickly changing the subject, 'I take it you've found a suitable gown for the ceremony?'

She nodded, her colour rising. The silence between them appeared to lengthen unnaturally. Once Aleyne thought of mentioning Ellis, then thought better of it. He bowed formally and left her.

How she managed to get through the remainder of the day Aleyne could not have told afterwards. From outside she could hear the noise of the town returning to normal life: shutters being unbarred, cartwheels clanking over the cobbles of the market-place, carpenters dismantling the wooden platform used during the morning's grim work, men bawling orders as, already, preparations for the departure of the King's army were under way. For her there would be no return to life as it had been before. In one or two short hours everything would be changed.

She stood docilely while Kate attired her for her wedding and even managed to smile when she was handed a scratched iron mirror so she could survey her maid's handiwork. The gown's rich material glinted in the candle-light. It sheathed her smoothly from shoulders to waist and fell in heavy folds to the ground, the hem and tight long sleeves as well as the deep V of the neckline edged with silvery grey fur. Her hair fell unbound in a heavy brown mane, as befitted her maiden state, beyond her shoulders almost to her waist, and round it Kate had bound a circlet of cloth of silver, also adorned with seed-pearls. Aleyne's face looked pale through the reflection of the tarnished metal, her eyes larger than usual, shadowed. She handed back the mirror, thanking Kate for all her pains. It could not matter to her in the slightest whether or not Sir Dominick was pleased with the appearance of his bride.

Taking place as it did in the evening, the wedding ceremony took on a dream-like propensity. The King met her at the west door of the Abbey, where she was escorted by Sir Dominick's squire and four of his men-at-arms carrying flaring torches, for now the light was beginning to fade. Edward smiled his approval and, taking her arm, led her to one of the Abbey's side-chapels to her betrothed's side. He looked strange to her, for once resplendent in sapphire-blue velvet, and the altar candles gleamed on the gold of his chain and the cloth of gold of the King's splendid houppelande. The golden light flickered on the pyx and chalice and illuminated the

jewel-like colours of the window above them. Beside Sir
Dominick she glimpsed the slighter form of the Duke of
Gloucester, also clad magnificently in a doublet of
sculptured green velvet. An emerald glimmered sombrely
in the folds of his velvet cap and, like the King, he wore
a bejewelled chain.

She murmured her responses obediently at the quiet
prompting of the chaplain, and felt Sir Dominick place
the ring symbolically on each of the fingers of her left
hand until it rested finally on the third at the end of the
chant, 'In the name of the Father, and of the Son, and
of the Holy Ghost, Amen.' Together they knelt as the
army chaplain blessed the marriage, and with the royal
brothers they took nuptial mass. The King kissed Aleyne
soundly on both cheeks as he led the wedding party into
the central nave of the Abbey. The Duke of Gloucester
smiled his congratulations and stooped to kiss her
fingers.

'I wish you every happiness, Lady Allard.'

The small party repaired to the Abbot's lodgings,
where again he'd served a sumptuous repast for his
sovereign's pleasure. Aleyne picked at the rich delicacies, only partially aware of the King's scarcely veiled
bawdy encouragement to the bridegroom. How different this day had been from her imaginings, so far from
Risby. She had thought her father would have been with
her, her own dearly loved servants packing the small
village church—and Ellis. Dear God, she must not think
of Ellis, not tonight. Afterwards—there must be some
way she could help him.

She was brought to the full realisation of her position
as, with a resounding clang, the door was closed on her
and Kate in the master bedroom of Sir Dominick's
lodging. The bantering which had accompanied their
departure from the Abbot's house returned sharply to
her mind in all its stark meaning.

Kate could feel her mistress's violent trembling as she
lifted her hands to remove Aleyne's circlet. She steered
her young mistress into the one chair and, kneeling before

her, took Aleyne's chilled fingers into her own warm grasp.

'There's nothing to fear; a little pain perhaps. It will soon pass. Are you ignorant?'

Aleyne shook her head. Her old nurse had taken it upon herself to enlighten her charge on the matter of a young bride's duties, hardly trusting Lady Risby to handle such a matter skilfully or with gentle compassion. Now the need for endurance was suddenly upon her with all its attendant terrors.

Kate chattered cheerfully as she undressed Aleyne and turned back the clean holland sheets smelling sweetly of lavender and rosemary.

'I chivvied the men into finding all we should need.' She bent and kissed Aleyne gently upon the forehead. 'Allow the familiarity. I believe Sir Dominick to be a true and courteous knight. Be happy, my dear.'

Aleyne clutched at Kate's fingers again convulsively, then swallowed hard and managed a tremulous smile as the maid withdrew.

She lay alone for some time, listening for each slight sound from outside the door. Would she have felt so apprehensive if the man she had been waiting for had been chosen by her father—Ellis, perhaps? The thought disturbed her. As much as she enjoyed being with Ellis she had not thought of him as a prospective bridegroom, had not pictured herself waiting for him as she was now for Sir Dominick.

Her fingers tightened on the sheet as she recalled that first encounter with Sir Dominick at Broadway. He had terrified her and yet—there had been an excitement, a strange, frightening awareness of the needs of her own body when he had pressed her close in his drunken ardour——

Dear God, let him not be drunk tonight! She had watched him covertly at the feast. He had been abstemious and, like her, had picked absent-mindedly at the food. He had been frowning. Why? Were the King's lewd comments abhorrent to him or was he angered at the

thought of bedding her, the heiress whom he'd asked for
only because she was to bring him a considerable
fortune? Perhaps he had thought to be in other, more
welcoming arms tonight.

She started up as he entered, paused to glance across
at her sitting up in the huge bed, then moved beyond it
to a faldstool beneath the window.

'It appears Kate managed to find everything needful
for your comfort. I regret all has had to be prepared so
hurriedly and—that today's events have placed a shadow
on what should have been, for you, a joyful occasion.'

Her throat ached with unshed tears too much to answer
him. How dared he suppose that marriage to him, under
whatever circumstances, could ever have been joyful for
her?

She averted her head as he undressed. She could hear
the chink of his ornamental chain as he removed it and
slung it across the stool.

'Kate did very well in preparing you for the ceremony
also. I was proud of my bride.'

Again she did not deign to acknowledge his
compliment.

The bed ropes creaked as they received his considerable
weight and her body stiffened as she was forced to use
every morsel of self-control not to deliberately recoil
from his nearness.

He said quietly, 'You have no need to fear me.'

'I am not afraid, simply unwilling,' this last through
gritted teeth.

'We have made a bad start in our understanding of
each other.'

'I am under no misunderstanding, sir. I know well
enough why you asked for my hand and why I was forced
to accept you.'

'Then can we not make the best of circumstances and
take pleasure in each other tonight?'

She withdrew from him as far as possible and he sighed
again.

'Aleyne, you are my wife——'

'I know well enough what is expected, sir. Just do not expect me to pretend to enjoy your attentions.'

He had not blown out the candle and she could see he was regarding her steadily. As yet there was no trace of anger in his expression. She kept her own eyes on his face, unwilling to gaze upon the bare massive shoulders. Unable to prevent herself, she shivered violently, and he bent forward to place a hand upon her shoulder.

'Come into my arms, Aleyne, willingly; it will be easier for you.'

'You are threatening me?'

'I have promised to be gentle with you, but you are a virgin, I take it——'

'How dare you impugn my honour?'

He smiled. 'Aleyne, it is because I am convinced of your virgin state that I am striving to be patient.'

Still she remained stiff, leaning as far from him as was possible. Pride kept her from attempting to jump from the bed. She would not submit tamely but he would not have the satisfaction of seeing her fear.

For moments his fierce dark eyes challenged hers, then he pulled her firmly into his arms so that she could feel the hard pounding of his heart close to her own. His lips closed demandingly on hers and she forced herself to remain passive. Despite her resolve she began to feel that mounting excitement she had so dreaded. A pulse in her throat raced and her heart began to beat as fast as his. His kiss lingered on her mouth, then he leaned away and cupped her chin in one hand.

'You are determined to play the ravished maiden, I see. Then I must compel obedience. On your own head be it.'

As she began to struggle away from him, really alarmed now, he drew her hard against him, one hand deftly imprisoning both hers. With the other he threw back the coverlet and gazed down at her naked form.

The candle glow turned her soft white skin to warm ivory. Her young body had still not matured to full womanhood, her breasts taut and firm but gently

rounded. She had arched her back, her whole being rigid
with shock.

'You are very lovely, Aleyne,' he murmured softly. 'I
had not realised how great my prize was.'

'Please,' she whispered hoarsely, 'blow out the flame.
Do not look at me——'

He laughed, still without a trace of anger. 'If you wish
it, my little virgin bride, but there is no shame in revealing your beauty to your husband.'

Without releasing her, he bent and blew out the candle,
leaving them in velvet black darkness. Aleyne was not
sure if she would have preferred to have seen his
expression in spite of her plea. She swallowed convulsively as his lips touched her throat near the racing pulse
then moved slowly downwards. She could not fight him
but she would not give way to the compelling need of
her body to welcome him, to relax in his arms and allow
a gentle languor, aroused by his lingering kisses, to arouse
her fully. With a determined effort she remained rigid
in his arms.

There was pain certainly when he took her at last, but,
as Kate had promised, it did not last long and, despite
all provocation, he was gentle with her. She gave a great
shuddering sigh when, at length, he withdrew from her.
She had become used to the darkness now and could
distinguish his slight frown as he leaned down to look
at her.

'There will be time, Aleyne, for me to teach you the
art of love, and you will learn willingly, I promise you.'

She closed her eyes as he leaned forward to kiss her
gently now upon the mouth and then he turned from
her to sleep.

Slow tears coursed down her cheeks. She was his now,
bound to him forever. He had consummated the marriage and made very sure of that. There could be no
possibility of an annulment. The problem she faced, she
thought as she lay on for hours, sleepless, was that her
own treacherous body had resisted her determination.
She had wanted him to continue his lovemaking. Was

she beginning to love this man, whom she both feared and resented as a fortune hunter thrust upon her by the King's will?

CHAPTER NINE

ALEYNE awoke with a sudden start. Her fingers were grasping the other pillow. Grey light was filtering into the chamber and she realised it was still early. She was alone. Sir Dominick had already gone to attend to the preparations for departure.

She lay still for a while, unwilling to summon Kate. She was not sure how she felt about the irrevocable step she had been forced to take. Heat suffused her body at the remembrance of the pleasure her new husband had given her. He had been very considerate, yet determined to hold her tightly within the marriage bond. Had his loving been a pretence, a necessary stratagem to allow him to possess her body without her being unduly frightened? Certainly he had taken pains to put her at ease. She could not have believed that such ecstasy of being existed. She had heard snippets of gossip from the servants on the manor, but nothing had prepared her for the devastating need for surrender which had swept through her body at his skilful touch. She was breathing fast, even as Kate's discreet tap came upon the door, and she sat up guiltily.

Her maid came in at her timid invitation and came smilingly to the bed.

'Well, my lady, I see you have not suffered too terribly.'

Aleyne flushed hotly and Kate gave a merry laugh.

'You have a fine handsome husband, my lady. You must not be ashamed of loving him.'

'Indeed Kate, I am not ashamed. As for loving Sir Dominick, that is a horse of a different colour.'

Kate chuckled again. 'I do not think you should talk of horses in his presence, my lady.'

Aleyne caught at her hand and they both burst into laughter.

Immediately she felt guilty again. What right had she to feel so absurdly happy when Ellis was still a prisoner and she herself little more? The King had given her into Sir Dominick's hands and he had exercised his right of control over her with more gentleness than she had a right to expect. She had treated him with a marked lack of respect from the beginning, and he had said honestly that his interest in the match was nothing more than his need to acquire an heiress, but he had extolled her spirit and he had said she was beautiful. Aleyne had never thought of herself as beautiful. Her brown hair and large grey eyes had appeared very ordinary indeed when set beside her stepmother's golden splendour. Now that she was his, Sir Dominick would doubtless consign her to his Yorkshire manor once he had presented her at court for a while as he had been directed to do. After all, she was the King's ward and he would be expected to show her off to the newly assembled Yorkist nobility.

Kate had brought water for her to wash. Deftly she swept up the soiled sheets from the bridal bed while Aleyne moved about the chamber.

'Have you seen—my husband?'

'Yes, my lady. He instructed me to hurry and finish our packing. The moment you are dressed I'll bring up the breakfast tray. Sir Dominick has already eaten.'

Aleyne felt a pang of disappointment. She would have liked to have eaten this first meal as a wife with her husband. She needed to see in his expression that he was not entirely dissatisfied with his bargain. She told herself, almost angrily, that she did not care if he was. He had Risby. He had no cause for complaint, yet a stab of resentment for his neglect of her insisted on making itself felt. She dressed with care for the journey. She would be the object of some avid interest from Sir Dominick's friends, she knew. She jutted her chin a little defiantly as Kate handed her a small iron mirror to examine the effect for herself. She looked well enough in the dark blue brocade gown and matching hennin. She was still determined to wear gowns not unsuitable to her mourning state, at least until she was required to parade herself at court in more peacock grandeur.

Both women looked up, startled, as a knock came on the door. Had Dominick decided to come to her so early, after all? Aleyne looked flustered, and Kate shook her head gently as she went to the door. She ushered in Sir Dominick's squire, Guy Jarvis.

'Good morning, my lady.' He bowed low to Aleyne and she saw he was carrying a small carved wooden box. 'Sir Dominick is still busied about the packing of the sumpter wagons, but he bade me come to you to express his regrets that he cannot take breakfast with you and to give you this.'

He handed the box into Aleyne's hands and, as if ordered to do so, excused himself and left at once.

Wonderingly Aleyne stared at the beautifully crafted box until Kate prompted her, gently, to open it.

Inside, on a scrap of purple velvet, lay a small gold reliquary on a golden chain. Aleyne lifted out the jewel and found it to bear the likeness of St Dominick in enamel, exquisitely done. Obviously the reliquary had been worn by Sir Dominick, possibly a gift from a close relative or friend, since St Dominick was clearly his patron saint, meant to protect the wearer throughout the stresses and dangers of life. Aleyne's eyes clouded with sudden tears. How could he bear to part with such a treasured possession? Yet he offered it to her. She knew what this symbolised: the traditional morning gift, offered on the first day of a bride's life, proving to her that she had pleased her husband in the marriage bed. Aleyne had thought the custom had fallen into disuse, yet possibly in Yorkshire, where Sir Dominick's manor was, it was still held to be important. She lifted the reliquary to her lips and Kate took it from her fingers and fastened it round her neck. She would wear it with pride. He had left her side early—duty kept him from her— but he had thought of her and wished to reassure her that the intimacy they had shared had meant much to him, too.

'Oh, Kate, this must have meant so much to him.'

'And shows that, already, you are important to him too.'

'He must have thought me very ignorant and gauche...'

Kate gave a barked laugh. 'He would have had more to complain about had he not found you innocent.'

'But I have been ungracious...'

'There has been much between you to breed resentment, but...' Kate shrugged again in that familiar gesture Aleyne knew well '...good marriages have flourished well, sown on more stony ground.'

She went to bring up Aleyne's breakfast and left her mistress fingering the reliquary and looking at her reflection in the iron travelling mirror.

Sir Dominick presented himself just as she finished eating.

'Are your mistress's belongings now packed and ready for loading on the sumpter?' he barked at Kate.

'Almost, Sir Dominick.' Kate curtsied respectfully. 'I'll put in the final things now and summon one of the men to take it down to the street.'

She hastened out and Sir Dominick eyed his wife thoughtfully. Aleyne noted that he looked a trifle flushed as if he had hastened climbing the stairs. She smiled suddenly, realising this great wolf of a man was as embarrassed by this meeting as she was herself. Oh, he had had women in plenty—servants, whores, women from the baggage train—but Aleyne suspected her husband had had little dealings with ladies of quality. He was in the train of a great nobleman, but most of his time in Gloucester's service had been spent in exile, possibly in penury while King Edward had been himself a pensioner at his brother-in-law Burgundy's court, then, later, in camps and on the battlefield. Now he had married an heiress, the King's ward, one who had spoken of his standing in a disparaging fashion. Between the sheets he had been the dominating force; now he was unsure of himself.

Aleyne felt a rush of tenderness for this man who was so sensitive to ridicule. Though she was as unused as he was to being in the constant presence of the greatest in the land, she knew he would find the need to dissemble and flatter foreign to his nature.

'Sir,' she said softly, 'I must thank you for my gift. It is very beautiful and I shall prize it always.'

He reddened, and avoided her eye. 'It was given to me by my mother when I entered Warwick's household as page. It contains a fragment of one of the saint's finger bones. I had little of value to offer you.' He touched the Yorkist chain he wore diffidently. 'This was a gift from His Grace at my knighting ceremony. I could not part with it—as you rightly observed, we Allards are not blessed with good coin in our coffers. The manor is small and well managed, but any gold I win now will be in payment for good service.' He frowned almost haughtily. 'I would not have you think that I serve the King's cause for mercenary motives only. I forged a close friendship with His Grace of Gloucester when we served together at Middleham. He was not one to despise a humbly born page who had been taken in by Great Warwick as a favour to my mother for services rendered to him by my father. From then on any cause he espoused would be mine also. Had the house of York fallen in this last encounter I would have been as unfortunate as those fugitives in the Abbey and would have accepted my lot with the same fortitude.'

Aleyne nodded. 'Is your mother living?'

'Yes. She will welcome you with open arms. She has been pressing me for some time to marry, though she had no hopes of a court match. She spends a great deal of time with my sister, Joan, who is married to a neighbour, Sir Ralf Liversedge. They already have two small sons.' He added sadly, 'I lost two younger brothers in infancy.'

Aleyne digested this information nervously. Whatever Sir Dominick said now, she was sure that his mother would be curious and somewhat wary of meeting her new daughter-in-law, though it seemed they would not have to wrangle over the management of the manor house. Indeed, Aleyne hoped not. She had every intention of spending as much time as possible at Risby, though she thought Sir Dominick would not be pleased by such determination on her part.

As if he read her doubts he said, 'She is a very gentle and loving lady, my mother.' A smile, almost tender, curled his lips, and again Aleyne was struck by this new aspect of his nature. She had thought him uncouth, dominating, arrogant, but was learning that much of his abruptness of manner was but a ploy to cover his diffidence in moments of uncertainty.

He returned quickly to his businesslike mood. 'I can have a litter provided for you, but I imagine you will prefer to ride.'

Aleyne flushed, mindful of the awkwardness between them over the matter of the hack Roland. 'Certainly, sir, I would much prefer to ride.'

'Good. I have had a palfrey provided for you also, but if you tire the litter can be brought up quickly. The King sets a hard pace.'

'I would like to take my leave of my groom, if time allows that.'

'We must leave on the hour. Will that woman of yours ride also?'

'I do not know if she can. I'll find out.'

He glanced briefly over her attire. 'I see you are suitably dressed. Keep your clothing as loose and light as you can—it's getting warm already.'

Guy Jarvis escorted Aleyne and Kate to the infirmary where she took her leave of Rob. He appeared to have taken to Kate and was mollified at the need for parting. His anxious eyes followed Aleyne as she left the cell-like room, and she promised him she would make arrangements for him to join her household the moment the infirmarian pronounced him fit enough to leave the Abbey.

Kate reassured Aleyne that she could ride well enough and added softly, 'I've found out from Will Scroggins that Master Dyer is to ride with us. He'll be well guarded. His wrists will be pinioned but he'll be in no great discomfort.'

Aleyne glanced at her sharply and nodded. What plans had Sir Dominick for his prisoner? She had been relieved that Ellis had not suffered with the other rebels in Tewkesbury Market-Place, but she still feared for his safety and must find some way of extricating him from the peril he had foolishly placed himself in.

She was astounded by the sight of the full force of the King's army when she was escorted to her palfrey by her husband soon after sun-up. Sir Dominick lifted his wife into the saddle, and Aleyne bowed her head at the Duke of Gloucester's salute as he rode past to take his place at the King's side. Guy Jarvis helped Kate to mount. Sir Dominick was riding the famed Roland, while his destrier, Oliver, was brought up with the other war-horses in the King's train. Like all the other nobles and knights in the company Sir Dominick wore full armour.

In the van went archers and pikemen of Lord Norfolk's company, then the King, flanked by his two royal brothers, Gloucester and Clarence; following him, his nobles and knights, esquires of the body, then lines of footmen in the blue and murrey of the House of York and, creaking behind this splendid company, the long train of laden sumpters and baggage wagons, cooks, camp-followers, all the ragtag of the army, trailing along on foot.

Aleyne rode by her husband's side in the King's household, her eyes taking in the splendour of the pennants, standards and the bright caparisons of the horses. Along the Cotswold lanes they rode, the hedgerows and ditches heavy with May blossom, trees flaunting their many shades of green. From cottages, villagers came to see the triumphant show. They waved and cheered, thankful that now there was little danger that their farms would be looted, their womenfolk raped. It was over. The Rose of Rouen was firmly seated again on the throne, and England rejoiced.

They crossed the Avon at the small market town of Stratford, where Sir Dominick obtained lodging at an inn for himself, Aleyne, Kate and Guy Jarvis, his men camping in the water meadows by the river. The King was graciously received by the mayor and the small town packed to overflowing by the large company.

Supper was served to Aleyne and Sir Dominick in their chamber by Guy Jarvis, who took himself off with commendable speed once it was over. Sir Dominick stretched his long legs as he rose from his stool.

'I'll see to the comfort of my horses and leave you with your maid.' There was a faint stain of red on his cheeks and Aleyne was hard put to conceal a giggle at mention once more of his favourites as he bowed and left her.

As Kate undressed her Aleyne questioned her about Ellis.

'I have found little out about him. It's impossible to be certain where anybody is in this crush but he's probably being guarded within the army camp.'

Aleyne creased her brow thoughtfully. 'We must find some way of helping him escape, Kate.'

The maid paused in the act of folding the brocade gown. 'That poses some danger and no little difficulty.'

'But if he reaches London he could well be brought to trial and die horribly at Tyburn. Once he is in the Tower it would be impossible to help him. It must be soon—on the journey, Kate.'

'I'll talk to Will Scroggins. We should wait for a town of some size. It would be easier for him to melt into the background then. Trust me.'

Aleyne's breathing came faster and heavier as Kate disappeared and she waited for her husband to join her. Surely, now she had little to fear? He had shown his gentleness, yet at his step on the landing she was almost panicked into leaving the bed.

He came in quickly and began to undress. If he noticed any reserve in her manner he did not refer to it. They might have been married for years.

'The horses have been fed and watered and well rubbed down. You cannot trust these grooms at inns.'

'No,' Aleyne said dutifully.

'Guy is a good lad but he lacks authority. It will come, of course.'

He joined her in the bed. 'Has your maid found a suitable place to sleep?'

'She made no complaint.' Aleyne supposed that Kate had gone to her Will, but she forbore to say as much.

'Billeting the King's party has made it nigh impossible for other folk to find lodgings. We are fortunate. Incidentally, my lord of Gloucester has informed me he will arrange for rooms to be put at our disposal at Baynards Castle, since I have no London lodging of my own as yet. Perhaps you would rather I take a house. I would have preferred you to leave for Yorkshire during the hot plague months, but I fear the King will insist on our staying at court for a while. Gloucester dislikes the prospect as much as I.'

He leaned towards the rushlight on its stool by the bed and then appeared to think better of it.

'You will not refuse me a sight of you tonight?'

She shook her head shyly and he chuckled low in his throat. 'You cannot imagine how absurdly proud I have been feeling all day with you beside me. I doubt if there's a man in the whole of the company who is not envying me tonight.'

'Sir...'

'Will you not call me by my given name?'

'Dominick?'

'That is much better, my wife. I told you we should deal well together. Can you not put your distrust of my motives aside now?'

'I do not think I distrusted your motives. I just did not relish being given over to you as a reward as if I were so much baggage.'

'That I can appreciate.'

'You would not have chosen me had the King not forced the issue?'

He put his head on one side slightly. 'I told you, back at the inn, I like nut-brown maids. In the rushlight your hair has the sheen of a ripe chestnut.' He put up a hand to stroke it and she drew back a little. 'You are not still afraid of me?'

'Yes...no, of course not,' she retorted indignantly.

He laughed again. 'Now you have full view of me, what is your opinion of the bargain?'

'I—I am not dissatisfied.'

'With that I must be content, for the moment.'

She was incredibly lovely, he thought, seated back against the bed-head, her huge grey eyes stretched wide in alarm, or was it confusion? She was shy, of course. He approved of that, but he sensed she had a passionate nature, once her natural reserve was breached. She had spirit, too. That he admired above all things. He released the long lock of her hair, leaned close and kissed her gently at first, then more demandingly. As he had guessed, she was shy at first, then began to respond. Her mouth opened sweetly to receive his, her breath came fast. He could feel the pound of her heartbeat close to his own. Jubilant in his own triumph, he drew her down into his arms...

Aleyne woke early as she felt her husband's body stirring beside hers.

She sat up, stretching and yawning, as Dominick sat beside her on the bed to pull on his boots.

'Do we have to rise so early?'

He laughed and turned to kiss her.

'I'm afraid, my lady, we must. The King waits for no man or woman once on the march.'

'Then I must be patient,' she said demurely and he laughed again.

'What did I say? You're a lass after my own heart and you will love the fresh cold air of Yorkshire. With luck we'll be home before winter and lie snug before our own hearth fires.'

She watched him leave with regret. He would breakfast as he went, snatching at bread and meat and ale as Guy procured it. She snuggled back within the bed to dream for a little time before Kate was sent up to her.

She was content. He was a hard master. Kate had told her of his reputation and she had found out for herself that he could be merciless with those who betrayed or tried to cheat him, but she thought he would be a fair lord for Risby without the malice and spite she had sensed in Sir Thomas Stoodley. She had seen enough of that gentleman's treatment of her servants to know how much he would have been resented. There was much to discover about her husband, but already she knew him to be a gentle and considerate lover and one who did not stint from assuring her of her worth. While busy in Gloucester's service he would be often absent from her side but she had no fear now that he would neglect her and turn to other, more experienced beauties for his entertainment. The King had done well by her. The wars were over and soon she would be mistress of her own household and, please God, the mother of a fine son or daughter.

Even while she dwelt on this attractive picture of her future life with Dominick, a little cold thrill ran down her spine as she remembered Ellis. She could not dismiss his plight from her mind. She bit her lip uncertainly. Kate had warned her how dangerous the attempt to free him would be. And Dominick would not forgive his wife if he discovered her complicity in such a plot. It was a terrible thing to deceive him just when they were beginning to understand and accept each other. Aleyne sighed. Yet there could be no other way. There could be no happiness for her while Ellis was in such peril.

She smiled resolutely, when Kate hurried in to prepare her for the journey.

*   *   *

On the ninth of May the King's army entered Coventry, where he announced his intention of summoning Parliament. Aleyne had found the journey exhilarating. The wind had freshened and the unseasonal heat they'd experienced in Tewkesbury had lessened. She had caught only one fleeting glimpse of Ellis—on their arrival, as he was hauled off by his two guards to a barn at the rear of the inn, the White Hart, where accommodation had been arranged for Sir Dominick's household. He assured himself that their bedchamber was clean and the serving wenches hurrying to meet his wife's needs, then hastened off to wait on His Grace of Gloucester.

Aleyne divested herself of her hennin, washed off the dust of the ride and lay down on the bed, the noises of the ostlers outside and the servants, scurrying about their business of serving the new arrivals, carrying to her through the opened casement.

Kate sank down on a joint-stool and looked around appreciatively. 'Well, we should be comfortable enough here, and the rest will be welcome. The King should be here some days while the business of Parliament is concluded.'

'Is the strain of riding telling on you, Kate?'

'Bless you, no, my lady.' Kate chuckled. 'I've been used to walking miles by the baggage wagons. I'm enjoying the luxury of travelling in Sir Dominick's well-managed household.'

'Do you think there will be more trials? Will the King summon Commons to ratify yet more death sentences?'

'He will demand they once more affirm their loyalty to him—that is his first priority. I doubt if more blood will be spilled. Be easy. Master Dyer should be safe enough for the present.'

Aleyne considered. 'Coventry is a town of some size and Sir Dominick will be kept busy waiting on the King and Gloucester. Isn't this the opportunity we have been waiting for, Kate?'

The maid nodded ruefully. 'Aye, my lady, it would seem so. I've been talking to Will.'

'He's the man who let me into the barn?'

'That's Will.'

'He'll help us?'

'If we make it worth his while.' Kate scratched her chin. 'The trouble is there are two guards. Will would have to arrange an accident for his fellow.' She chuckled as Aleyne's expression revealed her horror. 'Oh, nothing too final, just enough to render him *hors de combat*.'

'But the man is his friend. Will the sergeant agree to that?'

'He seems to think it can be arranged—for a price...'

Her voice broke off as a door banged below and a woman's voice, high and shrill, called something excitedly. Shutters banged open in the street and a babble of voices swelled in the inn corridors, spilling out into the courtyard entrance to join those of the townsfolk. Kate ran to the window and Aleyne joined her. The people were pushing and jostling for position. Obviously something of importance was happening to excite their curiosity.

Kate leaned perilously over the sill. 'It's a company of men-at-arms arriving—Sir William Stanley's men. I recognise them from their red jacks and...yes, now I can see his standard. There's a closed litter, well guarded.'

The two women withdrew a little into the room.

'Then it must be the Queen. He's captured her and is bringing her to the King. Could you see if the young Princess of Wales is with her?'

'No, the leathern curtains were drawn, but more than likely she is. Now I do pity her. She can be no more than fifteen, and a widow so early. Margaret is a malicious and ruthless shrew who can bring nothing but strife to the realm, but the Lady Anne...'

Aleyne recalled how Dominick had said Gloucester had true feelings for Warwick's Anne. How would he feel now that she was brought in a prisoner for the mob to gape at?

Kate plucked at her arm impatiently.

'That matter we discussed—are you resolved?'

'To free Ellis Dyer? Yes, of course...'

'Then now might be our best time. There will be much confusion and Sir Dominick will have his work cut out attending the Duke of Gloucester.'

Aleyne's thoughts raced. Yes, Dominick would be in constant attendance when the captive Queen was brought before the man she hated so fiercely and who had now brought her so low. Gloucester would be concerned for the Lady Anne and, if she was not in the company, anxious for news of her. Neither of them would have time for Aleyne—or for Sir Dominick's prisoner. This could be Ellis's last chance to escape.

'Kate,' she said, breathlessly, 'find Master Scroggins and bring him here.'

'Best, my lady, if we go ourselves and find him. There would be less possibility of connecting us with the escape when the hue and cry is up.'

Aleyne nodded as Kate snatched up two dark cloaks. Among the people below, who would note that they talked privately with Sir Dominick's sergeant-at-arms?

By the time they had reached the courtyard, it was deserted, the populace having followed Sir William Stanley's company to gape at his prisoners. Scroggins, still on guard, came at once at Kate's call. Aleyne waited anxiously as Kate drew the man aside, and he listened, withdrew, shook his head violently, then turned from Kate to regard Aleyne, chewing his nether lip thoughtfully. Kate plucked impatiently at his sleeve again and whispered more urgently in his ear. He hesitated, scratching his chin, then allowed himself to be drawn nearer to Aleyne where she waited in the shadows for his decision. He cleared his throat very deliberately.

'There's danger in this business, my lady. If Sir Dominick——'

'I know what I'm asking. If you are arrested, be certain I will plead your cause and, when I am in a position to do so, I will make this service well worth your while.'

He nodded, and Kate gave him a hasty shove in the ribs to help him make up his mind.

He was a pleasant-faced, thick-set man of uncertain age, weatherbeaten by the wind and sun while on the march, with a reddish thatch of hair and beard.

'Aye, I know that, my lady. Kate, here, is your surety. It's Jem Weaver we have to cope with.'

'Will he agree to help us, at a price?'

'He's young, my lady, and in awe of Sir Dominick, with good reason, I might add.'

'He's sharing your guard now?'

'Aye. It'll need the hilt of my dagger brought down hard on that pate of his to lay him out for a while. Best not to involve him in the decision. I can square it with him later.'

'You will make sure he comes to no real harm? Suppose he accuses you of this to Sir Dominick?'

He grinned. 'No, my lady, I knows what I'm doing and he's more afraid of me than he is Sir Dominick. I'll borrow your cloak now for the prisoner.'

Kate stripped hers off. 'Take mine—less noticeable.'

'Stay close and whistle, Kate, in case anyone comes suddenly back to the yard.' Scroggins signalled her towards the courtyard entrance. 'Can you station yourself near the rear door, mistress?'

'Yes, of course.'

Once they were in position he cautioned them to silence by a gesture, then knocked imperatively on the barn door. As he disappeared inside Aleyne forced herself to concentrate on the door and tried not to think about poor Jem Weaver's impending fate. Scroggins appeared at the open doorway again and beckoned her inside. Kate continued her watch by the courtyard entrance arch.

Aleyne sped across the greasy cobbles, skirts held high. The young guard was stretched face down on the straw and Aleyne stepped anxiously over his prone body.

'Never you fear for Jem, my lady,' Sergeant Scroggins said cheerily. 'He's got a right hard skull—had evidence of it more than once when we've both been caught up in brawls.' He was busy slicing through the ropes which hobbled his prisoner. 'Now, sir, we must lose no time.'

Ellis rose from a bale of hay and stumbled towards Aleyne. 'My dear, I endanger you by this——'

'Never mind that, sir.' Scroggins hurled Kate's cloak towards him. 'Put that on and keep your mind on getting yourself out of here. Leave my lady's safety to me and Kate.'

Ellis pulled Aleyne towards him and gave her a cousinly hug and kiss. His eyes told her he longed to do more but did not dare in the sergeant's presence. Aleyne withdrew herself from his embrace and gave him a frantic little push towards the barn door. 'Save yourself. That is all I want now. Where will you go?'

'To London and to ground in the stews of the South Wark, if I can get clear to there; then, who knows? To France, if I can.'

'I'll see that your mother is told as soon as that's possible.'

'Allard—he has not hurt you...?'

'No, no, and will not. Go now, quickly.'

Scroggins said urgently, 'You'll have to make it on foot, sir. I daresn't let you steal a horse. Into that crowd with you in the market-place and through to the town gates when the market folk leave.'

Ellis pulled up the hood of Kate's grey frieze cloak. Scroggins opened the barn door a fraction and looked out. Ellis looked back at Aleyne longingly, his face pale in the shadowed light.

'God guard you.' His voice was hoarse with emotion; then, as Scroggins beckoned him imperatively, he was gone.

They waited, silent and sweating, for any sound of outcry or pursuit. Jem Weaver groaned suddenly and Aleyne sank anxiously to her knees beside him, but Scroggins jerked her to her feet.

'Get back into the inn, my lady. He mustn't see you here. He'll be well enough, I tell you.'

'How will you answer for the prisoner's escape?'

He grinned. 'Careless, wasn't I? Left Jem here on his own, while I goes to find out what's happening in the

market square. When I comes back he's out cold on the
floor and the prisoner flown. It's obvious: one of they
Lancastrians still skulking in the town must have stolen
in and freed him.'

'But will you be believed?'

He grimaced comically. 'Bless you, my lady; Sir
Dominick never takes excuses from any of us.'

'Then he could——'

'I've been too long in his service for things to go too
hard with me. I'd not risk my neck else. Keep a close
mouth and guard yourself. Off with you now to Kate.'

Kate was waiting near the door and pulled Aleyne
hurriedly into the inn and back to their chamber. Quickly
she divested her mistress of her mud-spattered gown.

'We must get out of these clothes and be found resting.'

Aleyne's thoughts were on Ellis. What chance had he
on foot, without coin or even food? Would Sir Dominick
mount a hue and cry when he discovered the loss of his
captive, or would he be relieved of the need to bring a
former companion to trial for treason? At this moment
she would not allow herself to think what consequences
there would be if he discovered her part in all this.

CHAPTER TEN

SIR DOMINICK returned to the inn about an hour later.
He hurried into their chamber and drew Aleyne into his
arms. She was afraid he must be aware of the mad
pounding of her heart as he kissed her soundly.

'My love, I am sorry that I have had to neglect you
again and so soon. Something important has happened
and the King demanded my attendance.'

Aleyne's heart missed a beat. Had he been told already of the prisoner's escape? 'I was trying to rest for
a while but the noise in the street below woke me. Kate
and I went to the window but there was too much confusion. Kate went down and told me later the inn servants
were saying that the Queen has been captured.'

'Yes, that's true. She was taken at Malvern Priory and Sir William Stanley's men brought her in just now. The Lady Anne is with her and both are very distressed. His Grace summoned me to ask if you would wait upon Lady Anne. As your father was known to be in former service with her father, Warwick, he thought the lady would be glad of your company. Gloucester particularly requested it.'

'Of course, I would be glad to do her any service I can, but I am quite unused to attending noblewomen.'

'That will not matter in the least. Kate could go with you. Queen Margaret has two of her older women in attendance, but the Lady Anne seems to be withdrawing from them all.'

'Has she been told about the death of Prince Edward?'

He said awkwardly, 'No, I think not. Gloucester and I were hoping you would be able to break the news more gently than any other in the King's party. Clarence offered to do so, but Gloucester was anxious he should not be left to the task.'

Aleyne bit her lip doubtfully. She did not know the Princess of Wales, the former Lady Anne Neville, and the request Dominick made was a delicate one. Only too well, Aleyne was aware of the suffering the loss of a dear one caused. She was still unable to think of her father without a lump welling up in her throat. Would Great Warwick's daughter be a proud and haughty lady who would spurn any overtures of comfort Aleyne made to her? That would prove very likely. Yet she could not, in charity, refuse to do her best for the suffering young woman who must be in terror for her life.

'I will go to her at once. Where are the royal captives being held?'

'In rooms at the Charterhouse. The King is to dine there tonight and we are bidden to attend.'

'Will you escort me?'

'Yes, I'll summon Kate.' He turned as he reached the door. 'Aleyne, I'm sorry that I should burden you with this. God knows you have experienced enough disasters over the last few days without this business being added. I had hoped we could dine together quietly and continue to get to know each other. Everything is being so rushed for you . . .'

Aleyne smiled reassuringly. 'It is because so much has happened to me that I may be able to help Lady Anne. Do not disturb yourself for me. In spite of past differences, you have been kindness itself to me since the marriage and I do appreciate that.'

He reddened in the embarrassed fashion she was beginning to know well, bowed and left her.

As he escorted them through the Coventry streets Aleyne asked if he knew anything of the King's plans for the royal ladies.

'The Queen is to be conveyed to London very soon, presumably to join poor mad King Harry in the Tower. As to the Lady Anne, who knows? My Lord of Clarence was asking if she might be kept in his household with his wife, her sister. Doubtless the King will consider that suitable. It would be a convenient arrangement for the present. Her mother, the Countess, is still in sanctuary at Beaulieu.'

'The Lady Anne and her sister are co-heiresses,' Aleyne mused aloud, and Sir Dominick looked at her sharply. It was Aleyne's turn to flush hotly. The tactless remark had caused him to remember her own taunts at his wish to acquire her lands at Risby.

He scowled and looked away. 'It will be a matter for the lawyers to wrangle over. The Countess should be entitled to her dower share of the inheritance but there is the question of attainder. Since the Earl committed treason, by law the King must determine what is to become of the Warwick lands. He could withhold everything, but I think he will see fair play and see to it that both the Warwick ladies do not lose too much, despite their father's fall from grace.'

Aleyne considered that whoever married the youthful widow, and many would be anxious to do so, would not be acceptable to the Duke of Clarence. Obviously it would be to his advantage if the Lady Anne were to retire to some convent, either by her own will or the King's, and leave the whole of the Warwick fortune to him. Yet Dominick had said Gloucester had wished to marry Warwick's Anne. Had he genuine feeling for the girl, or had he, too, his eyes on the Warwick inheritance?

As they prepared to enter the Charterhouse, Aleyne squared her shoulders for her disagreeable task. At least this absorption in the affairs of his lord would keep Dominick away from the inn for the moment, and still unaware of Ellis's escape. Every second he could be kept from knowing made Ellis's chances better.

The King's guards admitted Sir Dominick, and the party was conducted to the rooms assigned to the prisoners. Sir Dominick knocked on the door of the room allotted to the Lady Anne. A woman's harsh voice called to him to enter and an old woman in dusty red velvet opened the door and stood back as Sir Dominick announced his name and errand.

Aleyne's eyes were drawn instantly to the forlorn figure who sat slumped upon the narrow truckle bed. The girl, for she could be no more, did not so much as lift her head as they entered.

Sir Dominick advanced and bowed. 'My Lady, I am Sir Dominick Allard. You might just remember that I was, for a while, in service at Middleham. My wife and her maid have come to offer you any assistance they can while you are here in Coventry.'

At mention of Middleham Castle the youthful widow lifted her face to his. Now Aleyne saw how lovely she was, fair as all the Nevilles, with very large blue, almost violet eyes, which were deep-shadowed with suffering. Her gown of green brocade was torn and dust-stained, and her hair tumbled untidily about her shoulders since she had discarded her hennin which lay crumpled beside her on the bed. Despite the fragility of her beauty Aleyne saw by the set of the chin and purposeful line of the mouth that this woman was no one's dupe and had inherited the determination and stubbornness of her famed

sire. Just now she looked as if she could take no more
blows of fate, and Aleyne longed to simply go to her
and put a comforting arm round her slim, dejectedly
held shoulders.

She curtsyed and looked meaningly towards her
husband, and then at the older attendant who was
standing in an attitude of haughty indifference, which
almost approached insolence, by the door.

'My Lady, I'm sure you would welcome a change of
clothing and possibly a bath if it could be procured. I
know you have been travelling for some time.'

The attendant's harsh voice spoke monotonously. 'I
have requested that a tub be brought but have been
ignored.'

Sir Dominick said quietly, 'I will see what I can do
for both royal ladies. Perhaps you would be of more
service to the Queen now that Lady Anne is to be attended by my wife.' His voice carried a steely note and
was not to be denied. The woman curtsyed and withdrew.
Sir Dominick drew Aleyne to the door and looked back
at Warwick's daughter, a concerned frown creasing his
brow.

'She is in a most disturbed state and that female appeared to constitute a gaoler rather than a companion.'

Aleyne's eyes followed his gaze. The Lady Anne had
sunk back again to her withdrawn and sullen attitude.

'She has been through so much. Leave her to me and
do not hasten the servants with the bathing
arrangements.'

His eyes caught her troubled ones and he inclined his
head slightly. Murmuring a wish to be excused, which
was not acknowledged, he bowed again and left the
chamber.

At a nod from Aleyne Kate went to the Lady Anne
and reached out a hand to the torn and dirtied sleeve.
She placed the bundle she had carried from the inn on
the bed.

'Will you allow me to help you off with this gown,
my lady?'

'What?' The girl looked up with a start as if she could not recall what they were doing in this chamber. She looked down, bemused, at the sorry state of her attire, and gave a little moue of disgust.

'I have no other gowns,' she said tiredly. 'I think the baggage must have been lost when we fled the convent in Tewkesbury.'

'I have taken the liberty of bringing one of my own mistress's gowns, my lady.' Kate looked up anxiously at Aleyne, who nodded again. For now, practical matters must take precedence.

The Lady Anne rose and turned for Kate to undo her gown's lacing, and Aleyne drew a bed-gown and the simple grey gown from the bundle, which Kate and she had both thought most suitable for the lady in her widowed state.

A knock came at the door and Aleyne frowned. She had not wished to be interrupted at this moment but she indicated for Kate to continue with her task while she went to the door. A page stood there with a bowl of warm water and a clean linen towel.

'I'm sorry, my lady, but with all the confusion a tub couldn't be found and the servants——'

'That will do,' Aleyne said briskly. 'Leave this with me.'

She took the bowl and towel from him and closed and latched the door. Outside she was conscious of the presence of the two sturdy guards further down the corridor. The Lady Anne might be the King's cousin but she was also recently wedded to his enemy and she was to be given no opportunity to escape him. Aleyne sighed. They were all the King's prisoners—she herself, Kate, Queen Margaret and this frightened young girl.

The Lady Anne had docilely allowed Kate to remove her gown and wrap her in the more comfortable bed-gown. Her nose twitched appreciatively at the aromatic herbal scent of the water, and she gratefully made her toilet. Aleyne herself brushed and combed the fair hair into a silky mass streaming below her waist.

'Is my husband held prisoner here?' she asked Aleyne at last. 'Or has he already been conducted to the Tower?'

Aleyne hesitated, and the large blue eyes turned on her enquiringly. There was a pause while Aleyne struggled to find the right words, then the Lady Anne said quickly, 'You were sent to tell me he is already dead?'

Aleyne's lips parted soundlessly and Lady Anne turned away from them and gave a heavy sigh. 'He was not executed, my lady,' Aleyne said hastily. 'I understand he was killed in the battle. His body lies in honoured state within Tewkesbury Abbey.'

'Has someone informed the Queen?'

'I do not know, my lady, but I imagine so, by now.'

Lady Anne turned and seated herself once more on the bed. 'There were executions, you said?'

Aleyne explained what little she knew, while Kate busied herself moving the toilet articles and discarded gown to a chest further off. Aleyne said, a little helplessly, 'I know what you must be going through, my lady. I lost my own father only a few weeks ago.' Too late she realised that her words had recalled to Anne that she had also lost her father on the field at Barnet.

'How long have you been married to Sir Dominick Allard?' Lady Anne asked, almost irrelevantly.

'Only three days, my lady.' Aleyne blushed and the Lady Anne smiled wanly.

'It seems it was not a forced match.'

'Indeed, it was...' Aleyne broke off awkwardly '...but—but—we are coming to respect each other.' Her eyes filled with tears as Lady Anne continued to stare at her wordlessly. She choked out, 'You must be feeling...'

'You never met the Prince?' Lady Anne's voice was very flat, perfectly steady.

'No, my lady.' Aleyne stared at her, puzzled.

'If you had done, Lady Allard, you might have had some understanding of what I am feeling now.' She glanced towards the grey gown laid out on the bed. 'I take it I am to be paraded before His Grace and the royal Dukes? Well, grey should be suitable for a grieving widow.'

Aleyne felt distinctly uncomfortable. 'Dominick said we were summoned to dine at the King's table. We had no black to hand...'

'And will Queen Margaret be there?' Anne's lips twitched as if in grim amusement. 'Well, it would be in keeping with King Edward's revenge. Do you know that, after the death of his father, she had the dead Duke's head put on Micklegate in York, crowned with a paper crown, so that he might preside over his principality of York?'

'I heard something of the sort but I hardly credited it, my lady.'

'Do so, Lady Allard. Neither the King or Queen Margaret is blessed with a merciful nature.'

The words were so bitter that Aleyne regarded her again, ruefully. It seemed that the Lady Anne had little affection or respect for her mother-in-law. Had she had any love for her young husband either?

Aleyne helped Kate attire her in the simple grey gown. Kate had managed to acquire a length of black veiling to swathe over the hennin, and the young dowager Princess of Wales was suitably clad for her ordeal at the King's triumphal feast.

Almost immediately a knock at the door announced Sir Dominick and he came in quickly, bowed, and shot his wife a glance of profound gratitude.

'My lady, I am sent to escort you to the hall.'

Lady Anne coolly offered him her hand. 'I am aware of your orders, Sir Dominick, and am grateful for your forbearance. You can be easy. Your lady has informed me of the Prince's death.'

Sir Dominick gravely inclined his head and the Lady Anne smiled again wanly. 'If it is possible I would be obliged if your lady could be spared to spend some time with me, at least until we are removed to London.'

'We would be glad to serve you, my lady. I still have
happy memories of my time at Middleham.'

'Ah, Middleham; the days there seem an age ago.'

Again Aleyne was struck by how mature the young
Princess appeared and mused that her terrible experiences had left their mark. Gloucester, too, she thought,
appeared older than his years.

As she walked with Kate and Guy Jarvis, only slightly
behind her husband as he performed his duty of pre-
senting before the sovereign the King's distinguished
prisoner, Aleyne realised she did not know her husband's age. He could be little more than twenty, she
thought, if that, since he had served with Gloucester and
Ellis at Middleham, but the bitter experiences of these
wars had robbed them of their pleasant youths. Like his
lord, Dominick was battle-hardy and cynical about the
blows of fate which might lie in wait for all of them.

There was a stir of interest within the ranks of waiting
noblemen and ladies when the Lady Anne entered the
hall led by Sir Dominick Allard. She carried herself
superbly, looking neither to right nor left as she walked
to the place assigned to her at the King's table. She
looked back anxiously for Aleyne, and Sir Dominick
stooped and spoke in the ear of the lady who had been
placed next to her. She and the knight accompanying
her rose and curtsyed and were escorted by the chamberlain, white wand of office at the ready, further down
the board. Aleyne took the vacant place by the Lady
Anne's side and Sir Dominick took his beside Aleyne.
Guy Jarvis stationed himself behind to serve them. Kate
had already moved to a place near the door with other
waiting-women.

The murmur of talk died down as the King entered
the hall, accompanied by his two brothers. Aleyne saw
Lady Anne catch at the table edge, pulling at the napery
so that the wine cups and platters set ready jarred. The
Duke of Gloucester halted abruptly, and Aleyne saw in
the glance they exchanged the strength of feeling there
had once been between the royal cousins. The Duke of

Clarence bowed to his sister-in-law mockingly and she acknowledged the gesture by a frigid inclination of her chin. The King paused before taking his seat and looked at Lady Anne gravely.

'You look very pale, cousin. Know that you have nothing to fear from us.'

She curtsied low and only Aleyne noted the glimmer of tears on her lashes and the very slight trembling of her lips.

'Your Grace is very kind.'

'How could I be otherwise, coz? I know well that your marriage, though unwelcome to us, was not entered into by any desire of your own. I take it you have been informed of the death of Prince Edward?'

'Yes, Your Grace.'

'He will be buried with honour inside Tewkesbury Abbey chancel. I have already made all arrangements.'

'Thank you, Your Grace.' The reply was respectful but toneless.

The King looked down at the slim figure thoughtfully, and, glancing up, Aleyne saw that the Duke of Gloucester was doing the same. It struck her with considerable force that both men might be asking themselves if their young cousin could be carrying Edward of Lancaster's child. Such a state of affairs could bring disaster to both their hopes. Aleyne followed their gaze but there was no hint of disquiet on the Lady Anne's strained young features. The King took his chair and, at an expansive wave of his hand, gossip resumed on all sides of him.

As yet no servitors had appeared with the first course, and Aleyne wondered uneasily when or if Queen Margaret was to make her appearance.

The doors at the end of the hall were suddenly thrown open, and talk immediately stopped again as all eyes went to the entrance.

A burly knight in red velvet advanced to the top table, leading a tall, gaunt figure by the elbow. There was a little gasp as the man half jerked, half urged his companion to the place before the King. The woman made no resistance, though, like the Lady Anne, she appeared to be only half aware of what was happening to her. Aleyne was horrified to see that she had made no effort to change the dust-stained apparel she had worn during her flight from the King's victorious army. Her gown of purple velvet had once been splendid, but it was now outdated and in a parlous condition. Had the Queen not been supplied with the means to make her toilet, or had she simply refused to take any part in this farce of coming willingly to the meal? Margaret had once been strikingly attractive, if not beautiful, her features strongly cast, line of mouth and set of chin showing a fierce determination to have her way in all things. Her eyes were downcast now, but Aleyne guessed they were dark. She felt the Lady Anne reach for her hand, and caught it willingly in her own and squeezed it comfortingly below the table-top.

'Well, madam,' the King said coldly, 'we meet again. Would it not have been wiser to take ship for France after your puppet Warwick's defeat at Barnet? We are informed that you were foolish enough to take the word of ambitious but incompetent counsellors. You see now to what unfortunate position you have been brought.'

The Queen's voice was a trifle harsh, not unattractive but still slightly accented. 'I have nothing to say to you, Edward of March. I wish only to join my son in whatever prison you have confined him.'

The knight by her side said sneeringly, 'Then you'll want to lie in your grave in Tewkesbury Abbey. Take care, old woman, that the King does not take you at your word, and send you to join him.'

Queen Margaret lifted her head and stared directly at the splendidly arrayed giant who faced her. Her lips parted and she mumbled something quite incoherent. Lady Anne half rose from her chair. Clarence's voice cut silkily across the embarrassed silence which had fallen upon the startled company.

'Her Grace does not appear to have been informed of her son's death on the field. Surely it was by your hand, brother, he fell, during the pursuit to the river, was it not?'

He looked sneeringly towards Gloucester. The Lady Anne gave an anguished cry. For the moment Aleyne's attention was on her and she did not see the humbled Queen crumple in an untidy heap before the dais. Dominick thrust back his chair with a muttered oath and rushed to tend the stricken woman. Gloucester joined him. Dominick looked up, his expression thunderous.

'God damn you, Stanley, that was ill done! The lady could have been told more mercifully.'

Gloucester said quietly, 'I'll give you a hand to convey her to her chamber, Dominick.' He did not stop to request the King's permission.

Edward said hastily, 'Of course, I had no idea...' He looked round for servants to lift the fainting Queen, but already Dominick and Gloucester had lifted her between them and were moving towards the door. Servants stood back awkwardly as they passed till the chamberlain hastened up to clear the way for them.

Lady Anne had risen agitatedly. 'Your Grace, may I be excused to tend Her Grace?'

Edward was looking distinctly uncomfortable. He had intended to humble his old enemy, true, but he had not realised she was unaware of her son's death, and her sudden collapse had embarrassed him. 'Of course, cousin.' He rose as she moved to follow her mother-in-law. Aleyne looked quickly to the King for permission to withdraw and, seeing him give a hurried nod of acquiescence, ran to join Lady Anne.

As Sir Dominick and the Duke of Gloucester carried their burden into the Queen's chamber, her ladies-in-waiting clustered anxiously round. The two men laid her gently upon the bed and backed to the door. Aleyne and the Lady Anne paused in the doorway. Gloucester halted and tried to take Anne's hand.

'Anne, wait just one moment. Let me explain.'

She withdrew her hand from his grasp as if a serpent had stung her. 'We have nothing to say to each other,

Your Grace. My father and husband are both dead, convenient for your brother's cause.' Her eyes filled with sudden tears. 'Yet, in spite of all, I did not think that you, of all men...'

Before he could prevent her she had swept past him into the chamber and slammed the door to in all their faces. Aleyne hesitated, but Dominick put a restraining hand on her arm.

'Let it be for the present, Aleyne. There is nothing you can do here. Lady Anne will summon you again if she has need of you.'

He turned uncomfortably to Gloucester, who stood in stricken silence, frowning at the closed door which barred him from his lovely cousin.

'There will be time to talk to her, sir. His Grace of Clarence's remark was most unfortunate at such a time.'

Gloucester's brows swept up in cynical interrogation. 'Unfortunate? That is what you think, Dominick?'

Dominick gave an embarrassed shrug and Gloucester turned and squeezed his shoulder. 'I'm sorry, old friend. As you say, all will be well when I have opportunity to speak with Anne privately. I'd best get back to this Death's Head feast.'

Dominick followed his retreating form with a concerned frown.

Aleyne said nervously, 'Do you think we should return, too?'

'Do you want to?'

She shook her head vehemently.

'Then we'll take supper at the inn.'

'But will you be missed?'

He shrugged again. 'I doubt it, and if the King is angered...well, no doubt we shall survive.'

Aleyne fell into step beside him as they left the Charterhouse, glad of the cool night air. It dispelled from her brain the sickly smell of the rich foods which had wafted up from the kitchens, the sharper scent of bruised herbs from the floor and the cloying, heavier scents of spices and musks which many of the nobles had used to sweeten their persons. Aleyne had observed, thankfully, that Dominick did not appear to follow their example. He exuded a fresh male scent of plain soap together with remaining traces of armour-oil and leather.

She could see, in the pale glare of a sconce on one of the town houses, that his expression was grim.

'I was so proud of you in that hall, sir—Dominick,' she amended hastily, as he turned to stare down at her. 'You tried to succour that poor woman, despite the fact that it could well have displeased the King and caused you to lose favour. I know she has the reputation of a shrewish termagant but no one but the hardest of hearts could have failed to pity her then. You did not hesitate but went straight to her.'

'Gloucester followed very quickly.'

She nodded. 'He, also, seems to distance himself from his brothers in all of this. The Lady Anne was very cold with him. Do you know if it was true what Clarence said, that he was the man who slew Prince Edward?'

'Who knows by whose hand that poor fool was killed? The rout was chaotic. Why, I might have been the one. The Prince was trampled under the hoofs of the pursuing destriers. His body was mangled. The Duke will not wish to talk of that to the Lady Anne.'

'You once implied that he loves her.'

'I more than implied it. I *know* he loves her, and, please God, he will soon be rewarded for his constant loyalty to the King and be given permission to wed her.'

Aleyne was about to mention the inheritance but thought better of it. She sighed. Anne's lot was similar to her own, yet, if what Dominick said was true, she might well make a happy match in the end.

It was obvious that something was wrong as they approached their lodging. Voices were raised in the courtyard and Aleyne recognised the gruff tones of Dominick's captain. Her heart almost stopped. Ellis's flight must have been discovered.

Sir Dominick paused in the entrance archway, his brows drawn together in a scowl.

'What is all this pother, Harry? Surely it is late to be disturbing guests in the inn?'

'Your prisoner has escaped, sir. I've only just now been informed, though I'm of the opinion it happened hours ago. The guard relieving the day-men discovered the facts and reported to me at once.'

'Which two were on duty?'

'Scroggins and young Weaver.'

'Bring both of them to our private solar,' Sir Dominick said coldly, 'and keep a close watch on them.'

Unwilling to leave Scroggins and Weaver to face the music alone, Aleyne followed her husband into the small solar placed at their disposal by the innkeeper. She was determined to stay until ordered to her chamber. As yet Kate had not returned but would soon do so, and all the maid's fears would be for her Will.

Dominick did not appear to see anything strange or unduly curious in her behaviour. He waited courteously until she was seated in the one comfortable chair and took his place behind her, thumbs tucked into his ornamental belt of gilded leather. Guy Jarvis hovered solicitously and Dominick nodded to the squire to serve them with wine.

Aleyne deliberately kept her eyes from Will Scroggins's face as he and the dejectedly boyish figure of young Jem Weaver were marched in to stand before Sir Dominick.

Dominick took a pull at his wine cup. 'Now, Scroggins,' he said in a deceptively mild tone, 'explain yourself. Where is your prisoner?'

The sergeant shifted his feet uneasily but Aleyne was aware that he had surreptitiously gestured to young Jem to remain silent and allow him to handle matters. The boy had made one ineffective movement of his lips as if he had decided to defend himself.

'I don't rightly know how it happened, sir. It were when there was all that excitement of the Queen being driven in. I finds young Jem, here, knocked out cold on the barn floor with a bump on his head as big as a plover's egg. Master Dyer was gone and the door wide

open, but since I saw nobody in the courtyard, seeing
as they'd all gone to see the captive Queen, I reckon as
how——'

Sir Dominick saw fit to interrupt what promised to
be a lengthy tale. 'But how was it that you were absent
from your post?'

Scroggins shot him an uneasy, almost appealing
glance. 'It were like I said, sir. We hears all the com-
motion and the prisoner, he wanted to know what it were
all about, so I decides to oblige him, thinking no harm...'
He swallowed nervously. 'Well, I let myself be persuaded and said I'd just go up the street and find out.
I were gone no more'n a few moments, sir, I swear it,
then—when I comes back, I finds——'

Sir Dominick signalled to him to be silent and fixed
his basilick stare on Weaver.

'And just what do you recall of this affair?'

'Me?' The boy was white-faced and sweating freely.
'Nothing, sir. He—they—must have come at me from
behind. All I knows is what Will says. When I comes to
he's kneeling by me, shaking and yelling and asking
about the prisoner.'

'I see.' Sir Dominick's tone still revealed no trace of
anger as he drained his wine cup and returned it to Guy
Jarvis. He spoke over his shoulder to his captain as if
the matter were of no importance. 'It seems a clear case
of dereliction of duty. Hang them both.'

'No,' Aleyne burst out, 'no, you can't!'

Dominick stared at her and his eyebrows rose in
surprise.

'Scroggins left his post. He knows the penalty well
enough. I've made myself sufficiently clear on the subject
over the years he's been in my service.'

'But Jem is innocent of blame.'

Dominick sighed. 'I see you still do not understand
these matters of discipline. Scroggins was undoubtedly
bribed, and, since the boy did not report the prisoner's
loss immediately it occurred, he must have been impli-
cated, most probably shared the ill-gotten gains. A pity,

I grant you, that the boy is so young and most likely
under Scroggins's influence, but desertion of one's guard-
post is a hanging matter. If my men were to see me as
too lenient my authority would be always challenged. I
understand your pity, my dear, but I must request that
you leave these matters to me without questioning my
decision.'

There was a steely note to his tone and Aleyne quailed
inwardly.

Jem Weaver threw himself on to his knees, his mouth
working, eyes almost popping from his head in abject
terror.

'Will, here, he wouldn't let me give the alarm. Please,
you must believe me. I didn't know he was going to let
the prisoner go.' The boy grovelled towards Sir Dominick
and the captain strode up to seize him by the elbow and
jerk him upright. Scroggins remained silent. He did not
look at Aleyne but she saw his eyes narrow doubtfully.
She stared at him, dry-mouthed. She had to speak, explain, as she had promised him she would, but could
not. She remained fixedly in her chair, her knuckles
whitening on the arms.

Sir Dominick shrugged. 'This tale is either completely
false or incomplete. Lock them up. Summon a priest
and hang them first thing in the morning.'

Young Weaver was dragged out by the captain and
Scroggins followed stolidly. Sir Dominick gave instructions to Guy to serve him and Aleyne with supper. The
boy was white-faced but he left immediately on his
errand. Sir Dominick strode over to a small folding camp
table which had been set up for his maps and papers
and began to gather them together to leave room for the
dishes. Aleyne watched the determined set of his
shoulders, her eyes wide with horror. Now was her opportunity, but she found she still had not the courage
to speak. Guy Jarvis will come in while I am in the middle
of it, she told herself wildly, but knew it was just an
excuse. She feared the revulsion of feeling her revelation
would bring to Dominick. They ate silently. Sir Dominick

appeared to be wrapped in his own thoughts. Aleyne
was unsure if the death sentence he had handed out so
summarily or the scene they had witnessed at the
Charterhouse was the reason for his reticence. She was
quite unsure of her ability to make conversation and was
relieved when he rose to leave her. He made no comment
on the fact that she had eaten scarcely anything. Clearly
he had put that down to her distress at the Princess of
Wales's plight or her concern for the two disgraced men-
at-arms.

'My dear, I must excuse myself for an hour. There are
matters I feel I should discuss with His Grace of
Gloucester. He should now have been excused from the
King's presence.'

She rinsed her fingers hastily in the bowl Guy held
for her.

'Of course. I will go up to our chamber. Guy, do you
know if my maid, Kate, has returned to the inn?'

'Yes, my lady. I saw her come into the courtyard when
I was ordering the inn servants in the kitchen. I think
she should now be in your chamber. If not I will send
her to attend you.'

'Thank you.' Aleyne rose and Sir Dominick stooped
to kiss her fingers.

'I promise I will not be long gone.'

Kate had turned back the bed covers and laid ready
her night-robe when she entered the chamber. Although
she was calm and controlled in manner there were signs
of redness and puffiness about the eyes. Aleyne closed
and latched the door and ran to take her maid's hands
in her own.

'You know?'

Kate nodded.

'Have you seen Will?'

'The captain will not allow it.'

'Kate, I promise, I will not let him die.'

The maid looked at her steadily and gave a shuddering sigh.

'I know, you are asking yourself why I did not speak out sooner. Oh, Kate, I could not find the words. I'm so afraid—oh, not that he will punish me, I could accept that. It's just that this understanding we have is so new—I cannot bear it to be snuffed out like a weak candle-flame.' She mastered her own tears. 'But—but I swear I will tell him.'

Kate led her gently to the bed and began to lift off her hennin.

'My lady, there is little point in ruining your own happiness. The chances are nothing you could say or do would save Will or the boy.'

Aleyne put out her hand to prevent Kate moving away with the head-dress. 'Nevertheless, I must speak. Do you think I could bear to let those two die with that on my conscience? Trust me, Kate. I think—I think he has enough affection for me to forgive this.' These last words were very shaky and Kate bit her lip doubtfully as Aleyne rose to allow her to unlace her gown.

Dominick appeared to have regained his spirits when he returned. Kate had left much earlier and Aleyne watched him undress with the same sense of dread as she had felt on her marriage night, and for a totally difference cause.

He sat on the bedside and smilingly surveyed her. 'You still look distressed, but so very beautiful.'

He reached out a hand to stroke a lock of her brown curling hair. 'All these disturbing events will soon be behind us. Try to put these unhappy thoughts aside.'

As he drew her into his arms she steeled herself to remain rigid, unyielding, so that he drew back, frowning.

'Do you still take me to task for my lack of mercy? I have explained. Aleyne, you cannot quarrel with me over every rascal in my household—or, for that matter, in yours either—that I am forced to discipline.'

'There is more to this than you think,' she said in a voice so low that he was forced to bend his ear to her lips. 'You cannot hang these men, Dominick. *I* was at fault.'

'You? How so?' He was frowning now, more in concentration than in anger as he tilted up her chin with one gentle finger to stare deeply into her eyes.

She swallowed hard and met that concerned gaze, dreading to see it turn into one of furious anger.

'I bribed Scroggins to free your prisoner. Ellis Dyer is known to me—my cousin. I could not see him brought to trial and die—horribly, at Tyburn.'

It was out and her lips were trembling but she held back smarting tears. His brows twitched together and his dark eyes grew stony, pebble-like, opaque.

'You say Ellis Dyer is known to you? You have strong feelings for the man?' He released her chin and, seizing her shoulder in a bruising grip, shook it hard.

'No, no, you don't understand! Ellis was my father's squire after he served at Middleham. We were brought up together. We are kin, nothing more.'

'Yet you risk my ire and a man's life to save him?'

'Ellis is like a brother to me.'

'Do you know he was caught spying behind Yorkist lines?'

'He—he told me something of it, but I…I know nothing of such things. I only know you were taking him to London to die.'

'Who said I would take him to his death?'

'Would you not have done?' She out-stared him now and he turned away from her.

'I don't know. I—I held my hand in Tewkesbury because I was not sure just how guilty he is.'

'Please, Dominick,' she was crying quietly now, 'try to forgive me. I know I—I betrayed you…'

'Aye, madam, that you did, and I find it hard to forget, let alone forgive.'

He stood up and moved moodily from the bed. She cowered back as if he would strike her as she feared he would have done in his lodgings at Tewkesbury.

'Why could you not have come to me honestly the moment you knew I held the man prisoner and explained your relationship?'

She bit her lip, confused by the directness of the question.

'I—I was afraid that—if—if you knew—you...'

'Would prevent you from taking the course you did. From the start you planned to deceive me.' The challenge was harsh and she bowed her head, her quiet tears now turning to anguished sobs.

'Well, it is done, and who knows what harm the man might do the King's cause.'

'What—what will you do?'

'Do?' He almost yelped the word. 'What can I do, madam? Should I reveal my wife's disloyalty to the world?'

'I can stand any punishment if——'

'If, madam? Do you dare issue conditions?'

'I can bear anything if—if you will reprieve Will Scroggins and Weaver. Dominick, please!' She held out her arms to him, her hair streaming in disarray, her face streaked and swollen with tears. 'Will Scroggins is Kate's lover. I beg you, for her sake...'

He faced her from the door, his expression still stony. 'For Kate's sake, aye, I'll reprieve Scroggins from hanging, though not from a torn back; for her sake alone, madam, mark me well, not for yours.'

She swallowed back her sobs. 'Where—where are you going now?'

'Why, to do your will, madam—where else?'

He snatched up hose and doublet from the chest where he had left them, wrenched open the door and left her.

She waited until she heard the ring of his spurs on the wooden stair supports, then she flung herself down on her pillows and wept bitterly.

CHAPTER ELEVEN

ALEYNE was dry-eyed but calm when Kate came to wake her. Dominick had not returned to their chamber.

'All should be well, Kate. Sir Dominick promised me Will would not hang.'

Kate's eyes lit up. 'Oh, my lady, thank you. I shall never forget this. Neither will Will. Was he very angry?'

Aleyne was about to reply when a harsh voice spoke from the door.

'Yes, Kate, very angry. Leave me with your mistress. Make sure everything is ready in the solar for breakfast.'

Kate curtsied and withdrew. Aleyne could see by the way the maid edged carefully round her master that she was relieved about her Will but deeply concerned about Aleyne.

Dominick did, indeed, look very fierce and, though Aleyne's heart was beating with sudden joy at sight of him, she quailed inwardly at the stony expression in those dark eyes.

He slammed the door shut and came towards the bed. 'I trust, madam, that you slept soundly knowing your dear coz was safely out of my custody.' The words 'dear coz' were almost sneered.

'No,' Aleyne said quietly, 'I did not sleep soundly. I wondered where you were. I am deeply sorry that I angered you but I cannot say I am sorry that Ellis is free either.'

'Obviously.'

'You did not allow me to finish.' Her chin tilted challengingly. 'You have intimated several times that now these wars are over men must seek to trust each other again. I cannot believe that the ignominious death of one man can ensure that the King sits safely on the throne again. King Edward is much too powerful now for rebels on the run to harm him.'

He seized her wrist in his fingers and bent close.

'Do not be so sure, my lady. Harry the Sixth lives still, and many disgruntled lords have fled the land. The King must make very certain now that England remains at peace.'

'By humiliating a helpless, defeated woman like Margaret of Anjou?'

'Just that. Margaret will never accept defeat till she lies in her grave.'

Aleyne stared up at him, horrified, and he released her wrist abruptly. 'Do not look at me like that. Edward does not make war on women but Margaret and the former King must be kept close.'

'In the Tower?'

'More than likely.'

'And the Princess of Wales?'

He shrugged uneasily. 'I doubt that Edward will keep the Lady Anne imprisoned. As I said, it is my fondest hope that he will arrange a marriage for her.'

'With Gloucester?'

'Certainly with Gloucester. Richard loves Anne and will be able to make her forget these troublous days.'

'And what if she is with child?'

Dominick turned to her sharply and it was his turn to look horrified. 'She did not tell you that?'

'No, she did not.'

'I pray the Virgin she is not,' he muttered uneasily.

'For Gloucester's sake, or because it would endanger the peace of the realm?'

'For both. Surely you can see that?'

Aleyne nodded, pushing back the heavy waves of her hair. 'It seems that none of us will be able to forget the consequences of these wars.'

'We must try. Before I send your maid up I want one thing settled between us: whatever there was between Dyer and you must be laid aside.'

'I swore to you there was nothing between Ellis and me.'

'Your father never suggested a match between you?'

'No, never.'

'And you yourself never wished for it?' He was staring at her so intently that she shifted uneasily on the bed.

'Never.'

'You spoke with him in the barn?'

'Only briefly.'

'And there were no words of love between you?'

She coloured hotly. 'He—he kissed me in parting, but only as a kinsman would.'

'You are my wife now and I will not have my honour impugned. If you do not keep that thought well to the fore of your mind I'll etch it so deep that you will never forget it. If I discover that you have disobeyed me in this and there has been any contact between you and Dyer I'll see he dies for it and take a whip to your buttocks. Do we understand one another?'

Tears smarted behind her lashes but she nodded tremulously.

He drew her into his arms fiercely and kissed her hard on the mouth as if he wished to satisfy himself that she belonged to him utterly and him alone. For a moment she remained passive, but his nearness overcame her and she found herself responding with as much ardour.

'Aleyne,' he murmured thickly, 'do not anger me so again. I need to trust you completely.'

'I swear to you I would not willingly go against your wishes.'

'Swear to me you do not love Ellis Dyer.'

She drew away, frowning. His furious jealousy disturbed her. This was no love-match but he had no cause to distrust her. There had never been anything more than cousinly affection between her and Ellis. Dominick Allard had claimed her hand, made her totally his. She had surrendered her body to him dutifully. From now on she was committed to him alone. Last night she had missed him, lain unsleeping, her whole being unaccountably aching for his presence, fearful that, in his justifiable anger, he would send her away to his manor in Yorkshire where she would not see him for months on end. Within these few short days she had come to accept him as a worthy mate and protector and had no wish to become a lonely and neglected wife. If they were to live harmoniously together it was necessary that he be completely satisfied that she was utterly devoted to his interests.

'You are my husband, Dominick, and will have my total support and obedience. That is your right.'

He gave a great, gusty sigh and sat on the bed's edge, smiling at her. The hard glitter had faded from his expression and there was a tenderness to the set of his mouth.

'We have wasted several hours and now I must be about my service to Gloucester,' he said regretfully. 'I dare not stay near you longer or I shall stand accused of dereliction of that duty. I'll send your maid up. Hurry and dress, my darling, so we can have an hour together before I must leave for the Charterhouse.'

Kate was eager for her news when she came to dress Aleyne.

'All is well. Have you seen Will yet?'

Kate shook her head. 'He may not be feeling too well,' she said grimly, 'if all I hear of Sir Dominick's discipline is true.'

Guy was waiting to serve them in the solar and Aleyne saw that his face was less strained. Likely, when Dominick was in a rage, his squire was wont to feel the force of his good right arm too. Dominick stood up to greet her respectfully enough and there was a grim little smile hovering round the corners of his mouth. She ate heartily, since last night's meal had been spoilt for her. As she watched him covertly over his bent head, Aleyne's heart quickened with her delight in him. If he had remained angry with her and had banished her to Yorkshire she could not have borne their parting.

When Guy announced that the Duke of Gloucester had arrived at the inn and was anxious to speak with his master they were both surprised. It was yet full early for the duke to expect Dominick to be in attendance.

He hurried in and with a hasty wave of his hand dismissed the need for Dominick or her to treat him with ceremony.

'I'm sorry to interrupt your meal, Dominick, but my need is urgent. I need someone to take the road to London ahead of the King and I thought it would save time if I saw you immediately.'

'Bad news from the capital, Your Grace?'

'Yes, we've heard from the Council. Rivers sent messengers to say the bastard Fauconberg is attacking the city. Since Warwick placed him in command of the fleet we've been concerned as to his movements. Apparently he landed first on the Kentish coast, has sailed up the Thames and insisted that King Henry be released from the Tower. Rivers has defended the city, of course, and the Londoners are holding their own, but he'll need reinforcements soon. The bastard's men have set fire to houses in Aldgate, Bishops Gate, even to London Bridge.'

Dominick had risen immediately the duke had entered. He listened thoughtfully and nodded.

'It will take less than two hours to have my troop ready to leave.'

Gloucester glanced doubtfully at Aleyne. 'There is your wife's comfort to be considered.'

Dominick hesitated only a moment. 'She can travel more surely in the Lady Anne's train. It will relieve your mind to have her there in attendance?'

Gloucester nodded and bent to take Aleyne's nerveless fingers. 'I regret that I must call on your husband's services and take him from you so soon, Lady Allard. It will be a comfort to me to know you will be with my lady cousin in the hours of her greatest need.'

Aleyne rose and curtsied. Her knees shook beneath her. It had been bad enough to think she might be parted from Dominick because of dissension between them, but now this ugly fear rose to daunt her. He was to go again into battle. She must not make him ashamed of her. She swallowed back her tears and faced the two men as calmly as she could.

'My husband is honoured to be asked to serve you, Your Grace.'

He smiled and, not for the first time, she saw how it lit up that narrow, normally grave young countenance.

'I was sure from the beginning that Dominick had found himself a truly courageous bride.'

She excused herself and returned to her chamber. She sat by the window numbly while Guy came to pack for his master. Dominick had so few personal possessions that his task was soon finished.

Aleyne continued to sit on silently while Guy armed Dominick for the ride. He dismissed the squire and came to join her at the window.

'This parting will not be for long, my dear.'

Her lips trembled at the tender note of his voice.

She rose and briefly touched the cold steel of his vambrace.

'Take very great care. The last time you left me for these wars I did not know how deeply I would be concerned if you did not return.'

'And now you do?'

She reached up to kiss him. 'Naturally I do, now. I am your dutiful wife.' She lowered her head, laughing. 'I feel I should bind a favour round this arm and I have nothing to give but...' Her fingers stole to the clasp of the reliquary, the mark of his love, but he checked her instantly.

'No, that must remain with you. It is dedicated to my patron saint and will guard you while I am gone.'

'Dominick, will there be great danger?'

'No, my heart, skirmishing only. Fauconberg is posturing. He knows he cannot win when Edward returns to the city. Richard feels he cannot leave the King's side at this critical time and it will relieve his mind to have a man loyal to his interests ready in London to receive the King on his ceremonial entry. He must be sure the city is quiet before that.'

'Do you take Will Scroggins?'

'Aye, he has a sore back but is well enough to ride. He can redeem his conduct by hard work and fighting if the need arises.'

'But can you trust him?'

Dominick touched her lips lightly with one finger. 'You really are concerned for my safety. Yes, Scroggins is loyal enough except where there is profit in defection.'

She frowned and he laughed. 'Seriously, my love, there is nothing to fear. I'll watch him too closely for him to have opportunity to take any reprisals. As for the lad, Weaver, I fear he is not so tough as Scroggins and it will take longer for him to recover. I leave him to guard you. He knows you saved him and that will be an incentive to see he does not leave your side. I shall be glad when your lad Rob can be returned to your service.'

He put both hands on her shoulders and looked deep into her eyes. 'You will not forget what was said about Dyer?'

She shook her head, her throat staining scarlet with hot blood.

He kissed her gently upon the forehead and she resisted the longing to cling to him tearfully. Knowing she was now a soldier's wife, she tilted her chin bravely and watched him go, smiling. After he had left the room and she had watched from the window while he mounted his hack Roland, and rode through the entrance arch, she gave way to her feelings and cried softly until Kate hurried in to comfort her.

Despite Dominick's reassurances about Scroggins's loyalty, Aleyne was fearful that the man would take his revenge for his master's treatment of him and then seek refuge among the masterless men who lived in the sanctuary of St Martin's. She could not, however, confide her doubts to Kate, who was happy in her Will's reprieve.

Gloucester had apparently spoken to the King regarding his wish for Aleyne to serve the Lady Anne, for Clarence made no objections, though Aleyne felt she was closely watched all the time she was in attendance. As the former Princess of Wales's brother-in-law, he had now had her placed in his charge until the entry into London. After that Anne would be in her sister's household.

The young widow received Aleyne with real pleasure. She had once more deliberately withdrawn herself from the presence of Queen Margaret.

'The Queen is closeted with her ladies. The depth of her grief shuts out any need for me to attend her,' Anne explained.

Aleyne still found it impossible to gauge the depths of her sorrow for the death of her young husband. Her former enigmatic remarks about his personality had left Aleyne bewildered. Anne did not confide in her new attendant about any fears she might have for her future following her arrival in London. Nor did she mention her mother, still in sanctuary in Beaulieu Abbey. She was delighted to learn about Aleyne's father's friendship with both the Duke of York and her own father and talked most often of happier days at Middleham Castle.

'It all seems so long ago now. The air is cold and clean there and we all went hawking together, Frank Lovell, Rob Percy, your husband Dominick, yes, Ellis Dyer and Dickon—the Duke of Gloucester,' she corrected herself hastily, but the slip revealed what Aleyne had been told: that there was truth in the story that Lady Anne and Richard of Gloucester had once been very close to each other.

The journey south was made without difficulties, Aleyne riding by Anne's side. Queen Margaret rode in a closed carriage, tightly guarded, and Aleyne caught only glimpses of her proud, tragic features. She had risked and lost everything in this final throw of the dice at Tewkesbury. That pathetic man, her husband, who awaited her arrival in the Tower, once more a prisoner, would be unlikely to offer her any assistance or real comfort. Aleyne doubted if Margaret would ever again attempt to thwart Edward.

Aleyne was pleased to see Will Scroggins ride out to greet her at St Albans, carrying messages from Sir Dominick.

Lord Rivers had driven the rebels across the fields to Stepney and taken many prisoners. The bastard Fauconberg had withdrawn to Blackheath and there was no immediate need to fear the possibility of more attacks on London.

'Sir Dominick has been in the thick of the campaign, my lady, but is well and completely unharmed. He bids me tell you he is waiting anxiously to receive you in your apartments at Baynards Castle.' Will bent his head to murmur conspiratorially, 'There's no need for you to fret yourself, my lady. There's been no news of the prisoner. Likely he made it safely to sanctuary.'

Aleyne nodded. 'Thank you, Will. I'm glad to see you well recovered.'

He gave her a grin and a knowing wink. 'Thanks to your good offices, my lady.'

'Do you ride back to Sir Dominick?'

'No, my lady. He gave me instructions to stay with you now. There may be some excitement when the King enters and Sir Dominick is anxious to ensure your safety.'

'Then you can join Jem and Kate further back in the train.'

He saluted her, grinned again, and rode to the rear of the company to join his companions.

The King entered London on May the twenty-first to be received with ecstatic rejoicing from the townsfolk. The position of honour in the van of the procession went to the Duke of Gloucester, following him Lord Hastings, then the King himself in gilded armour, a coronet round his helm. His welcome was the more vociferous since the populace knew he was to be reunited with his Queen and the baby Prince Edward, his heir, born only months ago in the sanctuary of Westminster while the King had still been in exile in Burgundy. It was a triumphant procession, standards waving, trumpets and clarions sounding bravely. At the rear came the Duke of Clarence with the Dukes of Norfolk and Suffolk and Buckingham guarding the pathetic chariot bearing the defeated Margaret of Anjou. She sat huddled, wrapped in a heavy frieze cloak, despite the heat of the early summer day. The Lady Anne had chosen to ride inside with her, but Aleyne, riding her palfrey in close attendance near the vehicle, noted that not one word passed between them.

The King was graciously pleased to knight the mayor, John Stockton, eleven of the city aldermen and Thomas Urswick, the recorder. The short ceremony took place in the meadows near Islington. Aleyne had been staring anxiously round for her first sight of Dominick and it was here that she saw him at last, riding towards her, accompanied by an older, distinguished-looking man she took to be Lord Rivers, the Queen's brother.

The chariot bearing Queen Margaret lumbered off to the Tower to the shouts and catcalls of the apprentice lads who lined the route. Aleyne, now separated from Lady Anne, was unsure if the Duke of Clarence had carried her off to his town house.

Dominick had ridden beside her for the remainder of the journey. He had kissed her in greeting but had been unable to speak more than a few polite words to her. Now he hustled her impatiently into position with the other members of Gloucester's household to take up residence at Baynards Castle, the present home of the King's widowed mother, Cecily Neville, the famed Rose of Raby.

Used to the relative peace of Risby Manor, Aleyne was utterly overwhelmed by the mixture of squalor and grandeur she found at Baynards. Their feet resounded on the great stone flags of the corridors, the groined ancient roofs bore down on her, grimed with the smoke of resined torches and braziers over the centuries. Her nostrils were assailed by the stinks from the river and the stale rancidness of unchanged floor rushes. Everywhere was noise—clanging hammers of farriers and armourers in the courtyard, the baying of hounds, frantic fluttering of jessed falcons, bawling of grooms and

esquires, cooks and scullions; and, inside, the shrill barks
of Italian greyhounds, and the raucous laughter of pages
and serving-wenches. Aghast, Aleyne drew back against
her husband. Not even at the inns at Coventry and
Broadway, or during the aftermath of battle, had she
experienced such a terrifying sense of inferiority and
insecurity.

He put his arms comfortingly round her. 'You'll get
used to this incessant racket. It's always so in the castles
of the great. The first time I experienced it was in the
Duchess of Burgundy's household. Middleham had never
been quite like it. It was busy, of course, but the
household members knew each other well and respected
each other. The Duchess of York keeps constantly to the
seclusion of her own apartments, rarely eating in hall.
The place will be packed tight as salted fish in a barrel,
but we have been allocated a small apartment in the
south-west tower, so we are fortunate.'

She followed anxiously, moving aside as pages and
squires brushed arrogantly by them. The rooms set aside
for their use were not large: a bed-chamber and an outer
room to serve as solar, where Kate must sleep on a pallet
by night. Guy must always find himself a corner in the
guard-room or hall, or, if required, stretch himself across
their doorway. The rooms were gloomy, arrow slits
placed too high in the walls to admit much light, but
there were wall-hangings to keep out the worst of the
draughts and the bed looked comfortable, though Aleyne
surveyed the mattress doubtfully, deciding that she and
Kate would examine it later and throw out the flea-
infested straw and padding.

As Kate set about the outer chamber with a broom
she snatched from the hand of a tousle-haired boy
lounging in the corridor, boxing his ears as she did so
to punish him for his pert reply to her demands,
Dominick drew Aleyne hastily into their sleeping-
chamber. Guy hovered, ready to help divest him of his
armour, but was quickly dismissed.

'Later. I'll send Kate when I have need of you.'

Aleyne, scarlet-faced, was drawn hungrily into his arms. She drew a hard breath later, as he released her.

'Let me look at you.' He stared intently into her eyes until she gave an embarrassed little laugh. 'It seems an age since I saw you.'

'I was so worried until Will Scroggins told me you were safe.'

He brushed aside her anxiety. 'I told you it was nothing—all skirmishing. Now, help me with this confounded breastplate buckle so I can hold you properly. I was too impatient to wait for Guy to do it.'

She struggled with refractory strapping, and the two of them laughed and kissed like children. Later he assisted her with her gown's lacing, unwilling to wait while Kate came in. The dubious cleanliness of the mattress was forgotten when Dominick pulled her on to the bed and she surrendered to the delight of having him close again.

Afterwards he struggled up and began to don his brown velvet doublet. 'Now don't be afraid to assert yourself. You'll be obeyed if you insist on fair service. Kate will know what you need and how to get it.'

Aleyne bit her lip uncertainly. 'Are we to eat in hall?'

'You may, if you wish. Guy will attend you. I'm sorry that I must leave you again so soon but I'm summoned to the Tower. The Duke wishes to inspect the state of the armoury.'

'Will you be late?' She blushed, conscious that already she was sounding like a complaining wife.

He grinned cheerfully, then made a grimace. 'Possibly. There's much still to be done. Fauconberg is not defeated yet, though he has retreated now into Kent. Summon one of the wenches to bring your food here if you prefer that. I know you feel very strange in this vast place, but it won't be for long. Gloucester is no more anxious to remain in London than I am. I'd have us settled in Yorkshire before the heat of the summer makes this place untenable.'

He gave her a parting kiss and she sank back on the bed, listening to his tuneless whistle as he navigated the steep spiral stair with ease.

Aleyne took Dominick's advice and ate in her own chamber. The food was cold by the time she got it and indifferently well cooked, but Kate procured clean sheets and they managed to change the offending bedding. Despite all the noise about her, Aleyne was glad to retire early. She felt more than a little aggrieved by her husband's desertion of her on her first evening in the castle. Indeed, the urgency of his lovemaking told her that he himself must be angered by the need for it. As she drew the sheets about her she pondered on the peremptory nature of Gloucester's orders. What was so important that the business could not wait until the morrow?

She sat up eagerly when she heard the click of the latch. It was almost midnight and the pallid glow of the rush-dip she had left burning revealed her husband's exhausted and strained features.

He came to the bed and began to undress. 'I'm sorry if I disturbed you.'

She shook her head and sat, hands clasped about her knees. 'No, I wanted to wait, but Kate was tired and Guy needed to find a comfortable place for the night, so I dismissed them. I must have dozed.'

He nodded. 'His Grace was kept in close council for hours.'

She reached out and touched his bowed head. 'Dominick, is something gravely wrong?'

He grimaced. 'Only that I must leave you again at first light.'

Aleyne gave a disappointed gasp. 'Is there still trouble in Kent?'

'Yes. We march for Sandwich. Fauconberg will go on making trouble until the King holds him prisoner.'

'Is the Duke of Gloucester in charge of the pursuit?'

'Yes, so naturally I must attend him.'

Aleyne frowned in the darkness. She felt cold resentment against the young Duke who must take

Dominick away from her again so soon. Surely it would have been possible to choose some other gentleman of his household? To please Gloucester Dominick had left her in Coventry. Now she must face these first frightening days at court without her husband's support. Was their life together always to be like this, subject to the whim of the King's younger brother?

Dominick was talking, and she switched her thoughts back to him. 'Guy will watch over your comfort and I'll leave Scroggins and Weaver to guard your person.' He gave a harsh little laugh. 'I can trust them to do that. They have already assured me of their undying loyalty to your service—not to mine, note, but yours!' She felt his body shake beside her with hearty laughter. 'You appear to have roused some spark of decency in Scroggins which I doubted he possessed. He has sworn to me that the idea of freeing Dyer was his alone and that you acquiesced after talking with the man.'

'That is not true.'

'I know that.' There was a frosty edge to his tone which made her give a little shiver of apprehension. Must Dominick always suspect her natural feelings for her cousin?

He sat up to gaze down at her as a portrait painter or image maker did before beginning work on his subject, and she saw the frown draw together between his brows.

'You still do not trust me?'

Instantly his expression cleared. 'Aleyne, of course I do. It's as Gloucester says: we are all driven to action against our natural desires and instincts. Dyer was my friend, yet lately I have come to distrust his motives.' He shrugged his shoulders. 'I've seen so much of betrayal and treachery these last months... There, I'll not try to track him down. Let him go his own way. He cannot harm the King's cause now.'

She marvelled at his change of mood. When he had last spoken of Ellis he had thought her cousin a danger to the Yorkist cause. Later she was to wonder at his abrupt decision to abandon his pursuit of Ellis Dyer.

'When this final bout with Fauconberg is over, will there be peace at last? Queen Margaret appears a totally broken woman, but would King Harry's imprisonment in the Tower be a focus for insurrection?'

'King Harry threatens no one's peace now. It is over. York is triumphant.'

'The Lady Anne is with her sister now. I feel she will be better away from Margaret's dominance.'

'I am not so sure. She and Isabel were never really close. Gloucester called at Coldharbour, Clarence's town house, before going on to the Tower, but he was unable to see Anne.'

'You mean she refused to see him?'

'I don't know the true reason. We were simply told the Lady Anne needed to rest in seclusion.'

'You do not think Clarence will keep her a prisoner?'

'Not if Gloucester has anything to do with it.'

Aleyne sighed inwardly. She and Anne had much in common. If the lady was to be won over to accept Gloucester's wooing he should be near her over the next weeks, yet the King was sending him on this punitive venture into Kent. Was Edward, too, intent on keeping his brother and cousin apart?

Throughout Dominick's lovemaking Aleyne sensed some urgent need, and strove to comfort him. It was during that unreal pre-dawn that she fell off to sleep, Dominick already fast off, his arms clasped tightly round her.

She woke as he was arming.

'Don't rouse yourself. I shall be clear of the chamber in a few moments.'

'No, this time I wish to come down and see you ride off.'

He sat down beside her on the bed's edge. 'A truly dutiful wife, eh?'

'Yes, Sir Knight.' She reached up to kiss him lightly. 'I know you are going to assure me there is no danger, but I do not believe you.'

'Best if I say nothing, then, except to give you this.' He reached for a small silk-wrapped package on the chest near the bed.

'Another gift? There was no need...'

Laughingly he tried to take it back. 'Very well, then, mistress, I'll sell it and buy a new falcon jess.'

She snatched it back. 'You will not!' Her fingers fumbled the silk impatiently and then she gave a little crow of delight at the dull glow of rubies set in a wrought-gold pin.

'Dominick, it is so beautiful. You have had so little time to think of gifts...'

He chuckled. 'At least you can be sure I was not spending the time enjoying the delights of the South Wark.'

Guy bustled in with some of the harness and began to buckle Dominick into breast-plate and greaves. As he bent towards her the chill of the metal struck through her body warm with sleep, and she wrinkled her nose at the now familiar smell of metal-oil and leather.

Dominick hurried his squire into the other chamber to allow Kate to help Aleyne dress. The castle was already waking to new life and Aleyne grimaced. It would be hard to sleep in this place and she doubted if she would ever adapt to it.

There was a twitch to Kate's lips as she admired the new brooch Aleyne proudly pinned to the front of her gown.

'I see there is more gallantry to the Wolf than we had imagined. I'd thought him devoted to fighting skills alone.'

'God keep those fighting skills sharp till he's safe home again,' Aleyne said fervently as she surveyed herself in the scratched iron mirror.

There was bustle and confusion in the castle courtyard, grooms leading out hacks and destriers, sumpter mules being laden with equipment for the expedition. Aleyne walked beside Dominick to his horse and stopped to fondle Roland's nose.

She forced a smile as the Duke of Gloucester emerged from a doorway accompanied by a tall, stately woman clad like a nun in unrelieved black. So this was the famed, beautiful Cecily Neville, widow of the Duke of York and mother of the King and the two princes. The faces of both mother and son were unwontedly grave while Gloucester acknowledged Dominick's bow and Aleyne's deep curtsy as he walked to his own mount. They stood together, heads bent in close talk, until he bowed to his mother and looked round the courtyard to assure himself that all was ready for departure. Aleyne met those clear grey-green eyes with an uncertain smile as he bowed in her direction, then, dutifully, he bent to kiss his mother's fingers. Her hand moved in a gesture of blessing over his bent head, then she stepped away as he mounted.

Dominick bent to kiss Aleyne. Tears pricked at her lashes but she held them back.

'God guard you.' Her words were formal but very real anxiety for him shone in her eyes and he nodded, his lips held tight.

'The Virgin keep you safe for me.'

The Duke held up one gauntleted hand commandingly, and the company filed out through the courtyard gateway.

As he stood beside her Aleyne was conscious of Guy's sullen resentment that duty kept him here beside her instead of with his master. She turned and looked steadily at him and he had the grace to look ashamed, his fair face flushing scarlet.

Missing Dominick terribly, particularly now that she was not needed to wait upon the Lady Anne, Aleyne forced herself to brave the bustle and confusion of the castle, and also agreed to Kate's suggestion that Will Scroggins should escort them to view the city.

They were impressed by the busy river traffic, the crush of people, carts and chariots, the overhanging shop and house fronts, especially upon the bridge, the never-ending fascination of the shops in the Chepe, noisy with the insistent cries of apprentices calling out their wares.

The stinks from the open kennels running down the middle of the streets caught at country-bred Aleyne's throat, and she would have slipped on the refuse or been doused by some careless woman leaning from an upstairs window to empty a chamber pot, had not Will Scroggins guided them cheerfully through all the filth; but, despite all, Aleyne found the capital utterly absorbing. In those packed streets humanity jammed together: noblemen escorted by liveried retainers, wealthy merchants in their furred mantles, physicians and students, men-at-arms and beggars—many exhibiting running sores and wounds taken during the recent campaigns—imploring alms. It was as if this cramped, evil-smelling city was the hub of England's greatness and its squalor.

It was on one such excursion to St Paul's that Aleyne and her party were forced back by a solemn procession of black-garbed monks and men-at-arms in the King's livery, who were using heavy wooden staves to good effect to keep off the jostling populace.

'Will, what is it?' Aleyne stumbled and Guy steadied her against a house wall lest she fall below the feet of the folk pressing anxiously forward to view the show. 'The people seem so quiet in spite of their curiosity. Some great man has died, surely?'

Scroggins called to Weaver to keep the women safe, and elbowed his way through the crowd. He was back very soon, his expression grim.

'It's the corpse of poor, mad King Harry. He died in the Tower, of melancholy, so they are saying. The King's men are conveying him to St Paul's to be exhibited to the crowds. It's the custom, my lady.'

Aleyne gave a distressed little cry. 'Poor soul. My father said he was always gentle. God receive his spirit.' She crossed herself.

Scroggins did likewise. 'Amen to that, my lady.' He looked round thoughtfully. 'We must get you clear of this. The crowds could get ugly.'

'I don't understand. Surely they mourn the King's passing, and will wish to do so decently and soberly?'

'Aye, my lady, and to express their doubts as to how he came to die so suddenly and conveniently after King Edward's entry into the city.'

It was difficult to press against the stream of folk avid to view the King's body, and Aleyne was exhausted and very relieved to arrive at Baynards Castle safely.

That evening for the first time she took her courage in both hands and went to the main hall to eat, Guy hovering close beside her and finally stationing himself behind her to carve and serve her supper. A haughty steward found a place for her and hastened off to deal with nobler folk, his white wand of office brandished high as a sign for all to yield place for his passing. Nervously Aleyne took her seat on the bench allotted, between two older women extravagantly dressed in jewelled brocades and fashionable butterfly hennins. Aleyne was conscious of her own dark gown, but she had donned Dominick's gifts of reliquary and ruby pin. There was a stir as the company rose to acknowledge the entry of the Duchess of York, who swept in and took the canopied chair of state. Aleyne noted how she carried herself like a queen and recalled what her father had said that some called her Proud Cis, though not to her face.

Aleyne enquired of her neighbour if the Duchess's unrelieved mourning was in honour of the passing of the late King Harry.

Dark eyes surveyed Aleyne shrewdly. 'Hardly. The Duchess has worn nothing but a nun's habit and wimple since the Duke was killed at Wakefield. She's hardly like to mourn the death of her royal cousin. But for him and that she-wolf Margaret, she would have been wearing England's crown instead of having to defer to her daughter-in-law, Elizabeth.'

Aleyne winced inwardly at the woman's outspoken waspishness.

'My father always asserted that King Harry was a saintly ruler. Many will mourn him genuinely.'

The woman gave a half strangled yelp of laughter. 'You think so? Certainly not His Grace the King, or that whelp of a younger brother.'

'My lord of Gloucester?'

The woman waved back her page and sank small sharp teeth into a venison pasty. 'You cannot deny King Harry's death is providential. York can wear the crown now without further fears of insurrection.' The hard eyes travelled over Aleyne's slight, tense form. 'You're Allard's wife, I think the steward said.'

Aleyne nodded.

'Hm. He was at the Tower with Gloucester, I understand, the night the King entered London.'

Aleyne's heart gave a sudden leap in her breast. How strained Dominick had looked when he had returned to her and how urgently he had needed her comfort.

She forced herself to reply calmly. 'Yes, my husband was helping to inspect the armoury and prepare for the expedition into Kent.'

'Well to get Gloucester out of gossip's way. Fortunate and convenient.'

'I beg your pardon?' Aleyne said frostily.

The youthful page behind them cleared his throat as if he thought to remind his mistress that her words were ill-advised.

'Gossip, what gossip?' Aleyne's voice was shrill with nervous alarm.

'You haven't heard?' The woman's expression showed malicious satisfaction at being the one to inform her. 'Rumour has it that the King died last night, while the Duke was in council at the Tower.'

Aleyne went white to the lips as the woman's words confirmed her own half-formed fears. Her fingers jarred her wine mazer. She forced herself to go on sitting throughout all the courses of the meal while her whole being screamed to jump up and flee the hall. The woman's voice droned on in gossip yet more scandalous, concerning one of the Duchess's ladies, and Aleyne was free to let her mind dwell on the horrifying implications of the woman's sneer.

Had King Henry been murdered, and by Gloucester, with Dominick's assistance? No, she could not believe it. That night after he had been to the Tower Council, what had he said?

'King Harry threatens no one's peace now. It is over.'

She had thought Dominick was talking of the former King's imprisonment. Now the words implied something infinitely more sinister.

Once back in her chamber she sent Kate to summon Scroggins. Undoubtedly he had been out and about in the city. When he arrived she made sure her door was closed, and asked Guy to guard it. Voice lowered deliberately, Aleyne demanded to know what was being said concerning King Harry's death.

'Are there veiled accusations of murder? Tell me the truth, Will.'

'Aye, my lady, and some not so veiled.'

'Who is held to be responsible—King Edward?'

He glanced round cautiously, as if even the thick walls of this chamber would not be sufficient to prevent them from being overheard. 'Aye, it's to the King's certain advantage.' His eyes were troubled as he read her distress in her expression. 'For the peace of the realm, my lady, a political necessity.'

'And the Duke of Gloucester is suspected of overseeing the deed?'

'He is Lord Constable of England and he was present at the Tower the night the King died.'

'But that is surely impossible. The King must have died yesterday, well after the duke left for Kent.'

'It's being rumoured King Harry died on Tuesday, the twenty-first, Ascension Day.'

'But the body could not have been kept fresh—in this heat . . .'

'The dungeons and cellars of the Tower are dank and chill enough, my lady, and there are skilled embalmers.'

A cold hand squeezed Aleyne's heart once again. That poor, confused, saintly man, done to death, perhaps hideously—not by Dominick on the Duke's orders! Sweet Virgin, not that!

'Have you been to St Paul's? Are there marks of violence on the dead King's body?'

'Not that can be seen.' He shrugged. 'You know how superstitious rumour spreads and feeds on so-called marvels. It's said the body bled before the altar, a sign of murder most foul.'

'Could that really be?'

'In my opinion, no, my lady. Corpses don't bleed after death, however they come to die, but people thrill to these tales; always have, always will.'

Aleyne sighed. 'Thank you, Will. You can go now.'

He frowned at her anxiously, then half shrugged and went to the door. Kate whispered to him for moments, then returned to Aleyne.

'Don't distress yourself, my lady. King Harry has been ill many times over these last years. You must not believe what is being uttered by malicious, lying tongues.'

'Kate, in your experience, can anyone die of melancholy?'

Kate hesitated. 'No, yet—it is possible, I suppose. Souls sick to the heart with no wish to go on do sometimes sicken with no outward cause and die. He had no future...'

'Who would say that? Had he lived, his supporters might have rallied.' Aleyne's voice choked. 'He wasn't allowed to survive.'

'My lady, it would be unwise to talk openly of this.'

'Kate, the castle...the whole city is ringing with these accusations.'

'But you are Sir Dominick's wife and he...' Kate broke off in confusion.

'I am Dominick's wife, and he is Gloucester's loyal gentleman and grateful to him for many favours, including a wealthy wife...'

After Kate had left her she lay awake for hours, troubled with dark and terrible thoughts. She had so longed for her husband's return; now she dreaded to face him with deep suspicion in her eyes. It could not be. Dominick, she knew, was a strict disciplinarian. She had heard him condemn Scroggins without a qualm, but to murder a helpless old man—no, she could not believe him capable of such an act, nor could she think it of Gloucester either. He had always been gravely courteous to her and considerate of her welfare. From the first the Duke had saved her from Dominick's fury.

Yet the Lady Anne thought him capable of deliberately seeking out her husband in the battle and dispatching him. Certainly the deaths of Henry and his sole heir made sure of the succession to the House of York once and for all, and it also made Anne a widow, her considerable fortune there for the taking.

What could she say to Dominick? Dared she voice her suspicions? She could not live contentedly with him if she believed him responsible for such a cold-blooded murder.

It was quite impossible for her to sleep. At last she got up, donned her bed-gown and sat by the window until she heard the castle stirring to life in the chill dawn.

CHAPTER TWELVE

KING HENRY'S death proved a nine days' wonder. His corpse, after the customary lying-in at St Paul's, was conveyed to Chertsey for burial. By the end of the month the new talking-point throughout the city was the news of the surrender of the bastard Fauconberg at Sandwich and the early return of the Duke of Gloucester with his prisoner. Aleyne anxiously waited for her first glimpse of Dominick.

As usual court protocol prevented an exuberant greeting, for which, for once, she was grateful. As she stood in the hall at Baynards Castle she watched the Duke being greeted by his mother and, as Aleyne curtsyed to him and he gently helped her to her feet, she winced from his touch. She could not dispel the torturing image she had had over these last weeks of the feeble King being done to death by the command of this youthful, grave young prince who had always treated her so kindly.

Dominick was held in talk during supper, his neighbours eager to hear the details of the Kent campaign so that he and Aleyne had little time together in private.

She had felt guiltily glad of the respite but the moment she dreaded, when she would be quite alone with him, could not be put off indefinitely and she steeled herself for his embrace as she had done Gloucester's light touch on her fingers.

Dominick dismissed Kate and Guy jovially, thrust their chamber door to and turned to face Aleyne.

'At last, my love, I have you to myself. Come on and kiss me, properly this time.'

Obediently she went into his arms and her traitorous body responded to him. Her mouth parted under his and her arms stole round his neck until with a little laugh he swept her up into his arms and carried her to the bed.

There was no talk. It seemed that he had sensed no reserve in her and she surrendered to him willingly enough. Afterwards, as they lay close, the revelry from the castle hall reaching them only dimly, he turned to look fully at her in the rushlight's gentle glow. His own dark eyes were gleaming with love, and she smiled tremulously as he took up her hand and gently kissed each finger.

'Well, have you missed me?'

Her answer was breathless. 'You know I have.'

A little frown formed between his brows as he bent even closer. 'Yet something is wrong. I can sense it.'

'No, I...'

'You have had news from Risby?'

She shook her head.

'Is the boy Rob well? Is he back with you?'

'Not yet, but a messenger came from Tewkesbury to say his leg is healing well.'

His frown changed to a heavy scowl. 'Is it Dyer? Have you heard news of him?'

'No, Dominick, nothing. I swore to you I would not try to contact him. Scroggins says...'

'And what does Scroggins say?'

'Only that he thinks Ellis may be yet in the sanctuary of St Martin's. Many of the Lancastrian knights have taken refuge there, it's said.'

'I saw you were not wearing my brooch at supper. Doesn't it please you?'

She stared up at him doubtfully. Since the news of the late King's death she had found the sombre, blood-like glow of the rubies strangely disquieting, almost as if they were drops of blood, and she had not worn it. Now she did not know what to say.

'I—I broke the pin. It will have to be returned to the goldsmith.'

'I'll see to it, send Guy in the morning.'

'No,' she lied, 'I sent Will Scroggins to the Chepe with it. The man said he was busied but I shall soon have it again.'

He accepted the tale readily enough and she made a mental note to see that Kate hid the jewel for the present.

As if aware of her reserve now he turned from her to sleep. She lay beside him miserably. This would not do. She could not tell him the cause of her distress. She had not the words.

She watched him carefully next morning when the subject of Henry's death was being discussed. He gave no sign other than to cross himself devoutly and enquire where the King's body had been bestowed. Aleyne left him in the hall to talk with other knights of the household and escaped to her chamber to work on a frontal she was fashioning. She jumped when the door opened abruptly and Dominick came in.

'You are very jumpy. Anyone would think I came to murder you!' His tone was light, but the brows were drawn together again in concern.

She forced a laugh. 'I'm sorry. I wasn't expecting you to leave your companions yet awhile.'

'We have been summoned into His Grace the King's presence at Westminster.'

'What can be wrong?'

'Wrong?' he looked bewildered. 'What should be wrong? Now the King is at liberty to concern himself about his ward's welfare, I imagine he merely wishes to see you to assure himself all is well.' He looked down at her plain gown. 'I think you should wear something more festive. I'll send Kate in.'

They went by boat to the Palace of Westminster, alighting at the King's steps. During the short journey Dominick asked if Aleyne had seen anything of the Lady Anne.

She shook her head. 'Will Scroggins says it's unlikely that the Duke of Clarence will allow anyone in the Duke of Gloucester's household to see her. It's being rumoured in the city that she is being kept a virtual prisoner. I thought it best not to try to see her until you were with me.'

'Scroggins has his ear close to the ground as usual,' Dominick commented drily, 'but he could very well be right. Clarence will not be best pleased if Gloucester is granted Anne's hand in marriage. He's no wish to share the Warwick inheritance with his brother. It will be necessary for Anne to guard herself. I think she fully understands that.'

Aleyne's gorge rose. Yet more talk of murder. 'Surely even Clarence would not dare to try and dispose of Warwick's daughter?'

Dominick shrugged. 'Greater nobles than the Lady Anne have died to serve the interests of those near them. Gloucester will be aware of the need to keep a close watch on Coldharbour.'

Aleyne thought bitterly, Could Anne be safer with Richard of Gloucester than with her sister's husband? In this den of royalty who could feel secure?

As they crossed the palace yard at Westminster Aleyne saw that it was crowded, like the outer yards of Baynards, with nobles, city dignitaries, clerics and notaries, whose sober garbs contrasted with the bright brocades and velvets of the courtiers. Obeying Dominick's instructions, she had dressed carefully in a gown of golden brocade trimmed with pale fur. Dominick hurried her through the corridors into the Chamber of Presence, its entrance guarded by two men-at-arms in blue and murrey, bearing the King's personal device of the sun in splendour within the petals of the white rose of York.

Aleyne curtsyed low to the King, who lounged comfortably in a padded throne chair, dressed, as ever, splendidly in a doublet of purple figured velvet, under a furred trimmed robe of cloth of gold. Beside him Aleyne glimpsed for the first time the famed beauty who had ensnared the King, it was whispered, by witchcraft: Queen Elizabeth, the former Lady Grey, whose marriage to her had cost Edward his alliance with great Warwick. The Queen, dressed in green brocade and cloth of gold, extended a hand to her to kiss. Rising and backing from the throne dais, Aleyne saw that Elizabeth was radiantly beautiful, though not a strand of that famous silver gilt hair was visible beneath the fashionable wiring of her butterfly hennin.

'So, my ward appears to be comfortably settled at Baynards, and is enjoying married life, I trust?' The King smiled at Aleyne expansively.

'Thank you, I am, Your Grace.'

'And looking quite lovely. The lady has blossomed within your keeping, Sir Dominick.'

The King signalled to the steward and leaned towards Aleyne, his chin on his hand, elbow resting comfortably on the padded chair arm.

'I was forced to request your presence as witness during this distasteful interview, Lady Allard. Please, sit down on the stool near you. Dominick will stand very close. I have summoned Sir Thomas Stoodley to answer the charges you laid against him. Do not be alarmed or embarrassed by these proceedings.'

Aleyne *was* decidedly alarmed. She had hoped never to set eyes on Sir Thomas again. Limbs trembling, she sat obediently, her hands clasped on her knee to keep them still.

Stoodley swept in as arrogantly as she remembered. Mentally she contrasted the flamboyant grandeur of his doublet of tawny velvet worn over green hose, and the sparkle of his gilded leather belt and chain with Dominick's quieter mole-brown attire. Yet her husband's air of dignified authority marked him as the more noteworthy of the two men.

The King deliberately kept Stoodley on his knees while his eyes ranged lazily over the man.

'How now, Sir Thomas, what is this I hear concerning your flouting of royal prerogatives?'

'Your Grace?' Stoodley's expression showed no alarm, merely respectful regret. 'I know of no way in which I have displeased you. If you will enlighten me as to my offence I will immediately strive to put matters right.'

'You *will* do so, Sir Thomas, I assure you.' The King's expression was bland but his tone cutting. 'It has come to my notice that you attempted to press your hand upon my ward, Mistress Aleyne Risby. The lady has attested to the truth of the affair.'

The King had waved him to rise and, in doing so, Stoodley saw Aleyne for the first time since entering the chamber. His blue eyes became wary, though his mouth continued to smile. He saluted her with a gallant bow.

'Mistress Aleyne, I am relieved to see you safe and well. My kinswoman, your stepmother, has been half out of her wits with anxiety for you, particularly since we heard of the problems following the aftermath of battle.'

The speech was so smooth and so blatantly insincere that Aleyne half moved from her stool to remonstrate, but the King forestalled her and his voice was ice-cold.

'Your liveried retainers took possession of Risby Manor House, Sir Thomas? For what purpose?'

'Your Grace, I beg your gracious permission to explain. Sir Godfrey's sudden death and the unsettled state of the realm...my cousin feared——'

'That some other would snatch the prize and possess the heiress.'

'Just so, Your Grace. I wished only to offer my protection——'

'The lady had first call on *our* protection, Sir Thomas. Did you forget that?'

'I dared not, sir.'

'I say you *did* dare. You spoke to our ward on the subject of marriage without our permission and, had she not escaped the manor house before your men surrounded it, she would have been forced into marriage against her will—and mine.'

Stoodley's confidence in his own ability to talk himself out of disaster was ebbing. He hedged, shrugging apologetically.

'I was over-hasty, Sire, but Lady Risby convinced me——'

'Lady Risby is equally culpable. Were she not a woman and recently widowed I would let the full weight of my displeasure fall upon her too. Had you men-at-arms for protection, Sir Thomas, they would have been more profitably employed in furthering the cause of your sovereign on the meadows of Tewkesbury, rather than in pressing a frightened maid into your bed.'

Aleyne saw Stoodley's shoulders straighten a mere fraction, and his fingers strayed towards his dagger. She knew he was too choked with fury to reply to the King's deadly rebuke.

'I have bestowed Mistress Risby's hand on Sir Dominick Allard. You will pay a fine of two hundred marks to the treasury and keep your retainers on your own land in future. You are excused, Sir Knight.'

Sir Thomas bowed low and backed. As he straightened Aleyne caught a shocked glance at his features. All false joviality had been wiped from that floridly handsome face, and the look he directed at her and Dominick was venomous. Dominick's grip tightened reassuringly on her shoulders.

She was still trembling when she again took her seat in the boat bound for Baynards Castle.

'Did you see his face?' she whispered huskily. 'He hates us, Dominick. He will never forgive us.'

'He knows he has forfeited royal favour but I cannot see why he should blame us for that. His failure to support Edward in these last two encounters will have ruined any ambitions he might have had.'

'I wish my stepmother were not still living at Risby,' Aleyne said. 'I would not like to find her there when I return.'

'I can send messengers ordering her to leave if you wish, but it is out of the question for you to travel to Warwickshire yet awhile. I'll not leave you alone on the manor while the country is so disaffected. In that neighbourhood, so near to Tewkesbury, there'll likely be bands of masterless men from the defeated army preying on defenceless houses.'

'Could you not take me?' She stole a glance at him, hoping he would understand her need to be from the intrigue-ridden air of the court.

'At Christmas, perhaps, or in the spring, when the Duke's need of me is not so acute.'

Her spine stiffened mutinously. There it was again, his extreme loyalty to Gloucester coming between them.

'Surely he would give you leave to be absent from his household for a while?' she said a little more curtly than she meant.

He frowned. 'Once the knotty problem of the Duke's marriage is settled he wishes to go north. Border raids are on the increase, since the Scots have taken advantage

of the recent insurrection. It will soon prove necessary
to teach the reivers a stern lesson. The Duke will need
commanders he can trust. Certainly he would excuse me,
were I to ask it, but I will not leave him now.'

'If the Lady Anne's suspicions regarding the death of
her husband still hold it may be that she never gives her
consent to the match,' Aleyne said sharply.

'Do you suggest that both you and she hold Duke
Richard responsible for Prince Edward's death?'
Dominick glanced quickly towards the boatman and
lowered his voice, but Aleyne could not fail to notice his
growing anger.

Her doubts over the last days rose up again in force.
She could not bridle her tongue now.

'His death was providential. Had he survived the battle
would he, too, have perished in the Tower with his sire?'

Dominick looked thunderstruck. He leaned very close
to her and whispered urgently, 'Do you wish to find
yourself in the Tower? Do not let me hear you frame
such thoughts again.'

'My being silent about them does not make them unfounded,' she snapped.

He lifted his hand and she thought, had it not been
for the boatman, he would have slapped her.

'Duke Richard is the most honourable man I know,'
he said softly, through his teeth. 'I command you never
to slander him in my presence.' His dark eyes bore that
opaqueness she remembered from the night he had discovered Ellis's escape. She was suddenly afraid of him,
opened her lips to protest, then closed them again and
turned away to look over the water.

'Your friendship with Duke Richard makes you
overlook his faults,' she said evenly.

'What faults? He has ever been exceptionally kind to
you.'

They were pulling into the steps on the wharf now,
and she waited while he assisted her from the boat and
began to escort her towards the castle entrance.

He pulled her sharply to a halt. 'Now, tell me what all this is about,' he ordered. 'Has this encounter with Stoodley addled your wits?'

She faced him directly. 'You were in the Duke's presence all night, before you both left for Kent?'

'Yes, you know that I was, or do you think I spent the evening in the South Wark?'

He was trying to make a joke of it. She sighed. In one way she might have felt less troubled if the two of them had indeed been sampling the wares of the South Wark brothels. She said tonelessly, 'Dominick, tell me that you were involved in nothing...dishonourable.'

He checked, becoming suddenly aware that this distress of hers was not due to some woman's whim, a trifling jealousy for the time he must spend from her with Gloucester.

'Do you believe me capable of dishonourable behaviour?' he questioned, a trifle harshly.

She dared not ask him openly about the murder. Surely, now that he was aware of her doubts, he would reassure her? She waited, her body tensed.

Abruptly he said, 'We shall be late for supper in hall.'

Her lips parted, but she had no words. She swallowed back the tears which came unbidden into her throat, and followed her husband into the castle bailey.

Aleyne was conscious of a restraint between them as they supped together. It did not lessen after Kate had been dismissed. For the first time they had been together since her marriage Dominick did not make love to her and she lay, tearless, at his side.

She had struck at his honour, that most precious of commodities, and she knew his fierce loyalty to Gloucester forbade him from decrying any royal conduct which she might criticise. She knew, only too well, that many wives were forced to accept a code of conduct adopted by their husbands quite different from their own, yet her very real respect for her husband was so deep rooted she could not bring herself to countenance any ruthless ambition in his nature. She wanted to believe him innocent, and she needed, terribly, for him to tell her that he was. That, she knew, he would not do, for an acceptance of the possibility of the duke's complicity would be to give rumour due credence.

In the morning he was coldly polite as he left her to report to the Duke. She wanted to call him back, assure him that she would believe anything he chose to tell her, but her pride forbade such behaviour.

Nothing more was said of the matter but the barrier between them seemed to grow higher over the next weeks. Often Dominick slept away from the castle and Aleyne did not dare to question if he had been on the Duke's business. Dutifully she played her part beside him at all the functions court procedure demanded, but her heart was heavy with its burden of unhappiness and deadly suspicion.

London was rife with gossip concerning the rivalry between the royal Dukes: Gloucester's demanding of the King the hand of the Lady Anne, Clarence's hotly denying him. Anxious to keep the peace between himself and Clarence, so newly patched up before Barnet, the King declined to give judgement. Aleyne wondered constantly how Anne was faring in her brother-in-law's household and remembered Scroggins's warning that the lady should guard herself.

The bastard Fauconberg was, surprisingly, graciously pardoned and, when the Duke of Gloucester set off for the North in mid-July, his erstwhile prisoner rode in his train.

Aleyne was not surprised when Dominick informed her coolly what he wished her to remain in London while he rode with Duke Richard. He treated her considerately but he was aware that King Henry's ghost lay between them, a cold bedfellow, and separation, for a time at least, would possibly allow a healing of the rift.

The Duke visited her and expressed his regret that he must take Dominick from her. She thought she read sorrow in those grey-green eyes, as if her respectful attitude, without warmth and troubled, disturbed even him.

'I can never thank you enough for the kindness you showed to Lady Anne during her distressing journey south,' he said quietly. 'On one of the occasions we have met since she spoke of it with gratitude. I hope, soon, when she is my Duchess, since Dominick will remain in my household, we shall both be able to reward you fittingly.'

Aleyne was bewildered. The young Duke seemed genuinely in love, and deeply honourable. Could he really be guilty of so dastardly a crime as she had accused him of to Dominick?

She stood with Kate and a mutinously disappointed Guy in the courtyard of Baynards as Gloucester's company rode out. Dominick spurred his mount towards her and reached down from the saddle to embrace her. She allowed herself to relax in his arms and lifted her face to his, her eyes swimming with tears.

'Take care,' she whispered hoarsely.

He forced a smile. 'Tell me that you trust me?'

'You know that I do—despite everything.' The final words were uttered in a tight little whisper.

He sighed, bent and kissed her again.

Her eyes strained hungrily for a last glance of her husband's armoured form beneath the Wolf standard, then she turned wearily back to her own chamber.

CHAPTER THIRTEEN

BY THE end of August Aleyne was thankful for the coolness of stone and absence of sun-glare in her small apartment. It had become unbearably hot, and plague was rife in the city. These days they avoided walking abroad in the stinking streets where rotting garbage and the carcasses of cats, dogs, and even diseased sheep and pigs lay abandoned, covered with swarms of flies. The Duchess of York had retreated to Berkhamstead Castle and Baynards seemed almost deserted, Gloucester's household gentlemen with him on the Scottish Border, and many other hangers-on at the Duchess's court had sought their own manors, fearful of contracting the pestilence.

When Aleyne complained of feeling mildly unwell Kate was at first concerned, then watchful.

'Have you missed your monthly course?' she questioned at last.

'Oh, Kate, not—the second is due now...do you think...?'

'It's too early to say yet. You have had a hard time recently and this can affect women. Have you suffered early-morning nausea? Are your breasts tender?'

Aleyne crimsoned. The changes in her body appeared to have happened to her all at once. She could not be sure and it would be pointless to inform Dominick till she was. Messages passed frequently between them by fast courier. She had received two letters from him, and returned him one. She was aware that her own had been somewhat stilted. It had seemed impossible to write how she missed him terribly and longed for his return to end this estrangement between them. He wrote that the Duke had been received joyfully by the city of York and that he had every confidence that the Scots would soon be subdued. Although his letters were by no means passionate, Aleyne was relieved to find a warmth there and was comforted.

She was cheered one afternoon when a cheeky page knocked on her door and ushered in a bashful Rob.

Aleyne was relieved to see that he walked well and that his injury was clearly mending.

'I had thought you had gone back to Risby,' she said, beckoning to him to come close. 'Does your leg ache at all? There seems to be no limp.'

'It's as good as new almost; gets a bit stiff, but they monks did a fair job of healing. I should have been here earlier for Sir Dominick left me coin for the journey, but—I decided to go to Gloucester first.'

Aleyne's chin jerked and, as Rob's eyes went hesitatingly to Kate, seated in the window embrasure with her embroidery, she nodded to him to go on, since her maid was in her confidence.

'Sit down, Rob, on that stool. Guy, Sir Dominick's squire, will show you where you can bestow your bundle and find you a sleeping place later. So you visited Mistress Dyer?'

'Aye, mis—my lady; I heard as Master Ellis had been taken prisoner then, later, how he'd escaped. Some men-at-arms were talking of it at the White Hart at Coventry where I was taking ale. It was then I turned tail and went to Gloucester—got a lift in a cooper's cart part of the way.'

'Mistress Dyer knows how things stand with me?'

'Yes, my lady, and she surmised you had a hand in Master Ellis's escape.'

'I did. She must be half out of her mind with worry. Later, when you are rested, Rob, you must go back and reassure her that we think Ellis is still free.'

'She's not in Gloucester, my lady.'

'Here, in London?'

'No, in Dover.' Rob fumbled beneath his leather jerkin and withdrew a small leather bag. 'She bade me seek out Master Ellis and give him this.'

'Gold? But Mistress Dyer was almost penniless.'

'She sold her house, my lady, is determined to go with him into exile, and sends what coin she has for his needs and for passage to France.'

'I don't know where Ellis is, Rob. He might well have left England by now. How will Mistress Dyer fare if she cannot find him?'

'I promised her I'd go to Dover with news if Master Dyer couldn't go himself.'

Kate grunted. 'Poking his nose into the sanctuary of St Martin's or the warrens of the South Wark could get the boy his throat cut.'

'Mistress Dyer is desperate, my lady.' Rob's adam's apple wobbled uncertainly.

'I understand that...' Aleyne nodded '...but you must need food and rest. We'll think of this soon, I promise.'

Guy received the newcomer politely but with some reserve. Aleyne, smiling wryly, realised that he feared his duties might be usurped by this bucolic servant who had already sustained injuries in her service. He resented being penned here when he should have been with Sir Dominick on the Border.

Aleyne discussed with Kate the problem of finding Ellis.

'I feel duty-bound to get his mother's message to him,' she said uncertainly. Her eyes caught Kate's and she looked away quickly. She had promised Dominick she would avoid all contact with her cousin.

Kate sighed. 'Will could make some enquiries for us, I suppose.'

'It must be soon. Rumour has it that the Duke is already on his way south.'

Kate grimaced. 'Aye, and when he gets here it will be to discover that his dove has flown the nest.'

'The Lady Anne—left her sister's protection?'

'It was being said in hall that she was being searched for, had left Coldharbour.'

'You think she fears this proposed match with Gloucester and has fled?'

'Or wishes it and the Duke of Clarence has taken steps to prevent it.'

Aleyne's facial muscles seemed to stiffen. 'You mean there's talk of—murder?'

'Who knows? That will be for Gloucester to discover for himself.' Kate gave a little barked laugh. 'It's likely there *will* be murder if he finds his betrothed has been done to death, royal murder or execution, however you'd regard it.'

Aleyne sat on alone, her thoughts in chaos. Had she misjudged Gloucester? If so her present misery was for nothing, and Anne—that brave, dignified, unhappy girl could already lie in her grave.

Kate returned to say that Will had already left to enquire in St Martin's sanctuary.

'If there's news of Dyer he'll sniff it out and he'll ferret
out any information he can glean about the Lady Anne's
disappearance. I doubt if Clarence would have dared to
act against her yet. More than likely he's shut her up in
some nunnery.'

'He couldn't force her to take the veil?'

'He could put a great deal of pressure on her, as I
know to my cost from my own parents' behaviour,' Kate
said feelingly. 'However, she'd take a sizeable dower with
her and that would not serve His Grace's plans. We have
to face the ugly truth that he needs the lady dead.'

Scroggins presented himself in Aleyne's chamber after
supper. She saw by his triumphant expression that he
had been successful.

'I've seen Master Dyer, my lady, and fixed up a
meeting at a certain tavern in the South Wark. I impressed on him the need to leave the city before Duke
Richard returns, for Gloucester's men'll tear sanctuary
and the hovels of the South Wark apart to find the Lady
Anne. Master Dyer could well be caught in that net.'

He hesitated and avoided Kate's eagle gaze.

'He sends his greeting, lady, and——'

'He asks to see me to say goodbye?'

'Aye, my lady, but that would be most unwise.'

Aleyne moved by him into the window embrasure. She
bit her lip almost until it bled. Behind her she could feel
the weight of Kate's disapproval. Of course a meeting
with Ellis would be unwise—and dangerous—and yet,
well escorted and dressed as a servant . . . He would leave
England and she would likely never see him again. In
the old days they had been so close. Was Ellis asking
too much of her?

She turned, her mind made up. 'Can you guide me,
Will?'

'Yes, my lady, but if Sir Dominick finds out——'

'I know what I ask of you, but is there real danger
of that? He is not expected for some days. Oh, Kate, I

know what you are thinking, but Ellis is as dear to me as a brother. I must see him this one last time...'

Will shrugged. 'I'll do anything you ask, my lady. You know that. But for you I'd lie in cold clay even now. If you promise to do just as I say, no harm should come of it.'

'Kate?'

'I go with you, of course.'

It was decided that Guy Jarvis must know nothing of it. Will would see to it that Jem Weaver would arrange for some problem in the household to engage Guy's attention. After some thought Will agreed that Rob could go with them, since he had seen Master Dyer's mother and had messages for him.

The following afternoon Will Scroggins escorted a party of three soberly but respectably dressed citizens across London Bridge on foot. He had chosen the time of day deliberately.

'It's so hot that most honest folk will be resting and the denizens of the South Wark are rarely up and about before evening.'

Aleyne's cheeks burned at the implication. It was so hot that she had not worn a cloak but borrowed a plain russet kirtle from Kate, holland blouse and apron, wimple and cap. A basket on her arm, she felt it most unlikely she would be recognised by any from Baynards who might be passing by. Will led them swiftly through the maze of narrow alleys where the overhanging storeys of the hovels met so close that they almost blocked out what air there was in this noisome district. Will indicated a shuttered tavern some yards distant. Rob, who was looking behind him, almost stumbled.

'Is your leg troubling you, Rob?'

'No, my lady, I wasn't looking where I trod. I thought—I'm imagining cut-throats behind every angle of wall.'

Scroggins halted. 'I'll wait here, my lady, just in case of trouble.'

'Should there be any?'

'I hope not, but you never know in this neighbourhood. Knock three times on the tavern door. She's a blowzy creature who keeps this place but close-mouthed if she's well paid. Tell her the sergeant sent you and give her a gold noble. She'll take you up to Master Dyer. If you need me Kate can give a shout.'

'We'll not be long.'

'I pray you'll not, my lady. This place breeds ears and eyes by the moment. I'd not have any word of this escapade reaching the master.'

A slatternly woman admitted them after Kate had given the agreed signal. Reeking of sweat and stale beer, the woman grunted her acceptance of the proffered coin and pointed to the rickety stair.

'He's awaiting for ye. Nobody'll disturb ye so long as you ain't too long.'

Aleyne hesitated and Kate said briskly, 'I'll stay below with Rob till you call. We'll take some ale and keep our eyes open, never fear.'

Aleyne lifted her skirts fastidiously and climbed awkwardly to the landing. The steps were greasy and stiff with filth. Despite the August sun outside it was pitch black there with the shutters closed, and she knocked urgently on the warped door she saw, only dimly, now facing her.

'Ellis, are you there? It's Aleyne.'

Bolts were drawn hurriedly and a triangle of light illuminated the gloom, then strong arms drew her into the fetid little room. Ellis faced her, laughing, the greenish light from the oxhorn window behind him falling on to his face. He looked well and suddenly older, as if his experiences in sanctuary had matured him too quickly. She was aware that she hardly knew this different, war-weary soldier. She had always been so much at home with Ellis, as she had with her father; now she was acutely nervous and wished that Kate had come up with her. Ellis drew her towards the window, turning her towards the faint light.

'It's good to see you, Aleyne. Allard is treating you well?'

She flushed, her voice unaccountably breathy. 'Very well.'

'I had to see you in person; could hardly ask such questions of that sergeant-at-arms. Allard is on the Scottish Border, I hear.'

'Yes, but not for much longer; that is why I came at once. I've brought you funds from your mother.' She searched within her basket and produced the leather bag of coin, then made to put the bag down on the greasy table-top, but he forestalled her deliberately, taking it and capturing and holding her fingers tight within his grasp.

'My mother should not have sacrificed her own comfort. I could have managed.' His tone hardened, became almost a sneer. 'One learns lessons in sanctuary on how to survive.'

'Why didn't you make for the coast at once? Oh, never mind, you should go now, Ellis. Your mother is waiting for you at the Old Oak in Dover. It will not be safe for fugitives soon in the city. The Lady Anne has disappeared and Gloucester will search every house. You are known to many of his men.'

'The Virgin protect the lady. What a misfortune it is to be born an heiress.'

'I've noticed it.'

Recognising the bleakness of her tone, he bent forward and cupped her chin in his hand.

'You are unhappy. I suspected it. Come with me, Aleyne. You must know I have always loved you and hoped to speak to your father when the time was right. What do we care for Risby or your inheritance? Trust me to provide for you and my mother.'

His hands were hard on her shoulders, his eyes boring into hers and with a strange hard intensity. She wriggled free of his grasp, her breath coming fast, oddly afraid of the one man she had thought always to trust to the death.

'No, Ellis, you mistake matters. You mustn't. This is sinful. I am Dominick's wife.'

He drew her close again and kissed the top of her head, gently this time, as if he was restraining his passion with effort.

'You cannot love him. You were sold into this match. God will not punish us for loving. In France or Burgundy we'll be free. He'll not pursue us. He has what he wants—Risby.'

She shook her head imploringly. 'No, Ellis, you don't understand. I have learned to love Dominick and I cannot, even if...'

She felt his body tense, his grip tightening cruelly again on her shoulders, then he pushed her very slightly from him.

'What is it?' White to the lips, she turned as the betraying click of the latch warned them both of an intruder. She froze as a hatefully familiar voice broke across her bewilderment.

'Well, well, a touching scene, on my soul, one which Sir Dominick would give his eyes to observe. A love-nest, and his innocent little bird, who was not to be forced into a hasty marriage bed, has learned much, it seems.'

'Stoodley?' There was venom in Ellis's question.

'Indeed, I am Sir Thomas Stoodley, as you rightly assume. Don't move for your dagger!' The last words were barked. 'My men could cut you down, Dyer, in a trice, and who would complain? You are Aleyne's cousin? Ah, and a wanted man, so I hear. It's fortunate for you at the moment that it's Lady Allard who interests me or I would find satisfaction and, no doubt, a reward in handing you over to the authorities.'

Aleyne stood defensively, her back against Ellis, the fingers of one hand caught and held in his. Her throat went dry with apprehension as she saw two men enter the attic and line up behind Sir Thomas, their daggers at the ready. The greenish window light glimmered on the steel. Warningly her fingers tightened on Ellis's. If he moved now he could die before her eyes.

Sir Thomas sauntered indolently forward, smiling that falsely genial movement of the lips while the eyes remained cold.

'So intent, my dear, that you did not hear us enter and deal with your "chaperons"...' the word was sardonically stressed '...and the avaricious lady who keeps this establishment, who unfortunately remained too greedy to know her own good? No,' he held up one hand in a gesture of mock consolation, 'do not concern yourself over her. Her troubles are at an end.'

'How—how did you come to find us here?' Aleyne forced herself to frame the words, her thoughts shying from the idea that Will Scroggins had informed on her movements.

'I've had you watched, followed your servants, waited my opportunity. When that boy of yours rejoined your service I thought it possible for you to fall into my hands.'

'Why? Why should you do this?'

'Because, my dear Aleyne, I allow no one to make a fool of me. Maud should have warned you of that. Now, I suggest you allow your leman to release you. Stand apart from him. One scream and my men will butcher him instantly. I imagine you would not care to see that?'

She shook her head and stepped aside from Ellis. He tried to cling to her fingers but her pull was imperative and he let her go regretfully.

She faced Stoodley, chin up defiantly. 'Do you intend to kill us?'

'How could you believe me to be such a barbarian? I want you as my guest for a while, both of you, provided your swain behaves in a reasonable manner.'

'What have you done to Kate and Rob?'

'Both are safe, the woman somewhat bruised—she's quite a hell cat—but the boy was taken so easily by surprise that he was simply overpowered.'

Stoodley bowed mockingly to Ellis, who remained silent throughout their exchange, his eyes narrowed thoughtfully. Aleyne shot him a curious glance. How Ellis had changed over these last months since Barnet! Once, like Rob, he would have rushed, blundering, to her defence; now, a veteran campaigner, like Dominick, he waited to see what new form this game would take. Having decided on his policy, he docilely allowed Stoodley's retainers to bind his wrists behind his back while another of them menaced him with drawn dagger.

Stoodley suavely invited Aleyne to sit on the truckle bed.

'Uninviting, I grant you, but it's more convenient if we wait until darkness falls before moving you. I'll send up your maid. Is it necessary to ensure your silence?'

Already Ellis had been gagged. His eyes appealed to her mutely and she shuddered, shaking her head.

'Then my men will keep guard outside. I'll go below and order the arrangements. The boy will stay with us.' It was an implied threat that Rob would prove a hostage to ensure Aleyne's compliance. Stoodley nodded to his men and Ellis was bundled out. Aleyne heard his unsteady progress as he was pushed down the stair. She got up and backed nervously to the window but Stoodley made no move to approach her. He gave a final mocking salute and withdrew.

Moments later Kate was hustled in, her guard cutting her bonds and giving her a brutal push towards her mistress. Kate's wimple and blouse were torn and she had a badly bruised lip. The left side of her face was swollen. The door banged to hard as the guards left them alone, and Aleyne clung to Kate tearfully.

'Forgive me for getting you involved in all this.'

'Let be, let be. Don't blame yourself,' Kate said with forced cheerfulness. 'I've known worse handling.'

'Certainly I blame myself. Stoodley would never have dared snatch me from Baynards Castle. Sweet Virgin, what can he hope to gain? I'm married. Is it revenge? Why didn't he kill me at once?'

'Men like Sir Thomas do nothing without hope of profit,' Kate said soberly. 'He may plan your death, but not until your husband is also below ground.'

Aleyne's eyes widened in shock. The man was mad. How could he win in such stakes? Dominick was an experienced fighter and went always armed and escorted. He ran no risk—unless he thought his honour threatened. He would come after her, especially if he believed her untrue. And Ellis was kept alive to further bait the trap.

She rocked on her feet and stumbled to sit on the bed. Dear God, not only had she brought disaster to her servants but she had placed Dominick in jeopardy. She loved him. Beyond all things she wanted him to come to her, deliver her from her own foolhardiness, but she was being used to lure him to his death. She buried her face in her hands and sobbed unrestrainedly. Kate waited until the worst of the storm was over than knelt before her and took both her hands.

'Listen, my lady, you mustn't despair. There is a hope—just a possibility—that Will Scroggins is still free.'

Aleyne lifted a tear-stained face. 'What? But how—how could that help?'

'I don't know. Will's no fool. He stayed outside because he feared something like this might happen.'

Aleyne was silent and Kate stared back at her fiercely.

'I know what you're thinking: that Will would do anything for ready coin, that perhaps he planned this. I don't believe he would put me in peril...' She broke off and stood up, her hands clasping in anguish. 'He wouldn't,' she repeated, 'and he has told me many times how much he thinks of you.'

'You really love him, Kate?'

'Aye, I do, and...'

Aleyne gave a deep sigh. Neither would put into words the thought that Will Scroggins might well be found dead in one of the open kennels.

Kate said determinedly, 'If he saw the Stoodley men break into the house he could at least inform Sir

Dominick who was responsible. The men were wearing the Stoodley livery.'

'But you said yourself that my husband's death is what Stoodley wants.'

Kate's lips formed in a secretive little smile. 'Do you tell me you don't know your own man's worth, my lady? Sir Dominick Allard is no fool to walk into a trap so simply. Stoodley underrates him and the power of his lord.'

'Gloucester?' Aleyne breathed.

'Aye, Gloucester. Between them they will think of a way to free you. Take heart.'

'Tell me what happened. Rob is not badly hurt ... and the proprietress?'

Kate shrugged. 'No, Rob should do well enough but for some rough handling; as for the woman, she was half drunk and made the mistake of blustering at Stoodley. He was in no mood to be thwarted. Her throat was cut.'

'How many men were there? Could you tell?'

'At least six. Four of them came into the house. I imagine there'll be two more outside. Any one of them could have disposed of Will.'

Aleyne shrugged. The thought of what had happened to the landlady and what might have happened to Will Scroggins made her sick to her stomach. She retched weakly and Kate glanced at her sharply.

'You said nothing of your—suspicion to Master Dyer?'

'About ...?'

'About the child?'

'No, he wanted me to go with him. I was about to tell him why I could not when Stoodley burst in.'

'You must keep your doubts to yourself.'

Aleyne's eyes searched Kate's face in sudden dread.

Kate nodded. 'The possibility of a child, an heir, would make you worthless to Stoodley. You understand?'

'Yes; oh, yes.'

Kate stared through the dirty window. 'I cannot lose the idea that Stoodley will want to leave some trail for

Sir Dominick. For that reason Will might have been left
to escape. We should know soon about that. If Rob or
I are allowed leeway...' Her voice broke.

Aleyne went to her and they clung together, weeping
bitterly.

CHAPTER FOURTEEN

DOMINICK was staring through the fine-glassed window
of the Abbot's lodging at St Mary's in Leicester when
the Duke of Gloucester entered the room and flung his
gauntlets upon the well-polished table.

'We can leave within the hour. The Abbot begs us to
take dinner with him. It will delay us but the weather is
good and it will please him. We are making excellent
time.'

Dominick turned and smiled. 'I think you are as
anxious to reach London as I am, my lord.'

'We both know why.'

'That last messenger gave you no more news of Lady
Anne?'

'Nothing. Edward informs me that Clarence swears
he has no knowledge of her whereabouts.'

'And you do not believe that?'

The duke shrugged. 'It is to George's advantage to
keep Anne and me apart.'

'But the King has promised that you shall be
betrothed.'

'Aye, but he delays making the announcement. I can
understand his need. The peace is hard won. He wants
no dissension between his brothers to mar it.'

'My lord, your loyal service to him over these last years
has made you very dear to the King. In the end, he will
override your brother's objections and grant you the
hand of Lady Anne; I am sure of it.'

The Duke sighed. 'I will not force Anne. What if she
is unwilling? You saw how distant she was to me in
Coventry.'

'The lady was in shock, my lord, had only that moment heard of her husband's death.'

'And my dear brother had just implied that I and I alone was responsible, as if, in that bloody retreat, I deliberately sought him out and cut his throat.'

Dominick was silent and the Duke moved moodily to join him near the window.

'You have been very reticent about your lady, Dominick. There is no estrangement, is there? I thought you very satisfied with the marriage I made for you.' He hesitated, then gazed out over the Abbot's flowered pleasance. 'I noted some reserve—no, more definite than that—a coldness in her attitude towards me.'

'Your Grace is mistaken——'

'No, Dominick, I think not. The lady resents your loyalty to me. Is that the cause of the coolness between you?'

'I have been forced to leave her so often——'

'Come, Dominick, I have never given you cause to fear speaking honestly with me. She would prefer you to leave my service, true?'

'She knows I will never do that, my lord.'

'But why this sudden dislike of me? I thought she trusted me to do well by her.'

'Like most women she is sometimes swayed by gossip. She will quickly understand that scurrilous talk is rife in noble households...'

'Like Anne, she believes me responsible for young Edward's death?'

'It is possible she and the Lady Anne talked of it,' Dominick said cautiously.

'Aleyne is attached to the Lady Anne? I was glad of that; had hoped she would be happy in our service.'

'And I'm sure she will be, Your Grace. Marriage is still new to her and the proximity of court officials and the intrigue that poisons the air of castles.'

'Dominick, I think you have not confessed, even to yourself, that your feelings for Aleyne run deeper than you could ever have expected from this marriage, made, in your opinion, only to advance your interest, and now, I am sure, become much more dear to your heart.'

Dominick turned from him, his fingers toying distractedly with the jewelled hilt of his dagger. When he spoke at last his voice was harsh with emotion.

'Yes, I truly love her, Your Grace. She is everything I admire in a woman: brave, spirited and wonderfully honest. That first time in the inn at Broadway I should have recognised her true nobility, and then when I accused her of stealing my horse, while any normal woman would have broken down and cried for mercy and spilled out the truth of who she was and why she was there even then, her first thought was for that maid of hers, Kate. She stood up to me and declared stoutly that if I needed to hang someone it should be her alone. She was so beautiful, her hair and clothes dishevelled, distressed by all the fearful sights she must have seen out there on the field at Tewkesbury, anger and grim determination shining out of those glorious eyes of hers. I was so angry I could hardly speak. She had defied me, made me look foolish—I had never met a woman like her before. She left me utterly confused, as if I were some bucolic buffoon from her own village. My first thoughts were to distance myself from her. When I knew—who she was—I saw no prospect of marriage with her—yet you made that possible and I shall be forever in your debt. I love her with every fibre of my being, yet...'

'It is your friendship for me that now comes between you two? Dominick, you fret against the need to be here with me. Well, you must reassure her, stay closer to her for a while. When we get to Baynards I will release you from service. Take her home to Yorkshire. I may be forced to remain in London until I am assured of Anne's safety.'

'You are gracious, as ever, my lord, but Aleyne must learn now, rather than later, that *my* decisions rule our household. Certainly I will not leave the capital until your hopes are certain. Aleyne will not wish to do so until she can see for herself that the Lady Anne is happily settled.'

'I pray you are right, Dominick, and that it happens speedily. Now, write to your lady, and hold nothing back. I know you, old friend; your letters are as full of battle news as my reports to the King! Tell her you love her and are longing to hold her in your arms. The courier will reach her a day or two before we do and it should put her in the mood to greet you more lovingly.'

Smiling, he picked up his gauntlets again and Dominick moved to hold the door for him. He would just have time to dispatch his letter before they took the road south.

Sir Thomas took the precaution of having both women bound, gagged and blindfolded before hustling them below stairs and out into the cooler night air. Aleyne strained her ears for sounds which would tell her of the nearness of Rob and Ellis, but there was nothing. She was hoisted roughly into an evil-smelling cart. She edged along so that she might sit with her back supported against the canvas covering. Sensing Kate's presence opposite, she flinched miserably against the jolting as the driver whipped up the horse and the vehicle lumbered off across the cobbles. She tried to retain some sense of direction but she had no knowledge of the South Wark and did not really know the north part of London well either. Surely Sir Thomas would find it difficult to pass through the town gates at this hour? Was he merely moving his prisoners a short way from one hovel to another? They appeared to have been travelling for some time before the cart jolted to a halt and, unable to steady herself, Aleyne was thrown sideways. Coarse hands fumbled at her body and drew her from the vehicle. She found it hard to stand, and her breath sobbed out her panic against the muffling of the scarcely clean linen her captors had wound around her mouth. A push sent her sprawling and other hands pulled her to her feet.

'Be gentle with her ladyship, man. Sir Dominick will take it hard if his bird injures her wings.'

Aleyne found Sir Thomas's grasp more hateful than her rougher guide's, but was forced to allow him to lead her into her new prison. Stone flags were cool beneath her feet and strewn rushes came sweeter to her nostrils. She was ordered to watch herself on steps, a door was opened before her, and she felt the sudden draught of air; then she was urged forward. A hand fumbled the blindfold behind her head and she blinked in the dim light of a kindled rush-dip. Sir Thomas released her gag and she drew in thankful gasps of fresher air. Kate was urged in and her bonds released. When Sir Thomas himself cut the ropes which bound Aleyne's wrists she gave a sudden gasp of pain as the blood coursed freely once more.

He bowed mockingly. 'I regret I must leave you, but you will find most things suitable for your comfort. Never fear, you are well guarded.'

She turned away, unwilling to grant him the satisfaction of a reply.

The room was clean, even luxurious. Bruised herbs mingled with the clean strewn rushes, the shutters were drawn, but Aleyne guessed they must be somewhere south of the city, since she was sure they had not crossed London Bridge.

The mattress on the bed on its heavy roped supports smelt fresh and dry and the coverlets, though not of the best quality, were clean and skilfully darned. There was no other furniture in the chamber but two joint-stools and a small table on which stood the rush-dip.

'I'll see food is sent up.' Sir Thomas left them and she heard his muttered word of command to the guard outside, then the ring of his spurs against the stone of the entrance hall.

Used to adjusting to whatever fate had in store, Kate settled Aleyne on the bed and drew off her walking-shoes.

'You must first eat, then try to sleep.'

'I couldn't, Kate.'

'Think of the child,' she said very softly, then, more clearly, 'Sir Dominick will not thank you for starving yourself. We must pray you took no harm from the jolting of that diabolical cart. The driver was either a simpleton or a madman, going at such a pace in the dark.'

One of Sir Thomas's sullen-featured men brought them meat, coarse rye bread and ale.

Aleyne snapped, 'Where are Master Dyer and my servant?'

The man lifted his leather-clad shoulders in an insolent shrug and slammed out.

Kate reassured her. 'Since they were not with us in the cart they might have been left at the tavern, unless...' She coaxed Aleyne to eat, and to please her Aleyne complied. Worn out by their suffering and gnawing fears for their companions, the two finally fell asleep, huddled together on the bed.

Breakfast next morning was coarse fare but acceptable, and they were brought water and towels for washing. Kate's bruises showed purple and yellow but the facial swelling was already subsiding, though Kate confessed the split lip was still painful.

Aleyne peered from the unshuttered window at the two men in salets and jacks who guarded the house wall. The building seemed to be within a clearing and Aleyne could see dense trees all around. Possibly it was some hunting lodge. Built of timber supports over plaster and lath, the house appeared sturdy, there was quite a drop from the window, and the men outside were too close and watchful to afford them any opportunity to escape.

Just before the sun topped the trees Sir Thomas rode out with three of his men, returning several hours later. He did not come up to their chamber, and the day dragged endlessly. Aleyne's mind dwelt constantly on Dominick, her longing to see him and dread that he might come soon to his doom. She worried about the fates of Ellis and Rob and Will Scroggins. She did not dare speak of him to Kate. If Will had perished how could Dominick even know of her abduction?

Even before dusk a man secured the shutters. Rush-lights were brought in and they sat in the dimness, listening to the evening birdsong from the wood. Aleyne thought she heard sounds of arrival, a horse's hoofs muffled on the grass, a quiet word from one of the guards, and the noise made when the main door was opened and closed.

Soon after Sir Thomas's sergeant unbarred the door to admit a scared-looking girl carrying a steaming ewer of water and clean towels.

'Sir Thomas requests that you dine with him below stairs, mistress. I'll return for you both in half an hour.'

Aleyne was relieved to know Kate would be with her. She did her best to set to rights her appearance, brushing down her kirtle, combing her hair and helping Kate to pin together the torn portions of her blouse with an enamelled pin Aleyne had worn for the meeting with Ellis. It had been a gift from his mother.

Later, she swept aside her skirts from proximity with the sergeant and preceded him down the stairs.

The lodge was well appointed and furnished. The large hall tapestry was probably French.

Aleyne, with Kate in attendance, was ushered into a room to the right of the stair, where the trestle had already been laid with a fair linen cloth for supper. The room was bright with wax candles, and Sir Thomas, at the far end, was talking to someone, probably the new arrival, now partially hidden from Aleyne by his burly form. Intent on his business, he did not turn as the door opened to admit his prisoners and Aleyne was left waiting, while the sergeant seemed unwilling to interrupt his lord and announce her.

'I tell you we are safe enough. The lady can be conveyed here easily from the Chepe. The foolish chit was trusting and glad enough to find a refuge in the cookshop. Who could possibly know of our involvement? She can be dispatched simply, and the woods keep their own secrets. Let Gloucester look where he will. My Lord of Clarence will protect us, and the rewards are considerable. Who knows, His Grace aims high and King Edward is hardly like to dance to my tune.'

'Thomas, are you mad?'

Aleyne rocked on her feet as she recognised her stepmother's well-known tones.

'To deal with some country chit without noble kin is one thing; treason, quite another. Need I spell out to you details of the fate dealt out to convicted traitors? Do you really imagine Edward will ever again trust his drunken sot of a brother? Can you believe Gloucester will ever give up his search? They say he's besotted with the lady, prepared to sacrifice the greater share of the Warwick inheritance to possess her. Those captains of his will ferret out those responsible for her murder and——' Lady Risby broke off, dumbfounded blue eyes staring at Aleyne. 'Sweet Virgin, Thomas, I know now you really are mad! How could you bring her here at such a time?'

Stoodley swung round and bowed mockingly, the cozening note leaving his voice as he greeted his prisoner.

'Aleyne, how good it is to have you again to eat with me. Like old times, at Risby. A surprise for you, eh, to be reunited with your loving stepmother? Come, kiss each other, make up your differences. Raised voices sour the wine and toughen the meat.'

Shuddering with revulsion, Aleyne was forced to relinquish her hand for him to kiss. She lifted her chin challengingly as her stepmother moved from the shadows to regard her, anger burning scarlet roses in her cheeks. Lady Risby had discarded mourning. Though it appeared she had only recently ridden in and made a hasty toilet, she looked as beautiful as ever in a gown of dark green silk, a jewelled belt gleaming sombrely at waist and hip which Aleyne thought quite magnificent. Those emeralds had never been given to her by Aleyne's father, nor had the emerald pendant swinging on its heavy gold chain or the jewelled clasp which ornamented the front of her fashionable truncated hennin.

'Maud, my dear, will you take the place on my right, and Aleyne—Lady Allard, I should say—will you sit here on my left? I've not forgotten our other guest. Will you join us now, sir? I regret I have kept you waiting.'

Aleyne caught back a horrified gasp as Ellis Dyer stepped from a shadowed window embrasure to seat himself opposite. He had obviously made an effort to put to rights his appearance and, though still clad in the leathern jerkin and plain hose he had worn to meet her in the South Wark tavern, he looked fine enough. His very movements and attitude proclaimed the fact that he no longer regarded himself as a prisoner. He bowed his head to Aleyne over the table and she stared back at him in utter bewilderment.

Stoodley looked in amusement from one to the other of them.

'How pleasant it is when men of good sense can come so simply to an understanding. Wouldn't you agree, Lady Allard? Master Dyer has decided that he and I are of one mind concerning the advancement of our interests. One has to do the best one can for oneself in these trying times.'

Aleyne's lips trembled as her eyes silently implored Ellis for some explanation of his apparent volte-face.

Ellis reached for his wine cup and drank deep.

'It is as you say, Sir Thomas. You are out of favour at present. My hopes were doomed at Barnet. An attempt to redeem my fortune by appealing to my former friendship with the Duke of Gloucester failed at Tewkesbury. King Edward, it seems, has no wish to employ me, largely due to the intervention of my lady's husband, so I look to His Grace of Clarence.'

Aleyne managed to find her voice. In her own ears it sounded unreal, brittle.

'I'm glad my father did not live to see this day, Ellis Dyer. He put great trust in you, held you in deep affection. It would have broken him to see you turn traitor to your King—worse, batten on the weak position of the lady who has most claim to your loyalty. The Lady Anne's father was true lord to you.'

Sir Thomas's blue eyes became steel-hard. 'How unfortunate you heard so much. This poses problems, but none are insuperable.'

Lady Risby snapped, 'I see one obvious solution to this one.'

'You may be right, my dear, but not yet. Our little caged bird might yet be persuaded to sing to our tune.'

'I assure you, Sir Thomas, nothing will prevent me doing what I can to save the Lady Anne, as long as life is in me.'

He shook his head gently. 'Yes, but you do see our point, Lady Allard? However, we have time yet, and it is bootless to disturb ourselves by dwelling on the pain of unfortunate necessities. Let me help you to a slice of fowl breast. My cook is an expert, I promise you.'

The smell of the food threatened to choke Aleyne, her throat already swollen as it was with unshed tears for Ellis's duplicity.

He glanced up at her briefly and continued to eat heartily as if unconcerned by her shocked disapproval of his conduct. Lady Risby, Aleyne noticed, appeared to have little appetite. Sir Thomas did not allow Aleyne's distress or Maud's anger at her presence to disturb him in the slightest and went on chattering genially to Ellis.

At length he pushed back his chair and rose, extending his hand to his cousin.

'I think it is time our bird was returned to her cage. You and I, my dear, have much to discuss with Master Dyer. Shall we adjourn to the solar?'

His sergeant came to Aleyne's elbow, ready to escort her upstairs. She sat very still in her chair, staring hard at Ellis, who had risen to accompany Sir Thomas. She thought she detected, for one fleeting moment, a shadow of guilt, or shame perhaps, cross his face, then he bowed to her gravely.

'You must understand, Aleyne, in the sanctuary of St Martin's one learns how important it is to survive. I intend also to prosper. I regret that you must suffer by it.'

'I regret that I ever thought well of you,' she retorted bitterly as she rose and submitted to the sergeant's prompting that she leave the room now. Kate, who had eaten at a table near the door, rose and joined her mistress. Proudly, unwilling for Lady Risby to triumph over her despair, Aleyne swept from the room, her spine rigid. She waited until the door of their chamber was barred before collapsing, sobbing, on to the bed. When Kate came to comfort her Aleyne noticed that her maid's cheeks also were wet with tears.

'Kate, it is unlike you to despair. What have you heard?'

'I asked after Rob at table. They said he had been left bound in the stable but when a servant went with his supper he'd managed to escape. His bonds must have been badly tied, they thought.'

Aleyne's heart ached for Kate. 'Then it is as you said earlier: he was given opportunity to get away, to reach Baynards and bring Dominick into the net, so we must believe that Will Scroggins...'

Kate said dully, 'Since Rob was allowed to go, Will must be lost to us.'

'Kate—oh, my dear!' Aleyne embraced her and they rocked together, each in an agony of grief.

'So, Ellis will save his skin by conspiring with Stoodley to help my lord of Clarence solve his problem and keep the Warwick inheritance entire.' She had told Kate succinctly what she had overhead and surmised from it. 'They know I would betray them. They cannot afford to let me live.'

'Sir Dominick will come, my lady, you know that.'

'Yes, I know it, and to his own destruction. Will he come to avenge his honour, or because he truly loves me? I could have misjudged him over the matter of King

Henry's death, both him and Gloucester. If I have done
so could I now be misjudging Ellis?'

The eyes of the two women met and exchanged
meaning glances. Kate's fingers reached for Aleyne's and
gripped them hard.

CHAPTER FIFTEEN

DOMINICK dismounted hurriedly in the courtyard of
Baynards Castle and hastened into the building, brushing
aside servants and courtiers alike who impeded his progress towards his own apartment. The Duke had ridden
on to the Tower, where he had heard the King was in
council. Dominick was in a fever of impatience to see
Aleyne. It had not been possible that a returning courier
could bring him an answer to his message—there had
been no time. He would read that in his wife's expression.
During the remainder of the ride south from Leicester
he could think of nothing but his need for her. Richard
had assured him that he could take time now to be with
her constantly, even return to Yorkshire if he thought it
best. He must make her understand his loyalty to
Gloucester, have her know the man as he did himself.

The room was empty. Some discarded embroidery lay
on a chest where Aleyne had left it, but there was no
other sign of the owner or of Kate. He stopped, disappointed, in his tracks, then hurried on into the bed-
chamber. This, too, was untenanted as he had expected,
since it was nowhere near time for Aleyne to retire. He
returned, frustrated, to the small solar, and flung himself
on to a stool to wait for her return. Surely she had gone
into the city to buy some frippery and would be well
escorted? He rose and paced to the window, peering
down over the busy courtyard as if he could hasten her
appearance by his own longing for sight of her.

It seemed hours while he waited, then he rose and descended the stair to the great hall. Servants were setting
up the trestles for supper, but the Duchess of York was

seated near the window oriel, examining some fabric samples with her ladies. She glanced up, smiling, at Dominick's entrance.

'So, my son is home. I haven't seen him. I've returned to London to greet him.'

He knelt to kiss her hand. 'No, Your Grace. The Duke is at the Tower but should be here very soon now.'

'He is well?'

'In excellent health, Your Grace, and anxious to see you.'

'As you are anxious to see your Aleyne.' She frowned slightly, noting his concern. 'There is nothing wrong, Sir Dominick?'

'My wife is not in her chamber, Your Grace. As you say, I am too impatient for sight of her.'

The Duchess nodded understandingly. 'I do not recall seeing her at supper last night, but there, she does not always eat in hall. I think she finds the atmosphere here somewhat too formal. I have tried to put her at ease, but things will be simpler for her now you are home.'

He excused himself and returned to their chamber. The sunlight was fading now and Aleyne should be back if she intended to make her toilet before going down to the hall. He was too restless to eat, and paced the small chamber, picking up small articles and garments that spoke to him of her presence: a book of hours he had presented to her soon after their arrival in London; a veil, half hemmed, possibly Kate's work. He was reassured. Since Kate was not here she was with her mistress. Aleyne could come to no harm with her faithful maid in attendance.

He half turned as the door was jerked open abruptly and Guy Jarvis hastened in.

'Sir, I have only just heard of your return.'

'Where is your mistress, boy? Surely you should be in attendance?'

The boy's face paled and he came slowly towards Dominick, his teeth torturing his nether lip.

He hesitated, then blurted out, 'I do not know, sir.'

'Don't know? God's blood, what do you mean, lad? I set you to guard Lady Allard. Have you allowed her to go unescorted into the city? Where have you been all day?'

Dominick had risen and caught Guy by one shoulder so cruelly that the squire bit back a cry of pain.

'I have been into the city with two of our men, searching, sir.'

It was Dominick's turn to pale. He released his grip on his squire, then put both hands on Guy's shoulders and turned him towards the window where he might read his expression.

'Tell me, lad, and quickly.'

'God knows, I fear to tell you, sir, but I haven't seen Lady Allard since soon after noon yesterday.'

'The maid is with her?'

'I presume so, sir.' The boy closed his eyes momentarily as if he feared to see the mounting fury in his master's black eyes. 'I served her at dinner. She dismissed me, and Jem Weaver came to say there was some trouble in the stable. Two of our men were involved in a brawl with some of the castle servants. I went down to sort out the problem and deal with offenders. It took some little time, and when I returned to report to my lady again she was not in the chamber and one of the castle pages said she had left with her maid and Will Scroggins, and that groom of hers who was injured.'

'Wait a moment—the groom, you say, the boy we left at Tewkesbury?'

'Yes, Sir Dominick, he arrived the previous day and I found him a sleeping place——'

'So you presumed they had gone shopping?'

'Yes, sir, I had no reason to believe anything else— then.' Guy swallowed. 'I was alarmed when she did not arrive at supper, nor...' he paused and swallowed again '...nor did she come ...nor did she come back last night.'

Sir Dominick's dark eyes bored into him, the heavy brows drawing together in a black scowl. 'God in heaven, boy, why did you not raise a search?'

Guy hesitated then raised his head and turned as the door opened behind him and the Duke of Gloucester strode into the room.

'My mother tells me you are concerned about Aleyne,' he said without preamble. 'Is she not back now?'

'No, sir,' Dominick shook Guy's arm imperatively, 'she is not, and this fool tells me she was absent last night and he made no fuss about the matter.'

Guy licked dry lips. 'Sir, I thought—I thought you might not wish me to make it public knowledge that...'

Dominick swore roundly. 'Go on,' he commanded.

'Will Scroggins was involved in that affair over Master Dyer and... and I wondered—only wondered, sir, I...'

'Dyer?' Gloucester's level brows drew together in some bewilderment. 'Ellis Dyer? What has he to do with all this?'

Dominick sank down tiredly on to a stool and rubbed a hand over a chin he had forbore to shave. 'Ellis Dyer is Aleyne's cousin. I held him prisoner after Tewkesbury. He was taken behind our lines. He swore he wished only to serve you, wanted to speak to you. I kept him bound in a barn at Coventry. Aleyne was instrumental in freeing the man.' He turned away. 'They have known each other since childhood. There was a closeness between them...' His lips tightened.

'And you think the fellow may have taken refuge in sanctuary and Aleyne has gone to see him?'

'It seems to be what my fool squire thinks.'

Gloucester looked from Guy to Dominick. He waved the boy out of the room and seated himself opposite his friend. 'You cannot believe Aleyne has run from you to this man?'

Dominick lifted his shoulders and let them fall in a weary shrug. 'What else am I to believe? You know well, sir, there has been a restraint between us and she was forced to the match against her will. Though she denied it, I have no way of knowing what there was between her and Dyer before he left to serve Warwick.'

Gloucester shook his head. 'Had there been any such understanding Mistress Aleyne would have informed the King of it when he gave her to you in marriage.'

A little flare of hope lit Dominick's eyes. 'Then how do we account for her absence since yesterday afternoon?'

'I hate to suggest that some harm might have befallen her.' Dominick stared at him blankly, and he added, 'Dominick, I have evidence that this sort of thing happens. Anne is still missing. My captain informs me he has searched in all the rat runs of the South Wark to no avail. Lady Allard is too honourable to deal you such a blow. I would wager my soul against such behaviour on her part. If she has failed to return to you it is because she has been prevented. We must take steps to find her without delay.'

Dominick's eyes became opaque again. 'Sweet Virgin, forgive me that I ever entertained doubts... My first thought was to... She may, even now, be in terrible danger. We must alert the watch...'

'Wait, man; let us think. Is it possible that she might have wished Guy Jarvis out of the way in order to leave Baynards without him?'

Dominick's teeth showed white as he bared them. 'Aye, more than likely. Then she *did* go to Dyer.' He wrenched open the chamber door and barked a command for Guy to come back.

'This brawl in the stables—who did you say summoned you?'

Guy's face flamed with sudden understanding. 'Jem Weaver, sir.'

'Find him, lad, and bring him here at once.'

Guy went at a stumbling run.

Dominick's fist smacked hard against his palm. 'If she went to Dyer it was likely only to bid him goodbye. If that is the case he may well have abducted her...'

Gloucester said quietly, 'Why did you not hand the man over at Tewkesbury, Dominick?'

Dominick turned and stared into the narrowed, concerned grey-green eyes.

'I—I cannot explain. I distrusted his motive in wishing to be brought before you.'

'You mean you feared harm to me?'

Dominick shook his head. 'I don't know. At Middleham—I never completely trusted him. He was a man, like myself, with no fortunes, a way to make in the world. After Barnet he had no hope of preferment. He asked to see you, trading on past goodwill—yet, for the sake of those days when we had ridden together as comrades, I did not wish to see him suffer with the other prisoners. The King was in no merciful mood—I hoped tempers would cool by the time we reached London and it would then be safe to hand Dyer over for judgement.'

'And Aleyne feared for his life and helped him to escape?'

'Yes, that night Queen Margaret was brought to Coventry.'

'You punished her?'

'No, but she knew how angry I was and I forbade her ever to see him again, and——' he sighed heavily '—she promised she would obey me. Scroggins and Weaver had been bribed to allow the escape and I reprieved them from hanging when she begged me to do so. It is possible Scroggins discovered where the man was hidden and informed her, but I cannot imagine what prompted her to go counter to my wishes and try to see him again.'

'Do you think Scroggins might have been in Dyer's pay?'

'Scroggins is a scoundrel but I believe he is devoted to Aleyne, and the maid, Kate, is his leman.'

'Then be comforted. He is unlikely to have delivered them deliberately into any dangerous situation.'

Dominick was back to his restless pacing again. 'That is what I fear most now. Why isn't Scroggins back? If Dyer didn't abduct her against her will she might have consented to go with him willingly or—as you suggest...' His voice trailed off in horrified alarm. 'God's wounds, how can I find her if all your efforts have failed to find the Lady Anne? What are *my* chances——?'

Guy Jarvis came into the room, breathless after the run up the spiral stair. 'Sir, Weaver is not to be found. His companions say he didn't sleep near them last night and they think he was not in the castle, but a wounded man has been brought into the guard-room. One of the watch found him in an alley in the South Wark. Sir, it might be Will Scroggins—or Weaver.'

Dominick was past him and out of the chamber before either he or the duke could say a word. Both hastened after him, though considerably more mindful that they might well break their necks on the steep stair if they kept to his pace.

Dominick thrust open the guard-room door and went to stand by the simple pallet near the wall. Will Scroggins lay, breathing stertorously, blood seeping from a bad wound on the crown of his head. His jack also bore ominous signs of dried blood, indicating that he might have been stabbed in the breast. The watchman came towards Dominick, anxiously twisting his greasy hat in his hands.

'We didn't know if we should bring 'im 'ere, sir, but 'e were a soldier, we could see that, and it did seem likely...'

'He's one of my men. When did you find him?'

'This morning, sir, about noon. Nobody 'ad been in that there alley at that time. People 'o lives near there, they don't get up early becos——'

'Quite. Was he conscious when you found him, or at any time since?'

'No, sir, my lord.' The man looked even more disconcerted as the Duke of Gloucester pressed into the small chamber. The watchman edged carefully by the fine velvet of his doublet, eyeing his gold chain, with its white boar pendant, in awe.

'No word, nothing?' Dominick pressed determinedly.

''E did moan when we lifted him. You see, at first we thought 'im dead——'

'Yes, yes, but did he say anything?'

'Nothing as we could make any sense of, my lord. 'E did mutter something about "my lady" and "sorry"; I thought——'

'Thank you for your trouble.' Dominick impatiently signalled to Guy to reward the fellow with a coin, and bent solicitously over his injured sergeant.

'He seems to have lost a deal of blood. There's no doubt whatever that the party was attacked and Aleyne abducted, but, dear God in heaven, to where? She could be miles from the South Wark now, or buried so deep in one of those crowded hovels that I'll never find her.'

The Duke winced, and Dominick swore inwardly at his own lack of tact. Richard had been searching for weeks now for his Anne, with no success, and his alarm had mounted to the same fever that was tearing Dominick apart.

The Duke said quietly, 'Guy, send one of the men for my army surgeon. Dominick, we can do no good here. When Scroggins regains consciousness he may be able to tell us more of his assailants. Come to my chamber and take wine. You'll be in the way here.'

'I'll follow as soon as I know how badly Scroggins is hurt, sir.' Dominick swallowed noisily. 'I must know if he is ever likely to...' he turned away '...if he will recover. He lay for too long before he was discovered.'

The Duke nodded and left the guard-room as his surgeon hurried up, clasping his bag of office.

As he was about to enter his chamber one of the pages cleared his throat as if anxious to give a message.

'Am I asked for, boy?'

'Yes, Your Grace. A man enquired at the guard-room and was conveyed into the presence ante-room. He seems to be a gentleman, sir, for he speaks well, though he is not extravagantly dressed.'

'He gave no name?'

'Dyer, sir, I think it was.'

The Duke started. 'He asked for me specifically, by name?'

'Yes, Your Grace, he humbly begs audience, said the matter would brook no delay.'

'Bring him up immediately, then go to the guard-room and ask Sir Dominick Allard to come here quickly.'

The boy bowed low and hurried off.

Ellis Dyer was brought to the Duke's presence under guard. He fell on his knees before Gloucester. 'My Lord, I need help urgently, for a lady in distress, Aleyne, Lady Allard——'

'You know where she is?'

'Yes, Your Grace.' Ellis looked pointedly at his guards and the Duke signalled for the men to await his instructions outside the chamber.

Before Ellis could rise, Dominick burst into the room and seizing the kneeling man by the throat shook him as he would a rat.

'Where is she?' he demanded through gritted teeth. His free hand moved restlessly to his dagger hilt.

'Dominick,' the Duke moved to his friend's side, 'don't choke the life out of the man before he can tell us.'

Dominick released Dyer, who fell sprawling at their feet then rose, unsteadily, his face purple, his hand clutching at his throat. At the noise of the disturbance the guards had hurried into the chamber, their eyes on their erstwhile prisoner, while Dyer continued to breathe hoarsely in an effort to recover his breath.

'Leave us,' the Duke snapped. 'Sir Dominick and I are perfectly capable of defending ourselves if need be.'

The men withdrew with the white-faced page, and the door was closed.

'Sit down, Dominick, and you, Dyer. You need a drink, man.' The Duke poured wine, and Ellis took the goblet in shaking fingers and drained it. Dominick, glowering, continued to hover over his victim until the Duke gently but firmly ordered him to sit.

'You were about to tell us, Dyer, the whereabouts of Lady Allard.'

'She's safe, for the moment.' Ellis turned nervously at a hiss of concentrated fury which escaped Dominick's lips. 'My lord, can you persuade Sir Dominick to hear me out in patience?'

Dominick gave a grunt of compliance at the Duke's look of enquiry, and Ellis began. He spared himself nothing, explaining how Scroggins had contacted him with news from Lady Allard, and his own deep desire to see her.

'She brought me the means by which I could leave England, and I begged her to go with me into exile.' He looked uneasily at the growling Sir Dominick. 'I had loved her, Your Grace, since childhood, and had hoped that some day my fortunes would improve and I might go to her father honourably and beg for her hand. That was not to be.' He paused. 'She rejected me, Allard, out of hand, told me she loved you...' His brown eyes closed for a moment in pain at remembrance of the revelation of his lost hopes. 'Then Stoodley and his ruffians burst in. I swear I had no notion that Scroggins had been followed. Apparently Stoodley had some grudge against you, Allard, and had been lying in wait for some means of revenge. Later I heard how he had felt himself humiliated in front of you both, before the King.'

Dominick grated, 'Then he means to kill her?'

'Not while you live to inherit. That would hardly be to his advantage. He planned, from the start, on your going to the rescue. The boy, Rob, was allowed to escape to draw you to the house where he holds her. It's a hunting lodge in the woodland off the Kent road, some four miles east of Blackheath. I doubt if the boy has reached London yet, on foot as he was.'

He put out a hand to stay Dominick, who had lurched to his feet.

'Stoodley has at least a dozen men guarding her, possibly more, since he has even more ambitious plans for the place later.'

Dominick leaned across the table to stare into Ellis's eyes. 'How can we trust you to tell us truth? How was it, if you were taken prisoner, that Stoodley allowed you to leave the lodge?'

Ellis gave a half-smothered laugh. 'Perhaps because men of Stoodley's kidney judge others by their own standards. I am a wanted man, have no future under a Yorkist King, have been treated badly by a former companion.' He glanced meaningly at Dominick, his mouth twisting wryly. 'I'm in need of ready coin and, last of all, I knew he'd kill me out of hand if I didn't fall in with his plans. He doesn't fully trust me, of course. He had me followed, but I dealt with that problem.'

As both men stared at him, he added, 'I left the fellow dead in a ditch, lay in wait for him to pass me on the road.'

Dominick said starkly, 'What are Stoodley's intentions regarding Aleyne? He can hardly acquire her manor now.'

'He could if he managed to force her into marriage with him after she became a widow. He still hopes for that; hence his need for you to attempt a rescue.'

'Surely the man knows the King would not allow such a marriage?' the Duke expostulated.

Ellis smiled. 'But what if another King sat on England's throne?'

'Ah, so he plots treason and thinks you ripe for it, too?'

'Aye, Your Grace, I managed to convince him of that. It was not too difficult.'

Dominick snarled, 'You had time on your ride here to consider the best course of action. Let's hear it. I take it you do not favour a frontal attack?'

'No, Stoodley's hatred is so great he might just dispatch Aleyne if he thought you might storm the place rather than surrender.'

Dominick sucked in his breath sharply.

'I must go back with some instructions from—other gentlemen in the plot.' Ellis frowned slightly in the Duke's direction. 'Believe me, sir, I have no intention of dealing you false. Allow me first to deal with the urgent business of freeing Aleyne, Lady Allard, and I will reveal everything to your satisfaction. Even if his man doesn't return to him Stoodley may trust me long enough to allow me to expedite Aleyne's escape, or at least give her some protection should the worst happen— if Sir Thomas should threaten her life. I'll contrive to deal with the guards in the hall and admit Dominick, who will then help me deal with the rest and get Aleyne to safety.'

'To re-enter that house alone courts certain death,' the Duke said quietly. 'Stoodley is bound to be suspicious.'

'Yes, sir, but Sir Thomas does not take into account my love for Aleyne, which defies danger. He knows no such emotion. She does not return my love, but that does not bar me from endangering myself for her, as she risked all to save me.'

'It will be crass folly for you to contact and plot with Lancastrian nobles,' Dominick said, 'who may know your connection with Middleham and your former friendship with Duke Richard.'

Ellis shrugged. 'I must supply Stoodley with some proof that I am fully committed to his cause.'

The Duke nodded thoughtfully.

'Then go about your errand, Master Dyer, and Dominick and I will see to the provision of a raiding party. We give you until one hour past midnight to reach Lady Allard and warn her what is afoot. At midnight itself, Dominick, you will deal with the sentries on watch outside the lodge and pray that Dyer can find some means of admitting you secretly. In the meantime my men will draw into the wood, keeping well clear of the lodge, until either one or both of you returns with the prisoners or we see a fire arrow fired by you. My captain will remain close by for your call in case of need. If necessary he will fire an arrow to us to draw us in for attack. If neither of you reaches us or we receive no signal by two hours after midnight we'll move in regardless. I

pray heaven, gentlemen, that the ladies will be clear of
the house by that time.'

Ellis looked briefly at Dominick, who nodded.
'Agreed.'

'Then with your permission I will leave, Your Grace,
and meet up with your party in two hours' time, just
past the east gate of the city. Without me with you you
could mistake directions, for the lodge is well secluded.'

He rose and bowed, then the Duke rang for his page
to see him out.

Dominick watched his departure sourly. He sighed. 'I
still wish to God I could be the first to enter that house
and get to her.'

Gloucester touched his shoulder comfortingly. 'I know
that, man, but by so doing you could doom Aleyne. I
fear we must trust Ellis Dyer. Though it angers you to
know it, I think his love for Aleyne will bring her safely
through this peril and back into your arms.'

CHAPTER SIXTEEN

A SLIVER of moon shed little pallid light when the
company of men-at-arms drew up at the Duke's signal
a mile short of Blackheath into a small copse. Gloucester
went apart with Dominick and Dyer for a final con-
ference. All the men, including the Duke, wore drab
clothing—jacks and riding boots, without livery.
Dominick, in a fever of impatience, still insisted that the
arrangements did not please him.

The Duke put a steadying hand on the shoulder of
each man. 'Let us be of one mind, gentlemen. God knows
I'm as anxious as both of you to have this matter safely
concluded.' He waited, and Dominick bowed his head
submissively. 'We are decided on our course, then? We
give Ellis one hour past midnight to warn Aleyne what
is afoot and admit you, Dominick. If I hear nothing by
two hours after midnight I'll order the attack.'

Ellis looked towards Dominick, who nodded.

'Then God guard you both. My captain will be well behind you.'

Dominick and Ellis mounted up and rode for the next mile in silence. Ellis eventually drew rein and pointed ahead.

'Watch yourself from here. This is where I disposed of the spy. Don't concern yourself too much. I hid the body well. It shouldn't have been discovered yet.' He turned to look directly at Dominick. 'I love Aleyne, always have, but she loves you. She made that very clear and—I cannot swear to it, but I suspect she is carrying your child.'

Dominick's chin jerked in surprise.

'Her woman watched her like a hawk while we ate with Stoodley and Lady Risby.' He shrugged. 'I could be mistaken, so do not pin your hopes on it, but it's an added incentive to get her out of that house before the attack.'

Dominick nodded grimly. 'What will you do when this is over?'

'Join my mother in Dover and sail for France, if I'm allowed to.' Ellis grimaced ruefully. 'I never seriously nurtured hopes that Aleyne's father would give her to me. I know Aleyne is fond of me, as a brother perhaps, or dear friend. Her affectionate regard must be enough for me.'

'If I misjudged you at Tewkesbury you have my apology.' The words were stiffly uttered, but Ellis knew them to be sincere. He held out his hand and the other grasped it.

Ellis said, 'This has been a sorry time, when loyalties have not been clearly defined. I swear I meant no harm to the King or Gloucester. Our comradeship at Middleham meant much to me. After the Earl's death I wished only to join the Yorkist army.'

'That friendship meant much to me too, and to all of us.'

Ellis saluted him and rode off towards the hunting lodge, while Dominick dismounted and drew his horse into the concealment of low scrub, aware that Rawlings, the Duke's captain, was still close, alert to his every need.

Sir Thomas Stoodley welcomed Dyer genially, though he had retired to his chamber. He donned a furred bed-gown and came down to the solar.

'I had given you up for tonight. Sit down, man, and take wine. Shall I send the boy for food?'

'No, sir. I stopped in a certain cookshop in the Chepe and was royally served.'

Stoodley chuckled. 'Well, what did His Grace of Clarence have to say?'

Ellis proffered a thumb ring with the enamelled crest of the Neville black bull. 'He greeted me warily, as I had expected, but in the end accepted me as your agent when I told him about my difficulties following Barnet. He sympathised. After all, he too had changed sides. He's anxious to have the business speedily concluded before his lady gets wind of the affair.'

Stoodley grinned. 'Understandable; the Duchess will be inconsolable when she hears of her sister's death, yet the whole of the Neville inheritance should console her, eh, don't you think?'

'The Duchess of York is to leave London for a short visit to the King's hunting lodge at Sheen on Monday. Clarence tells me that she has requested that young Gloucester escort her.'

'And he will prove a dutiful son, I've no doubt. Very convenient for our purpose.'

'Gloucester's men are still active about the city, searching for his cousin, so we should have a care. Incidentally, I heard it bruited that the lady might well have her own reasons for fleeing her brother-in-law's house.'

'Oh?'

'It's rumoured she could be with child by Edward of Lancaster.'

Stoodley whistled sharply through his teeth. 'And is she?'

'I saw no sign of it, but the rumour is to our advantage. It could be thought she destroyed herself or fled the country to keep the child safe.'

'An heir to the Warwick estates would certainly complicate matters, and the birth of a grandson to saintly Harry, God rest his soul, would hardly please the King. Well, Dyer, we do him a favour, and he will never know it.'

Stoodley rose and ordered a sleepy page to put a chamber at Master Dyer's disposal. At the moment of parting, he turned. 'Did you see Hardwick in the city?'

'Hardwick?'

'My sergeant. He followed you in. There were items I needed from the city, not ones I could trust some serving-man to procure.'

'Ah. No, no one passed me on the road. He's still roistering on the South Wark, I don't doubt.'

Stoodley's eyes narrowed. 'Possibly, though I hope he returns tomorrow or I shall fear some harm came to him.'

'Surely the man can look after himself?'

'I should have thought so. I give you goodnight, Master Dyer.'

Aleyne lay wakeful. Kate had finally cried herself to sleep, desperately afraid for Will Scroggins. Aleyne wondered about Rob. Had he made it in safety to the city and reached Dominick? The Duke's party must be back at Baynards by now. Was Stoodley aware of that and had he deliberately released the boy to draw Dominick to his death? She prayed silently that Dominick would leave her to her fate. He must know that she had disobeyed him and gone to Ellis. He would despise her. She caught back a sob of despair. She could not wish for Dominick to come here, yet she needed so much to explain to him, show him how deeply she cared. She knew now that nothing Dominick could ever do or say could stop her loving him, and her heart told her that he was incapable of anything dishonourable. That very thought nagged at her peace. It would be dishon-

ourable for Dominick to ignore Stoodley's challenge. He
would come, and her desperation grew because of it.

Her thoughts turned on Ellis. She had believed him
incapable of treachery, yet she had heard him plot with
Stoodley to murder Anne of Warwick. He had everything to gain by an alliance with Clarence, yet was he
so blind to honour that he could leave her in Stoodley's
hands? He had said he loved her, begged her to leave
Dominick and fly with him to France. Had that been
pretence? Had he been in league with Stoodley from the
beginning? She racked her brains as she thought what
advantage Stoodley could get by her husband's death.
True, she would be a widow, but the man knew how she
loathed him, would never agree to marry him. Yet, if
the King was to be supplanted by his brother Clarence,
she could not overlook the possibility of being forced
into it against her will. Stoodley was capable of anything, even the murder of his sovereign, and she did not
doubt from what she had heard that Clarence was con-
templating replacing his brother upon the throne. After
all, when he had supported Warwick the golden lure of
the English throne had been the spur which had led him
on; that, and the hope of the great Warwick inheritance.
Gloucester must be warned. Her chin jerked as she
realised that subconsciously it was Gloucester she trusted
to cleave to the King's cause loyally, with Dominick by
his side. Neither man would stoop to murder. She had
been foolish to harbour such a thought for one moment.
Dear God, she must have opportunity to tell Dominick
how she had misjudged him and his lord. Somehow she
must win free of this place without endangering
Dominick's life. She must not despair. Dominick had
told her that one of the things he most admired in her
was her spirit. There must be a way, there must...

Ellis lay for a while, fully clothed, on a truckle bed in
a small chamber off the hall. He listened intently till the
household settled finally to rest. He had noted that a
man was stretched across the threshold of Aleyne's

chamber but he had no idea where Lady Risby was accommodated. It was hard to judge the passage of time. He was impatient to put his plan into action but Dominick must be given time to get into position.

He rose at last and checked that his dagger moved easily in its sheath, removed his shoes, and moved steathily to the door. He half expected to stumble across a page or man set to guard his chamber, but there was no restriction to the door's movement as it opened with little sound, though to his strained ears its faint jar screamed aloud a warning to the household.

The hall was deserted. Ellis checked, puzzled. There had been a man on watch there earlier and it was unlike Stoodley to be incautious. Possibly the fellow had taken himself off in search of ale or to relieve himself. Ellis drew the bolts of the outside door. It was too early yet for Allard, and there was a man on watch outside Aleyne's chamber to be dealt with first.

It was easier than he had thought. The man was slumped, yawning, with his back to the wall. Soft-footed on the stair, Ellis was able to spring and dispatch him before he could utter anything more than a surprised gurgle. He had learned quickly, within the sanctuary, where to thrust his dagger for the swiftest and quietest effect, and found the deaths of the spy set to follow him and this other man-at-arms astonishingly simple and expedient. He crouched down against the stair-rail over his victim as the guard below tramped back into the hall. Apparently sure of his companion, the man did not so much as glance upwards but, grunting, took his seat again on a bench within sight of the door.

Ellis waited as long as he dared and fumbled with the bolts of Aleyne's chamber door. As nothing appeared to alert the man below, he ventured inside. The room was in darkness, shutters barred, rush-dip extinguished. He moved in cautiously, fearful of stumbling against furniture. He barked his shins on the bed-foot and held his breath to prevent himself calling out. The gentle even breathing of the two women told him he must take great

care not to terrify either Aleyne or the maid into sudden
screams of panic. He could not silence both women at
once. He was growing accustomed to the gloom but
needed more light. The door was firmly closed behind
him and he found tinder and flint and kindled the dip
by the bed, holding it high above the sleepers. The faint
brush of movement or sudden gleam awakened the one
nearest to him.

'Quiet, for love of the Virgin,' he whispered hoarsely.
'Trust me. It is Ellis Dyer.'

'Ellis?' Aleyne's face loomed up at him out of the
darkness, then her tone sharpened. 'What are you doing
here? Dear God, what further insults am I to stomach?'

'Keep your voice low, you'll waken the household.'

'I *intend* to waken the household!' She was thoroughly roused now and her alarm had changed to fury.

He put one hand over her mouth, struggling to restrain her. Kate woke and gaped owlishly.

'Tell her to trust me, woman,' he snapped. 'She must,
or she'll doom us all. Aleyne,' he hissed into her ear,
'could you so doubt me as to believe the act I put on
for Stoodley's benefit? I am your friend, will always be
so. I'm here to help you. Will you keep silent if I remove
my hand from your mouth?'

'Do as he says, my lady,' Kate whispered, her eyes on
his bloodied dagger.

Trusting to what he read in Aleyne's eyes, Ellis released her and she gave a quickly suppressed gasp as her
gaze followed Kate's to his weapon.

Hastily he wiped the blade on the bed coverlet. 'Don't
be afraid. I had to silence the guard. I want you both
to dress quickly. Aleyne, your husband is waiting outside
for you, and Gloucester has a company of men near by
to come to our assistance. If you obey me implicitly I
can get you clear of the house before Stoodley can be
aware of the coming attack. If he wakes we'll be trapped,
and, rather than give you up, he'll kill us all. Do you
understand?'

She nodded, white-faced.

'Good. I'll wait near the door. Be very quick. At any
moment Dominick will come barging in to your rescue.
I had the utmost difficulty in preventing him from doing
that from the first.'

Once aware of his need, Aleyne flung back the covers,
and Ellis, his back turned from the women, could hear
the swish of material as they struggled to assist each other
dress. There was a warm soft breath against his cheek
as Aleyne joined him near the door.

'We're ready, Ellis. I'm sorry I panicked.'

'Take off your shoes.'

'We didn't put them on.'

'Good. Now I must deal with the guard in the hall.
Wait here till I come for you, or, if I call, both of you
come running. Don't stop, whatever happens to me. Run
out to Dominick, who'll get you clear, then signal to the
Duke's men. Stand back while I open the door.'

'Ellis——' she squeezed his arm lightly '—God guard
you.'

Kate extinguished the dip and they stood waiting,
hands clammy with fear, as Ellis cautiously opened the
door. He emerged on to the landing and stared down
into the dark well of the hall.

'Hey, there, boy, bring me wine; I can't sleep.'

Ellis checked and swore under his breath. Stoodley
bawled again imperatively.

'Where is the varlet? Wine, in the name of the saints.'

The guard in the hall jumped to with alacrity, as
Stoodley pushed open his downstairs chamber door and
stood, a tall, shapeless form in velvet bed-gown, limned
against the light from within the room.

Ellis drew a sharp breath. In Christ's name what was
he to do now—tackle Stoodley while the guard was gone
to the buttery and signal to the two women to run for
it, praying that the main door still remained unbarred?
Stoodley would prove no easy prey and would shout for
reinforcements even while he grappled with his as-
sailant. He'd not take Stoodley by surprise as he'd done
the others. He had to move, take the initiative, but

Stoodley had emerged into the hall now, and his shout to his page had wakened another sleeper. Lady Risby appeared on the landing from the chamber which adjoined Aleyne's prison. Behind her, a tousle-headed maid held up a candle.

'Tom, what is it? Is there trouble...?'

The candle-flame revealed Ellis to her shocked gaze. The maid screamed shrilly and her mistress snapped a warning to Stoodley.

'Tom—Dyer, at the girl's room. I warned you...'

Stoodley muttered an oath and went back into his chamber, undoubtedly for his weapon. Ellis stood, uncertain how to act. The moment of indecision almost cost him his life, for the guard, returning to the hall, let fall the wine cup and launched himself at him. This man was a veteran and fully alert. His sword was in hand as he mounted the stair and Ellis had worn no sword lest its betraying clink alert the sentries. He had relied on his dagger only and now lacked the advantage of reach. They closed and fought, panting and clumsy in the restriction of the narrow stair. Ellis heard the man grunt as his dagger found its mark on the guard's wrist, but the man was well protected by his leather jack. He was heavy set yet light enough on his feet. Ellis fought on doggedly, fearing that Stoodley would come to the man's assistance in moments. He hardly felt the stultifying blow which sliced through the fine wool of his doublet, numbing his right arm from shoulder to fingers and forcing him to drop the dagger. There was a sticky wetness down his arm, confusion of noise above him as Lady Risby's maid went on screaming hysterically, then, dimly, over it all, Aleyne's sobbed shout, 'Dominick, oh, dear God, Dominick!'

Stupefied, Ellis felt his attacker slump on his knees on the lower rung of the stair and, before he himself fell forward in a faint, registered the hilt of a dagger protruding from the man's back and knew it had been aimed unerringly by Dominick Allard as he had burst through the main doorway.

Dominick glanced upward and barked a command.

'Keep that idiot maid quiet before she brings other guards to the house.' He swung round instantly as Stoodley appeared from his chamber, sword in hand.

Aleyne waited for no more. She sprang at her stepmother, one leg thrust out as the older woman made for the stairs. Further squawks of alarm and rage told her that Kate had settled on the maid in obedience to Dominick's instructions.

Lady Risby was hampered by her voluminous night-robe and went sprawling. Aleyne seized her by the wrist and her stepmother spat at her furiously, too winded to scream. They struggled together in an undignified tangle of arms and legs, breathing heavily, each straining for mastery. Aleyne felt hot tears as her stepmother pulled her hair almost from its roots, then relief came suddenly as Kate wrenched her clear.

'Let me, my lady. I'm more used to holding my own with women. Fetch me some torn sheeting.'

Aleyne scrambled up and dashed back into her chamber, wrenching frantically at the holland sheets, tearing with teeth and fingers as she dashed back to the two women. Kate had Lady Risby's wrists twisted hard behind her back and the woman was sobbing with pain and exhaustion. Aleyne helped as Kate pinioned her wrists then tied another strip round Lady Risby's mouth to gag her, a difficult task as she was twisting her head from side to side in frenzy.

Maid and mistress clung together as the sound of methodical clang of sword on sword went on from below as Dominick engaged his enemy.

'The door,' Kate gasped and, struggling by the inert forms of Lady Risby and Ellis on the stair, she raced down to bar it against any men-at-arms coming to Stoodley's assistance.

Aleyne hastened to Ellis. She had found the maid unconscious and neither knew or cared if the woman was still breathing. Ellis's sleeve was soaked with blood and,

as gently as she could, Aleyne bound it tightly with strips
of the torn sheet. Kate hurried up. 'How bad is he?'

'I don't know. His right arm feels broken. He's still
in a faint.' Aleyne stood up, her kirtle stained and torn.
She clung for a moment to the stair-rail then moved to
go to where she could see Dominick still engaged in
deadly combat with Stoodley. Her hand went to her
mouth as she held back a desperate cry of fear.

'Leave them,' Kate warned grimly; 'you'll only hinder
Sir Dominick.'

'There may be others——'

'None in the house,' Kate said evenly. 'I think, between them, Sir Dominick and Master Dyer dealt with
all the opposition.'

She drew Aleyne down on to the steps and they sat,
hands clasped in each other's, waiting. Kate's fears were
for the unborn child but she would not frighten her mistress further. Sweet Virgin, let her not have been hurt in
that struggle with that Risby vixen.

The men in the hall were tiring. Stoodley had given
up taunting his antagonist. From first to last, Allard had
said no word but set about his task of beating back his
enemy with steady determination, his lips drawn back
in a silent snarl of fury. There came a half-gurgled
scream. Sir Thomas staggered backwards, sending a
trestle flying. His body jerked oddly like a puppet Aleyne
had once seen at the fair in Chipping Campden. His
sword fell with a final clang and slithered along the
flagged floor. His sword-hand struggled vainly to re-
possess it, but Dominick pressed on, swaying on his feet,
clearly as winded and exhausted. He stood over
Stoodley's body. His sword lowered until it arced once
then fell again. He looked up, panting, to see where Kate
clasped Aleyne close to prevent her from trying to
interfere.

Aleyne gave a choking cry, then, as Kate released her,
ran to him, sobbing. He dropped his sword and drew
her into his arms, where she cried hysterically and he

gently stroked her hair. At last she pushed free and
fought to regain mastery of herself.

'Oh, my love, I'm sorry. I could have endangered
you...'

Dominick staggered, smiling tiredly. 'He'll give no
more trouble, sweetheart. I made sure of that. Where's
Ellis?'

Her heart raced at the endearment and she looked to
the stair, where Ellis was staggering to his feet with Kate's
help.

'My arm's broken, I think, but I'll mend. You?'

Aleyne gave a cry. 'You're bleeding...'

Dominick shrugged. 'I haven't had time to take stock.
Some of it's Stoodley's. How many more men, do you
know?'

Ellis shook his head and Dominick gave a barked
laugh. 'It seems they took to their heels or were rounded
up by the Duke's men. I'll give the signal to move in.'

When he returned Aleyne poured wine from the court
cupboard and they sat in the solar, Aleyne insisting on
examining Dominick for any serious wounds. There were
several scratches, which bled copiously, but nothing
dangerous. Dominick had freed Lady Risby, who immediately ran to Stoodley's body and lay sobbing, his
head cradled in her arms. Aleyne felt helpless to offer
comfort. It seemed her stepmother had loved the man
too well. The woman had sought her life yet she felt
bereft of any enmity, merely an aching feeling of regret
for all that had passed between them.

Ellis was corpse-pale and obviously in severe pain.
Aleyne prayed that the Duke would have a surgeon in
his train. Kate and Ellis left her alone with Dominick
and she turned, lip trembling, to look at him, dreading
to see contempt in his eyes.

He was watching her very intently and she said hesitatingly, 'You must be very angry.'

'Because you went to Dyer?'

She nodded, her lower lip caught on her teeth.

He shook his head and drew her close once more. 'He told me how it is with you both. I should have trusted you, my darling. And now, is it true what he said—that you carry our child?'

Her troubled grey eyes met his dark ones. 'I—I am not sure yet, but I believe . . . that it is so. Oh, Dominick, I do love you, and what I said of you—and the Duke—I do not believe it now—and—and even were it true, I would love you still, my darling.'

His eyes shone with triumph as he bent to kiss the top of her dishevelled dark head.

CHAPTER SEVENTEEN

RICHARD OF GLOUCESTER'S men took charge of Sir Thomas Stoodley's hunting lodge in the early hours of the morning. The young Duke's expression was grim but relieved when he took in the sight of death and destruction. Lady Risby was returned to her own chamber, a prisoner, with her maid, now fully returned to her senses, to attend her. The Duke's men were set to put to right the house and collect the dead for burial. Duke Richard listened gravely to Dominick's brusque account of what had happened.

Aleyne waited impatiently for her husband to finish, then she rose and knelt at the Duke's feet.

'My lord, I think I know where the Lady Anne is,' she said softly.

He bent and drew her to her feet, his grey-green eyes shining strangely. 'My lady . . .'

'I heard Stoodley plotting with my stepmother and . . .' she broke off awkwardly as she was about to name Ellis, then pressed on. 'She is hidden in a cookshop in the Chepe, forced to work in kitchens and tap-room. They meant to kill her, my lord. You must go to her at once.'

Dominick burst out, 'But Dyer must have known this! Why did *he* not inform us?'

Gloucester's smile was understanding but a little grim. 'I think I know why, eh, Master Dyer? You were intent on saving Lady Allard first, isn't that it?'

Aleyne gave a distressed little cry.

Ellis said, shamefacedly, 'Aye, Your Grace, that is the sum of it. It was to the Duke of Clarence, your brother, that I went last night. I knew of the plot but I knew the Lady Anne would be quite safe for the present and Aleyne's needs came first.'

Gloucester nodded. He turned to issue brisk orders.

'We ride for London within the hour. Rawlings, have the men ready. One of them must go to the local priest and give notice of the burials. Dominick, are you and Dyer well enough to ride?'

Dominick rose at once. 'Aye, Your Grace, but Dyer should keep that arm still. It's broken but firmly strapped.'

'Lady Allard and her maid with Master Dyer can ride in the cart which brought them here. It is not the most dignified mode of travel but it must serve.'

Aleyne was about to protest that she was fit to ride with Dominick; then she saw Kate's warning look and nodded her acceptance of the plan.

Dominick and Ellis left to oversee the men with the Duke's captain, and Gloucester gently placed his hand on Aleyne's arm. Kate hastened out to find a cloak for her mistress.

'Aleyne—you will let me call you that in friendship?'

Aleyne's face flushed scarlet with shame and she curtsyed low. 'Your Grace honours me.'

'But I want your affectionate regard and your trust, Aleyne,' he said quietly.

'Your Grace takes me to task for——'

'Dominick loves you with his whole soul. He believes that you resent his loyal service to me.'

'Not any longer, Your Grace.'

He frowned in concentration. 'Will you go with me to rescue the Lady Anne, try to make her understand that she must trust me?'

'With all my heart, Your Grace. I—I wronged you in my thoughts...'

'I think I understand. Those matters must never be spoken of again. Only this I say to you: believe that Dominick is the most honourable of men. He would never stoop to a contemptible deed, not even to save his life, let alone to assist his fortunes.'

'My lord, he spoke of you in just such terms.'

'Great friendships were forged in those days at Middleham. Master Ellis Dyer was one of our number. Be sure that I will not forget him. I shall see to it that he has the King's pardon. Meanwhile it might be best if he goes to the court of my sister Margaret in Burgundy for a while with his mother. There are messages from me he can deliver to her.'

His grey-green eyes looked sternly into hers and she read his meaning. Better for Ellis and Dominick to see little of each other during the coming months. Ellis would not lose by this arrangement and she would be happy for him.

It was almost noon when Aleyne, escorted by Ellis, entered the cookshop in the Chepe. Richard of Gloucester had decided it were better, for the moment, if he waited outside, but his men surrounded the building and his sergeant followed Aleyne and Ellis inside, standing solid and watchful in the doorway. Aleyne had made only one stop, in a small draper's booth nearby, and procured a mantle for the Lady Anne's use.

'We wish to speak with the Lady Anne Neville.' Ellis's tone brooked no argument. The landlord blustered, his bushy brows rising in surprise. Had he not seen Master Dyer only last night and known him to have been in the service of the Duke of Clarence by the ring he'd worn bearing the crest of the black bull? He glanced nervously to Gloucester's sergeant, wearing the badge of the white boar, shrugged deprecatingly, and went to the kitchen.

Aleyne would never forget her first sight of the Earl's daughter as she came into the tap-room, pushed forward by the landlord, her expression one of abject terror. Her face was drawn and pale, her kirtle and blouse torn and stained, yet, even in those squalid conditions, she had struggled to retain some degree of dignity, for her face was cleanly scrubbed and her hair neatly secured beneath a linen coif.

Aleyne said gently, 'My lady, how have they dared to treat you so?'

Anne's expression was bewildered and she looked from Aleyne to Ellis, who unceremoniously took the landlord by the arm and hurried him from the room. Understanding his imperative glance, the sergeant moved outside and drew the door to behind him.

Aleyne drew the frightened girl to a bench near the hearth. Anne's hand was icy cold and the palm rough and calloused. Aleyne's cheeks flamed with anger as she thought how the girl had been shamefully used and humiliated.

'You know me, my lady. Duke Richard came the moment he knew where you were. He has been searching for you for weeks. He sent me to attend you.'

'Where—where are you to take me?' Anne's fingers fastened, claw-like, on Aleyne's wrist. 'Not to Coldharbour? My brother Clarence——' she drew a painful breath '—hates me, wishes me dead.'

'Duke Richard will see to it that you are taken wherever you wish to go, or are safest. Trust him.'

'No, no, not even Dickon. They all wish to use me, as my father did. He married me to Edward of Lancaster though he knew how I loathed him. For that the Lord has truly punished me. I bear the heavy guilt of his death, since Dickon killed him.'

'No, my lady. The Duke of Clarence said that only to alienate you from his brother. The Prince was killed during the rout. No one can be held responsible for his death. Those who say otherwise only do so to poison your mind against the Duke of Gloucester, who loves you well.'

'And Henry, that poor sick man...'

Aleyne's lashes pricked, heavy with her own guilty tears that she had also distrusted her own love. 'No man will ever say who perpetrated that deed, my lady, for it would be unsafe to breathe it, but I do not believe it was Duke Richard. My own husband was with him on the night it is said the King died, and I cannot believe anything so foul was done by either of them.'

Anne's lips parted involuntarily. 'You really love Dominick Allard, and yet, as men do me, he wished to marry you for your lands and manor.'

'If that was so in the beginning, I know he loves me now with all his heart, as you are loved, have always been loved.'

'I thought Richard loved me,' Anne whispered, 'yet he would not forsake Edward, not even for the promise of my hand.'

'Men deem honour before everything,' Aleyne said softly. 'These battlefields have taken their toll of hearts as well as lives.'

Anne's fingers tightened on her wrist again but not so painfully. She was beginning to calm. Gently Aleyne persuaded her to stand up, and she wrapped her in the silken mantle.

Anne smiled tremulously. 'You say Richard is here, outside?'

'Waiting to see you. He would not force his presence on you, despite his longing to hold you in his arms.'

Anne swallowed painfully. 'He—he would not force me back to Coldharbour?'

'No, my lady, he will not do that.'

Anne nodded shyly as Aleyne went to the door and looked at her for consent to admit the Duke.

'I look—dreadful,' she said tearfully and Aleyne smiled. Now, at last, Anne was exhibiting a woman's natural disinclination to be seen at a disadvantage by the man she loved.

'You look very well, my lady.'

Gloucester was pacing restlessly in the corridor outside, his spurs ringing on the flagged stones of the floor.

Aleyne said softly, 'Be very gentle with her, Your Grace,' and, as he burst impetuously through the door, she went to Dominick.

He drew her into his arms, then, holding her slightly away from him, gently kissed her tear-drenched lids.

'I hope those are tears of joy, Lady Allard.'

'She loves him, I know she does. Now, if only the King will give his consent to the match...'

'I think there is no doubt of that.' He drew her down on to a rough wooden bench near the door, while the sergeant, still on guard, looked impassively away. 'And now, my love, tell me you have taken no hurt by this rough journey nor that brawl you had with your stepdame.'

'I feel well, Dominick.' Her grey eyes clouded. 'I do not think the Virgin will let me lose my baby, not now, when my prayers have told her how much I long to place your son in your arms as the truest mark of my love.'

He bent to kiss her fingers humbly like a suppliant.

The Duke emerged some half-hour later. He was smiling.

'The Lady Anne has agreed to place herself within my charge. It seems best to take a lodging for her in the sanctuary of St Martin's. There she cannot be forced by anyone, not even me, to do anything she does not wish to do. Would you agree to guard her, Dominick, with a detachment of my men?'

'Certainly, Your Grace. Lady Anne will feel more content if Aleyne attends her.'

The Duke beamed his pleasure. His young face was radiant, less stern than Aleyne had ever seen it.

'Then all will be well. Dyer can stay in sanctuary also. I will go to Edward and demand that he gives me my due reward, Anne's hand, even if I have to forfeit all the Warwick lands to get it. I'll see to it that Dyer receives a free pardon and will soon be able to sail for France.'

That afternoon Aleyne found herself settled in a respectable small house within the sanctuary. That evening she was joined by a happy Kate, who bubbled with delight as she helped her mistress dress for supper.

'My Will has regained consciousness, my lady. He was so glad to see me that he kissed me there, before them all in the guard-room at Baynards, and asked me to be his wife.'

'In front of witnesses, too!' Aleyne said, her lips twitching at Kate's joy and astonishment. 'He'll never regret it, Kate, as I never regretted meeting you that dreadful day after Tewkesbury.'

They supped with the Lady Anne, who was already regaining her courage and regal bearing, and, later, Aleyne lay in her husband's arms.

'I still cannot believe that it is all over and that evil man dead,' she said reflectively. 'Dominick, was it all greed that brought Stoodley and Maud to their dooms? Will the King hang her, do you think?'

Dominick grunted his contentment. 'You seem to think she loved the man. Possibly he was still married when her father insisted on the match with your father. Her love for Stoodley might well have forced her into that unholy alliance. The King is ever gentle with women. She deserves to die, certainly, but may well be dismissed to some nunnery for her sins.'

'That may well prove a worse punishment,' Aleyne said thoughtfully.

'I'm glad to hear that Scroggins is recovering and intends to take Kate to wife. I'll make provision of a small dowry for her.'

Aleyne bent and kissed his chest where the dark hairs curled. 'Dominick, you can assure Duke Richard that the Lady Anne does not carry Edward of Lancaster's child.'

'She told you?' He sounded astounded.

'She told me she and Edward were never bedded. Apparently Queen Margaret forbade it. Anne thinks the Queen would have repudiated the marriage had Warwick won back the throne for her. She always hated the man, had no wish to see his daughter sit on England's throne.'

Dominick's lips curled derisively. 'What a grievous mistake that proved to be. Now there is no heir to Lancaster, no focus for insurrection.'

There was a silence and Aleyne stirred restlessly.

Dominick said at last, 'Edward made very sure Richard was well away from London while the deed was done. He knows his brother would not have wished to be involved in such a ploy.'

Aleyne remembered Scroggins's words that the late King Harry's servants had been paid up much later than the day he was said to have died. So that was it. York must be secure on the throne, even as a result of murder. She was glad to know in her husband's revealing words that certainly the King had been living when he and Gloucester took the road to Kent. Her suspicions had been utterly unfounded. She gave a little sigh, and Dominick sat up on his elbow to look down at her. His eyes gleamed in the candle-glow as he swept her up into his arms once more.

The first week in March and Easter already planned for. Aleyne turned from the window with a happy sigh to where Kate sat on a stool, her foot on the cradle rocker. Three weeks since Baby Dickon had made his arrival in his father's manor. The birth had been hard, a little premature, but with Kate, now a respectable married dame, and Dominick's mother to help and encourage her, Aleyne had come through the ordeal safely, exhausted, but jubilant at the knowledge that she had borne Dominick a son.

She had feared she would be homesick so far north of her beloved Cotswolds, but they had travelled in the glory of the autumn and she found the grey, solidly built manor, lying snugly within Wensleydale, welcoming and comfortable. Dominick's mother had received her joyfully and the manor servants had been delighted that she was already carrying Sir Dominick's child.

These months with Dominick had been wonderful, balm to her body and mind after the storms of the past year. She would not have believed that the Wolf who had fought so savagely to defend his mate and at his lord's side in mortal combat could become the considerate husband who would treat her with such gentleness and care. Now his pride and contentment knew no bounds.

Since Christmas the snow had been heavy on the hills and Dominick's mother had been unable to travel back to her daughter's house, but there had been a thaw three days ago and she'd departed, promising to return soon and exhorting Aleyne to continue to take good care of herself and the child.

Aleyne had no wish to be further cosseted. Last night she had taxed Dominick roundly for treating her as if she were one of those fragile glass mirrors she had once seen at court, imported at great expense from Venice.

'I am not ill. My body healed fast and I am gloriously happy and have a marvellous sense of well-being. I want everyone to laugh and sing and rejoice as I do, Dominick, and, most of all, I want you to hold me tight and love me.'

As she had lain gently cradled within his arms she had thought of those others she loved who had still not attained her new-found bliss. Ellis, who had sailed to France with his mother, she prayed would put aside his feelings for her and find someone he could love as dearly; the Lady Anne, still in sanctuary, now attended by ladies well trusted by the Duchess of York, and Richard of Gloucester. He had done so much to ensure Aleyne's happiness and she prayed that he, too, would have his heart's desire.

Dominick hastened into the solar, turning instantly to the cradle, his colour mounting in embarrassed pride for the tiny swaddled scrap who slept so comfortably after his wet-nurse had fed him and returned to her own child in the kitchen. Aleyne had heard sounds of arrival and a pin-prick of doubt touched her spine. She had a great need to prolong this period of quiet happiness but she knew if there was news from his lord in London requesting his presence Dominick would immediately answer the summons.

He nodded at Kate, who curtsied and left, then he drew Aleyne down on the high-backed settle near the hearth.

'Do you think little Dickon would take great harm if he travels with us, warmly wrapped and in a closed litter? I'm summoned to Middleham.'

Her anxious gaze scanned his face then her heart leaped with sudden joy. 'They're coming home, Richard and Anne—at last?'

'Aye, wed these past three weeks. I'm anxious to be at the castle to greet His Grace.'

It was but three miles to Middleham and Aleyne agreed joyfully.

She stood with Dominick within the gatehouse as the ducal party rode up the street. They had already glimpsed the long line of laden sumpter-wagons and riders approaching from the high turrets of the keep. The wintry sun shone out on the standard of the white boar as it floated free in the wind. Richard of Gloucester was bringing his bride home to the place where the two of them had met and loved for many happy years of their childhood. Dominick had told Aleyne how Richard had finally persuaded the King and his brother Clarence. The whole of the Warwick inheritance was to remain in George of Clarence's hands save the Earl of Warwick's most loved residences, the castles of Middleham and Sheriff Hutton. So, thought Aleyne, Anne is truly convinced that Richard loves her, even as I know my husband loves me.

The leading horsemen approached the gatehouse and rode through and now, at last, Aleyne could see the bridal pair. Anne of Warwick wore a mantle displaying the dual arms of herself and her husband—the Neville saltire, and the leopards and lilies of royal England. She wore, proudly, the ducal crown over her flowing golden tresses. Richard, at her side, looked radiant and triumphant, also wearing his own heraldic mantle. The crowds had lined the small town, cheering madly. Their own lady had come home to them, a royal duchess, and married to the man she loved.

Richard dismounted and lifted down his wife. He kissed her before them all and the cheering broke out afresh, then he led her by the hand into her own castle.

Dominick slipped to his knees to greet his lord, who lifted him to his feet with a glad laugh. He looked round quickly.

'Where is she, then, our little mother?'

Aleyne, blushing, came to his side to have her two hands grasped delightedly by Anne of Gloucester.

'How glad I am to see you, Aleyne. Little Dickon, he is well?'

'Very well, Your Grace, and is sleeping contentedly, I hope, in the nursery.'

Anne's joyful laugh rang out. 'Aleyne, you are the most fortunate woman in the realm. You do not know how much I envy you your little son. I hope to give Richard an heir soon, now we are home again.'

Aleyne's heart was too full for words. The storms were past. They were *all* home. Richard had turned from the poisonous, intrigue-ridden air of the court, and Aleyne was thankful that Dominick, too, was free of it. She took the hand her husband held out to her and, confident of the future, followed the Duke and Duchess into the castle.

THE DENMEAD
INHERITANCE
Janet Edmonds

At 23 Miss Libby Barton had resigned herself to being an old maid, and as companion to the Duchess at Copthorne, Libby derived much enjoyment of the crotchety, witty old lady.

So it was a total shock when Marcus, Viscount Charlbury, visiting at Copthorne, suddenly proposed marriage to her. For years Libby had loved Marcus from afar, and she *knew* that he had never truly noticed her, so what had prompted him?

The answer led to doubts and danger, but by that time Libby had already said yes . . .

Look out for the two intriguing

MASQUERADE *Historical*

Romances coming next month

SWEET SACRIFICE
Elizabeth Bailey

Miss Clementina Hythe, in an awful quandary, believed the only immediate answer was to run away from her relatives' home. But gently brought up girls cannot travel alone, so her only recourse was to dress as a boy.

So it was sheer bad luck that Jake, Lord Sothern, should cross her path and see through her disguise, even though she flatly refused to divulge her secrets – not until she discovered that Jake truly was the only one who could help, though his answer to her problems did seem a bit drastic!

JEALOUS HEARTS
Deborah Miles

Life wasn't easy in the Sydney of 1838, and Bregetta Smith found it even harder when her father died and her brother Jim fell into trouble with the law.

Sergeant Alistair Duncan had his duty to do, and the fact that he was deeply attracted to Bregetta couldn't be allowed to sway his sense of duty. But they did become lovers, until Bregetta's best friend saw fit to meddle – but there was still the question of Jim. What chance did they have, unless that problem could be solved?

Available in September

TWO

HISTORICAL ROMANCES

Masquerade historical romance
bring the past alive with splendou
excitement and romance. We wi
send you a cuddly teddy bear an
a special MYSTERY GIFT. Then, i
you choose, you can go on to enjoy
more exciting Masquerades every tw
months, for just £1.99 each! Sen
the coupon below at once to – Reade
Service, FREEPOST, PO Box 236
Croydon, Surrey CR9 9EL.

&

TWO
FREE GIFTS!

- - - - - - - - - - **NO STAMP REQUIRED** - - - - - - - →

Yes! Please rush me my 2 Free Masquerade Romances and 2 Free Gifts!
Please also reserve me a Reader Service Subscription. If I decide to
subscribe, I can look forward to receiving 4 Masquerade Romances every two
months for just £7.96, delivered direct to my door. Post and packing is free,
and there's a free Newsletter. If I choose not to subscribe I shall write to you
within 10 days - I can keep the books and gifts whatever I decide. I can
cancel or suspend my subscription at any time. I am over 18.

Mrs/Miss/Ms/Mr _____ EP04M

Address _____

_____ Postcode _____

Signature _____